STOLEN SOMMER

NORA SOMMER CARIBBEAN SUSPENSE - BOOK TWO

NICHOLAS HARVEY

HarveyBooks

Copyright © 2022 by Harvey Books, LLC

All rights reserved. This book or any portion thereof may not be reproduced or used in any manner whatsoever without the express written permission of the publisher except for the use of brief quotations in a book review.

Printed in the United States of America

First Printing, 2022

ISBN: 979-8423646615

Cover design: Covered by Melinda

Cover photograph of model: Drew McArthur

Cover model: Lucinda Gray

Editor: Andrew Chapman at Prepare to Publish

Author photograph: Lift Your Eyes Photography

This is a work of fiction. Names, characters, businesses, places, events and incidents are either the products of the author's imagination or used in a fictitious manner unless noted otherwise. Any resemblance to actual persons, living or dead, or actual events is purely coincidental. Patti Weaver's name is used with permission in a fictional manner.

PROLOGUE

Human beings take things from each other. It's been that way since cavemen clubbed each other over the head for the last rat carcass sizzling on the fire. Survival may have been the original motivation, but as man has evolved, his reasons for taking someone else's crap have expanded. Greed and power have long since been the primary forces behind individuals – and nations – losing their precious possessions to their neighbours. But occasionally, a unique motivation drives someone into risking their livelihood, and their freedom.

1

TAKING OTHER PEOPLE'S THINGS

Residential security systems had come a long way in recent times. Hollywood loved to portray tech-savvy thieves with futuristic gismos tapping into an access point and foiling the high-dollar electronics. As it turns out, the alarm people aren't stupid enough to put the control units outside of the alarmed area. Artistic licence works in movies, but not in real life. Regardless, once Fernando had picked the lock on the side door of the beachfront mansion, he walked right in.

He stood in what the estate agent likely called a 'boot room'. In this case, an area the size of most people's living rooms where the homeowners and guests could clean up before entering the main house. Shining his torch to one side, he saw a large shower and bathroom area akin to a health club locker room.

Fernando took a pair of shoe covers from his rucksack and slipped them over his black trainers. The blue polypropylene distinct in its contrast to his black trousers, long-sleeved turtleneck shirt, and balaclava. The air conditioning inside the house was a welcome relief from the balmy Caribbean night. He glanced up at a red light, just below the ceiling in the corner of the room. He guessed the camera had low light sensitivity, but the resolution would be poor, giving little away.

Through the doorway, he entered one end of a long kitchen. Before him stretched an open-plan expanse encompassing the dining area, living room, and some kind of bar and games room. Fernando switched off his torch. Subtle mood lighting cast a pale blue glow, accenting meticulously placed furniture and design features. The effect was stunning. He wondered what kind of ego spent that much money for the benefit of anyone who happened to pass by on a boat. It was only visible from the ocean through floor-to-ceiling windows overlooking the Caribbean Sea. He glanced around. Everything about the home reeked of luxury, opulence and excess.

Two wide, curved, open-riser metal and dark wood stairways wrapped around the back of the living room, going up to a balcony which spanned the area like a bridge overlooking the ground floor below. Fernando hurried up the steps, noting several more discreetly placed cameras. Grinning to himself, he wished he'd faked a limp or some other obvious physical attribute. As he walked along the bridge towards the master bedroom, he glanced down to his left, where the open foyer ended with arched double entry doors.

The bedroom took up the whole east section of the first floor. The same full-length windows presented what Fernando imagined being a magnificent view of the ocean. In the darkness, soft lights around the pool and the ironshore coastline beyond faded quickly into blackness across the calm water. He stared for a few moments, looking for boat lights, but saw none.

Switching his torch on once again, he kept the beam low and away from the windows. Looking around the room, he verified the bedroom didn't have any security cameras. At the back of the room were two arched doorways. Fernando opened the door to the right with a gloved hand and shone his light around. It was the biggest bathroom he'd ever seen. He closed the door and moved to the second option. This door opened to an equally large dressing area

DEDICATION

This book is for the Rains family.
Thank you all for your love and support.

and walk-in closet. Although closet was a misleading term. Clothing store perhaps. He wondered how anyone could remember the clothes they owned with such a collection.

Quickly entering the room, he moved to the left, leaning over a purple couch, and carefully pulled on the end of a sturdy picture frame containing an original Wyland painting. The artwork swung away from the wall, hinged from the opposite end. Fernando took a headlamp from his rucksack, turned it on, and slipped it over his head. He glanced over his shoulder and saw the telltale red light of a security camera in the opposite corner. He checked over his other shoulder and made sure there weren't any more. There weren't, as he'd been briefed. Moving slightly to his left, he blocked the camera's view with his body as he set about opening the wall-mounted safe.

The home's security system was elaborate and very expensive, so unsurprisingly the safe was of similar quality. Two-foot square, the thick metal door looked dauntingly impenetrable. Fernando felt a bead of sweat running down his back despite the cool, heavily air-conditioned room. His nerves were more settled than during his first job, but the next few seconds would determine everything. If he couldn't open the safe, then as hard as he'd tried, he knew a trail of clues had been added for the authorities to follow, for nothing.

Fernando held his breath while he tapped on the keypad of the digital lock. Hesitantly, he tugged on the handle, and the door swung open. Relief flooded through his body, and he fought back the urge to yell and raise his arms in victory. Don't give the camera anything useful, he reminded himself as he began pulling items from the safe.

Time is the first enemy of a burglar. Minimum time inside was the golden rule, so he knew he shouldn't sort through the items. But he did anyway. Carefully shielding his wrist from the camera, he pulled back a sleeve and glanced at his watch. 9:16pm. He had fourteen more minutes until his drop-dead time. Fernando continued dividing the contents of the safe, scattering them across the couch and putting only the items he wanted into his bag.

He barely heard the distant sound of a garage door opening over the low drone of the air conditioning. Fernando froze. The massive three-car garage was a separate building, with the owner's office above. Was someone arriving home early, or was the sound coming from a neighbour? He couldn't tell from inside the dressing room.

Leaving his rucksack, he rushed into the bedroom, where a window overlooked the courtyard. One of the garage doors was closing behind the tail of a red Porsche, and an elegantly dressed lady in her forties walked towards the house.

Fernando ran back into the dressing room and hurriedly shoved two more small jewellery boxes in his bag before slinging the rucksack over his shoulder. He scrambled from the closet and out of the bedroom door to the bridge. Below, he heard the digital beeps of the front door code being entered on the keypad. Realising he didn't have time to make it downstairs, he sprinted across the bridge to the other side of the balcony, where guest rooms were located.

The front door opened, and the woman stepped inside, humming an upbeat tune to herself. She closed and locked the door before heading for the kitchen and dropping her handbag on the island counter. From his position in the shadows above, Fernando could see the woman until she went to the fridge, built into custom cabinets directly below him. She was an attractive lady with auburn hair and a shapely figure, well presented in a form-fitting designer dress.

He watched her walk towards the bar and game room area, trying not to stare at her backside and keep his focus. She flicked on a light in the bar, rolled a ball across the pool table as she walked by, and began making herself a drink. Fernando realised that when she was done, she'd be walking back in his direction and, with the slightest glance up, he'd be seen. Treading as softly as possible, he made for the stairs which would lead him back into the dead centre of the living room.

She was beyond his view around the corner in the bar, but he had no way of knowing when she'd re-emerge. At the bottom step, he heard a pool ball rolling across the felt and careening into another ball, the clunk echoing around the house. Knowing she was coming back, he slid behind a huge pillowy U-shaped couch. Crouching, he tried to calm his breathing. What would she do next? Either sit on the couch or head upstairs to change, he imagined. At some point she would set the alarm in 'stay mode', and once she did, he was stuck inside, or forced to disarm it before he ran. Neither option felt appealing.

What happened next, he didn't expect. The doorbell rang. He heard the woman set her glass down on the kitchen island, her gleeful hum returning as she padded across the tile floor. Fernando risked a peek over the couch. Without giving himself time to second-guess the decision, he stood and briskly walked across the living room as the woman continued towards the entry. As he carefully opened the boot room door, he heard a squealed greeting as a girlfriend came inside. The voices died away as he closed the door and quietly left the house through the side where he'd entered.

2

DRINKING PROBLEM

My shift ended at ten o'clock, and I was ready. It felt like a long day, because it had been. I never slept much past sunrise, so by seven that morning I'd been freediving on the reef in front of the little shack where I lived. The rest of the morning I'd spent doing bullshit like laundry and cleaning. Sometimes I wished I had a dog for company, but based on my history, people close to me didn't fare too well, so I worried the same would be true for a four-legged soul.

The evening had been boring, with nothing of interest happening in the West Bay area. That wasn't unusual. Grand Cayman was a quiet island at the best of times, but Tuesday nights tended to be extra dull. Most of the tourists, who didn't care what day of the week it was, were farther south along Seven Mile Beach. The local West Bay bars, of which there were only a few, had their regulars bellied up, telling lies about their fishing conquests.

I was happy to sit in silence as we drove around, but my partner, Jacob Tibbetts, liked to chat. We get along really well and I enjoy working with him, but people's obsession with mindless banter confuses me. More accurately, it annoys me. All these stories about his wife, kids, and family were very pleasant, but am I supposed to remember all these details? People burden each other with all this crap and then expect the friend to recall their kid's football score from two weeks ago. I have enough shit to remember.

"How's the family?"

"Good, thanks."

See? Perfect. I was interested in their welfare, and now I know they're fine.

"How's the family?"

"My kid broke his leg jumping off the roof."

"Cool." I like kids that don't sit around playing on their mobile phones.

Also fine. I can remember to ask about his kid's leg in a few days. Of course, I wouldn't have to, as Jacob would keep me informed with a daily commentary on who signed the cast and how the kid gets about on crutches. Jacob's kid hadn't broken a leg, but it makes a good example. I'd really feel like shit if his kid broke a leg now.

'Careful what you wish for' is the phrase in English I believe. At 9:40pm we got the call from dispatch about a disturbance at Benny's Bar and Grill. We were at the north end of Watercourse Road, only a mile away, so we responded. Benny's was little more than a shack with a covered porch area alongside. They served tasty local dishes with fried fish, and in the evenings their patrons liked to stab and shoot each other. Not often, but if trouble happened in West Bay, odds were it was at Benny's.

As with most brawls, by the time we arrived it was all over. On TV, men face off and trade blows for ten minutes, whaling on each other. That's not how it usually works unless the fight is between a couple of UFC contenders. A punch or two is thrown, and it's over with. Generally, if we're called, it's because neither of the pugilists has left, so a general disturbance continues with little actual fighting.

As Jacob parked out front, we could see the place wasn't busy, but one guy was outside, slumped against the waist-high lattice work which bordered the porch. I couldn't tell if that was his usual spot at the end of the evening, or he'd been beaten into that position. As soon as we got out of our patrol car, the barman approached us.

He waved his arms around and did a lot of pointing while blathering about the incident. I didn't understand a word. I was slowly picking up more of the locals' heavily accented dialect, but this guy was talking too fast for me to follow. They spoke English, and I'm fluent in my second language, but Jacob still had to translate for me.

"He says dere's a crazy white guy inside dat punched this fella and now he won't leave."

I looked at the local man slumped against the lattice work. Now I was closer, I could see blood coming from a cut above his left eye. "Check on this one and I'll go inside," I told Jacob.

He looked at me sternly.

"I do white and crazy," I assured him and didn't wait for him to argue.

Benny's didn't blow their expenses on lighting. Under the covered porch was dingy and smelled of fried food and beer. My boots made disgusting sticky noises with each step. Two locals sat at one table to my right and they nodded their heads towards the only other person in the bar. He was a small man, pushing forty by my estimate, scruffy, unshaven, and staring at me.

"Jordy?" I asked, recognising the face and trying to recall his name.

"Jonty," he mumbled in reply. "And who are you, sweetheart?"

His northern English accent was slightly slurred, as though he was a bit tipsy, but he had the look of a professional drinker. Judging by the array of empty beer bottles on the table, he'd either had company or fifty per cent of his bloodstream contained alcohol.

"Constable Sommer," I responded. "I hear you had a disagreement with the fella outside."

Jonty shook his head. "Nah."

"The barman says you hit the guy," I persisted.

"Aye," he replied, his mouth curling into a slight grin. "I did that. But it were in 'ere, not out there."

"So you did punch the man?"

"We had a debate," he explained, looking up at me through tired, bloodshot eyes. "Then he tripped and his head hit on my fist. But I think we resolved our differences, love."

"I'm afraid there's been a complaint against you, so you need to leave the bar," I instructed, slightly amused, but ready to go home.

"Nah, I'm good, thanks," he said, taking a swig of beer as he looked me over. "Don't I know you?"

"AJ Bailey is a friend of mine," I replied, hoping the mention of our mutual friend might help his compliance.

"Aye, that's it," he said, wagging a finger at me. "You were on telly with all that kidnapping business a while back. AJ helped out, didn't she?"

"Yes," I reluctantly replied. Talking about my first big case after I'd joined the Royal Cayman Islands Police Service was one of my least favourite subjects. "Come on, we'll give you a ride home."

"Betta be arrestin' dat man!" the bartender shouted from behind me. "Dat my cousin he put a beatin' to."

"Get up, Jonty, let's go," I ordered, before turning to the bartender. "We're taking him to the station," I said, although I really had no interest in filling out paperwork and prolonging my shift.

"I'm fine, thanks," Jonty muttered, downing the rest of the beer and slapping the empty on the table.

I sighed and looked at Jacob, who was standing outside between the bartender and his cousin, who appeared to have woken up. I was sure his nap had more to do with drinking than the smack he took. Turning back to Jonty, I knocked one of his empty bottles off the table, where it crashed to the floor. He instinctively looked down and away from me, where the bottle loudly shattered into pieces. I moved behind him and picked him up out of his chair with an arm wrapped around each of his, pinning his limbs between us.

I was a little taller than Jonty, but at five feet nine inches, I'm taller than many people. He started to struggle but quickly relaxed, to my relief. I steered him out of the bar and Jacob held the back door to our patrol car open while I bundled the man inside.

"Betta be chargin' him!" the bartender demanded as we got in the car. I ignored him and Jacob started the patrol car.

"Where do you live?" I asked Jonty, who seemed quite content in the back seat.

"You can drop me at Kelly's," he replied.

"We're not taking you to another bar," I informed him as Jacob drove slowly north on Watercourse Road towards the middle of West Bay.

"You're no fun," he complained. "Take a right on Hell Road."

It still made me chuckle when people referenced Hell on the island. The ancient forbidding formation of jagged pinnacles made of black-covered limestone had become a tourist attraction, complete with a gift shop and even a post office. You could send a postcard home from Hell. Naturally, the road running past the small fenced-in area had been named to match.

The police radio crackled into life and dispatch alerted us to a burglary on North West Point Road.

"*Faen*," I grumbled, before responding over the radio while Jacob turned the car around.

"Where we going now?" Jonty asked from the back, apparently thinking this might be a bit of fun.

"Stop," I told Jacob, who pulled to the side.

"What we doin' wit him?" he asked.

I got out of the car and opened the back door. Jonty stared blankly at me.

"Get out," I barked.

Jonty didn't move. "Thought you were takin' me home?"

"Change of plans," I replied impatiently. "You can walk from here."

"I'd rather have a lift, thanks."

I reached in and grabbed him by the most convenient body part I found amongst his flailing hands.

"Owww!" Jonty howled as I dragged him out of the car by his ear. "Police bloody brutality!"

I released his ear and slammed the door closed. "Go home and quit getting drunk and punching people," I said as I got back in the front seat.

"I'll try not to punch anyone for a while," I heard him shout as we pulled away. "But the drinking part's gonna be a problem."

3

EVERYBODY LIES

The house was a modern white building on the water along North West Point Road, only a quarter of a mile west of my friend AJ's dock. As we pulled between the tall white stucco walls into the courtyard, it looked like it could be a condo complex, but I knew it wasn't. The place was obnoxiously huge. Ahead of us was the main building, and to the left was another structure the size of a large home with three double garage doors along the ground floor. Above was a guest house, servant quarters, or whatever rich people put above their oversized garages.

As we came to a stop beside a fancy SUV, a woman opened one side of the double front doors and waved frantically in our direction. She was fifty-something with a trim and curvaceous figure, complemented by a little red dress. I guessed a lot of money had been spent on upgrades to her figure and lack of wrinkles. The kind of money that hides the fact anything had been improved at all. She was strikingly attractive despite the circumstances.

"Are you alone in da house, ma'am?" Jacob asked as we stepped from the car and approached the entrance.

"Yes," she blurted. "Well, no. My friend is with me. Oh my god, do you think the burglar is still in the house?" her proper English accent rising a few octaves in panic.

"We'll search da house, ma'am. No need to be alarmed," Jacob assured her. "Are you da owner of da house?"

"Yes, yes. I'm Estelle Cosgrove," she said. "My husband is away on business in London."

I noticed the glass in her hand was mainly ice, with the remnants of a brown liquid swilling around as she waved us inside. Whatever it had been, she'd drunk it before the ice could begin to melt. Apparently Tuesday nights were a party night after all. I also caught the sparkle from the rock tethered to her finger. Carrying her wedding ring around all day must be quite a workout.

"What alerted you to a break-in, ma'am?" Jacob asked while Estelle led across an open-plan living space with fancy twin staircases rising to the first floor.

"The safe is open," she replied, pointing upstairs. "I was going to change clothes, and I noticed the safe door was open. Our stuff was spread all over the couch."

"Did you touch anything?" I asked, and she looked me up and down disapprovingly.

"No," she replied curtly.

I get those kinds of looks a lot. I'm tall, slender, with long blonde hair and blue eyes. Most people don't expect a nineteen-year-old Norwegian woman to be a constable in Grand Cayman. Guys tend to look at my arse and women seemed pissed off with me right away. It's a good job I don't give a shit or I might get a complex over it.

"Do you know how the burglar entered the house, ma'am?" Jacob quickly took over.

I glanced around the living area and noticed the friend leaning against the kitchen counter. She was a red-headed twin of Estelle. Same expensive look, jewellery, and I presumed the owner of the $100,000 SUV sitting outside. She, too, sipped from a glass with unmelted ice. It would be interesting to see if she'd try to drive away while the police were present. I doubted she'd risk it.

"I have no idea," Estelle replied, throwing her arms up. "I haven't seen any broken windows, but I haven't checked every room since I came home."

"I see cameras," I said, pointing to one discreetly tucked above bookshelves. "We'll need the recording."

The woman nodded an acknowledgement and took an attempted swig of her drink. Ice slapped against her upper lip and she handed the glass off to her friend, who walked towards the bar for refills.

"What time did you come home, ma'am?" Jacob asked as I began checking all the ground floor entry points.

"Nine thirty or thereabouts," Estelle replied.

"And how long had you been gone?" Jacob continued.

"Couple of hours, I suppose," she responded. "We had dinner at Ragazzis, then came back here for a drink and a chinwag."

"Did you set the alarm when you left?" I asked, coming out of a huge side entry room, complete with showers.

Estelle hesitated. "Of course," she finally replied, and I glanced at Jacob.

"Was it still armed when you came home, ma'am?" he asked.

She took a moment again to consider her reply. "No, I suppose it wasn't. I should have noticed, but Sandra was coming by and I must have been distracted," she said, taking her full glass from the friend we now knew was Sandra. "The thief must have disarmed the system."

I was sure she hadn't set the alarm and was now panicking about what the insurance company, and her husband, would have to say about that. Everybody lies. The guilty, victims, witnesses, everyone. If you're wearing a police uniform and talk to anyone for long enough, they'll lie to you. Authority scares people who have a secret. And every beating heart has a secret.

It didn't matter. The system stored a log, so we'd find out soon enough from the security company. What we wouldn't know was whether the doors had been locked or not. I couldn't find any signs of forced entry.

Jacob looked my way, and I gave him a nod, letting him know I'd checked the ground floor.

"We'll go upstairs, ma'am," Jacob said politely, "and once we've checked all da rooms, we'll have you join us."

"Alright," Estelle replied nervously, taking a sizeable gulp of her fresh drink.

We walked up one of the curving stairways and split at the top, Jacob heading into the master suite while I went across the bridge-like balcony to the guest side. We both switched on lights as we went, checking windows and anywhere a person might hide. The two guest bedrooms had their own en suite bathrooms and everything looked spotless and untouched. Probably just as the maid had left them. I crossed the bridge and met Jacob, who was staring at the open wall safe in a large room pretending to be a closet. The dressing area and endless built-in wardrobes occupied more square footage than my whole shack.

Our radios buzzed, and a voice crackled, "Tibbetts and Sommer, dis is Blake and Ebanks. We're outside da house. Over."

Jacob keyed the microphone clipped to his lapel. "Blake and Ebanks, dis is Tibbetts and Sommer, copy dat. All is clear in da house if you'd like to hold station. Over."

The two policemen who'd just arrived confirmed they'd remain outside the house, and we turned back to the open safe. It was above a couch which was coloured purple – something I hadn't seen before, which I guessed was its intent. Various papers and envelopes remained on the couch, but the safe was empty.

"Odd," I murmured, looking at the paperwork again.

"What's dat?" Jacob asked as he took a series of pictures with his mobile phone.

"This guy gets inside the house without leaving a mark," I said and pointed to what I now realised were stacks of papers. "Neatly arranges the contents of the safe to take only what he came for. Then leaves it like this."

"Plus he got past dat alarm," Jacob said, and I threw him a look. "I know," he grinned, "I doubt she set da ting."

We both heard a knock at the front door and walked out to the bridge as Estelle greeted someone. Detective Whittaker stepped inside and introduced himself to the homeowner. Roy Whittaker was in his fifties, tall, slender, with close-cropped hair and glasses. He always wore a neatly pressed suit, even when called out on short notice, late at night. Like tonight. He was also the reason I'd joined the police. The detective glanced up and saw us peering over the balcony.

"Evening, sir," Jacobs said. "Safe up here is the only ting we found so far dat's been disturbed."

"Please wait with your friend in the kitchen, Mrs Cosgrove, while I have a preliminary look," Whittaker said with a smile, then strode up the stairs two at a time.

"Sir," I greeted him.

"Constables," he responded as we led him to the room that resembled a mall clothing shop.

"Any sign of forced entry?" Whittaker asked.

"No, sir," I responded. "The owner claims she set the alarm and didn't pay attention to it being off when she returned from dinner around 9:30pm."

"Do we know what's missing?" the detective asked.

"No, sir," Jacob replied. "We were about to ask Mrs Cosgrove to come up here and tell us."

Whittaker nodded and looked around the room, so we left him to think for a moment and observe. Finally, he turned to me. "Thoughts?"

He loved doing this. I'd told him from the beginning I'd like to be a detective and he'd taken me at my word. At every opportunity, my mentor quizzed and tested me. I'd found it annoying when I first started, as I'd enough to learn and keep up with. But now, after the best part of a year since I began my training, I welcomed the chance to prove myself and move up.

"Priority on reviewing camera footage and alarm logs from the security company," I replied. "The side entry door was unlocked when I checked it, so I suspect entry and exit were made there.

We'll ask the owner, who'll swear it was locked. We should maintain an undisturbed external perimeter and have SOCO look for footprints and any other evidence in daylight." He looked at me patiently, so I kept going, ignoring Jacob, who was unsuccessfully stifling a grin. "SOCO can process the scene here, but the safe wasn't broken into, so the thief either cracked the digital code, knew it, or it wasn't locked either. I doubt he left any trace evidence. And I think the burglar was still here when Mrs Cosgrove came home."

Whittaker nodded slowly and looked around the room one more time. "Why does Constable Sommer believe our perpetrator was still here when the owner arrived, Mr Tibbetts?"

Jacob stopped grinning now he was on the hot seat. "Someting to do wit da way dese papers be all neatly arranged I believe, sir."

"And why does Nora think we won't find any fingerprints or trace evidence?" the detective continued, still looking at Jacob.

"She believe he a professional type, sir?"

Whittaker turned to me. "Any details you'd like to fill in, Constable Sommer?"

I took a step towards the left side of the couch. "He stood here and sorted through the safe's contents," I said, reaching towards the papers without touching anything. "That's why they're arranged in a slight arc." I turned and pointed to the camera over my left shoulder. "He used his body to shield what he was taking from the camera, which suggests he doesn't want us to know exactly what he took. Everything was precise and calculated, so I don't understand why he didn't put the papers back and close the safe. It could have been days or weeks before the Cosgroves even knew anything was missing. That would have guaranteed most forensic evidence would be long gone." I looked at the detective. "So, I think he was disturbed."

Whittaker paused thoughtfully for a moment. "I'll ask the sergeant if you can follow this case," he surprised me by saying. "If he agrees, this might be a good one for you to learn some of the processes we use."

"Okay," I replied, feeling a little excited inside.

"Go downstairs please, and ask Mrs Cosgrove to join me," Whittaker said, switching back to immediate business. "The contact number for the security company should be on each of the keypad terminals. Give them a call and alert them we'll need all the footage from this evening, as well as the sensor activity logs."

"Yes, sir," I confirmed and walked downstairs, trying not to smile.

"You can go up now, ma'am," I said to Estelle, who barely acknowledged me as she walked to the stairwell.

I looked around the room. An alarm panel was on the wall next to the front door, so I went over and took out my mobile. As I punched in the security company's number, which was on the unit as the detective had suggested, I noticed a framed photograph on the wall. My finger froze over the touchscreen and all the breath hissed from my lungs. In the picture, Estelle Cosgrove stood on the shore in front of their Grand Cayman mansion with her husband's arm around her waist. The man appeared a few years older than his wife, but in good health. He wore cotton shorts and a white Tommy Bahama shirt that was billowing in the ocean breeze. They were both smiling. I recognised the man, and the sight of him brought back a flood of nightmares.

4

ANNOYINGLY ADMIRABLE

I laid in bed and waited for the sun to rise. I'd been desperately tired by the time I'd come home from the Cosgroves' house, but sleep had still avoided me. It felt like I hadn't actually slept all night, but I knew I'd drifted off several times and caught patches of rest. Each time I awoke, images and thoughts leapt into my brain, denying me the chance to nod back off.

It was just before 7:00am and the pale light of dawn began peeling back the cover of darkness across the water. I considered going out for a swim and freediving the reef. My morning ritual always calmed me, which I badly needed, but not today. The anger and resentment I felt inside was important. I didn't want to brush it away. I'd worked hard to suppress so many emotions about my past, but the plaster had just been ripped from an unhealed wound, and I wasn't ready to cover it over so quickly. I doubted I could, even if I'd wanted to.

I threw my uniform in my rucksack and dressed in running shorts and an old T-shirt. The ocean called to me as I stepped from the front door onto the deck of my tiny shack and caught the breeze off the water. Usually, being alone was fine with me, and often preferred, but occasionally I craved company. Out of habit, I set a pebble between the door and its frame, my own crude security system. It was no alarm, but it told me if anyone had opened the door in my absence.

Very few people knew where I lived, and I preferred it that way. In my past I'd hidden in various parts of the Caribbean, and while I didn't need to now, privacy felt more comfortable. Jogging through the woods behind my home, with a travel mug of coffee in my hand, I left my isolated world behind me.

I moved the towel from the seat of my old faded blue 1986 CJ-7 Jeep, and fired up the engine. She looked worn out, but ran like a sewing machine, thanks to the loving care of my late boyfriend, Ridley. I drove a little too fast – especially for a police constable – taking Birch Tree Hill Road through West Bay, pulling into the car park for Pearl Divers' dock.

Pearl Divers was a three-boat operation run by a wonderfully grumpy old sailor by the name of Reg Moore. He and his wife, Pearl, were the island parents to a few of us nomads. Sharing the dock was Mermaid Divers, my friend AJ Bailey's dive op. She ran a custom Newton 36 dive special with her friend and only full-time employee, Thomas.

I walked down the pier where dive tanks were being filled from an air line, which was plumbed down the dock from a compressor in a little hut they used as an office and storage. Reg's crew nodded hello as I passed by, and Thomas beamed his broad smile.

"Hey there, are you on day shift?" AJ asked me from the deck of her boat.

My friend is shorter than me, as most women are, thirteen years older, and far more approachable. She has shoulder-length blonde hair with purple streaks and artistic full-sleeve tattoos decorate both her arms. At first glance, she could be confused with the lead singer in an alternative rock band, but her ready smile and enthusiastic demeanour quickly dismiss any illusion of an angst-driven rebel.

For me, she's the big sister I never had, and the only person in the world I feel comfortable sharing some of my feelings with. Since Ridley's murder.

"Evening, but I'm going in early," I replied. "We have a debrief about a case."

"Ooh, is it the robbery I heard about?" AJ asked. "Did you get called there last night?"

I nodded. "Ya."

I knew she'd love to know more, but of course I couldn't talk about a case with anyone. Not with others around to hear, anyway.

"Got time to grab a coffee?" I asked.

AJ looked at her watch and then at Thomas. "You okay if I run to Fosters with Nora? Customers might start showing up soon, but I'll be back in fifteen minutes."

He poorly hid his grin for a moment and scratched the stubble on his chin. "Man, I don't know, Boss. S'pose I can get by best I can. Probably be mighty hungry by da time you're back."

AJ laughed. "You already had a breakfast pastry!"

"Workin' solo'll make me hungry again, I'm guessing," he replied, and his beaming smile returned.

AJ waved a hand at him as she stepped over the gunwale of the Newton and joined me on the dock. "I'll bring you a treat. Don't worry."

We left Thomas, his chuckles mixing with the sound of air hissing from the lines as he moved the manifold to the next six tanks. AJ knew to stay quiet until I felt comfortable talking, which took a lot, as she liked to chatter away like most people do. It's taken a year of training for her to embrace silence. Embrace is probably the wrong word. Tolerate is more accurate. But I embrace the quiet.

"Jacob and I were first on scene to the house," I finally said, once we were driving down the road in my Jeep. "One of the 'look how much money we have' homes just north of your dock."

"What did they pinch?"

"Looks like mostly jewellery, all from a safe," I said, raising my voice over the wind rushing through the open vehicle. "The wife came home to find the safe door open."

"That would be sketchy," AJ responded. It was typical of her to immediately sympathise with any victim. I wasn't so ready to feel sorry for Estelle Cosgrove. "I'd be freaked out if I came home and knew someone had been in my place," she added.

"She was, and she's going to be even more when we get the security camera footage," I said. "I'm pretty sure he was still in the house when she came home."

AJ squirmed in her seat. "Bugger that, thank you. I'm glad I live in a little cottage no one would ever want to break into."

"Anyway," I said, keen to move the conversation on. "The husband is away in England on business, but I saw a picture of the two of them." I paused, not for dramatic effect, but because it made me squirm to say the words. "I know him."

AJ's head whipped around to look at me, her hair blowing across her face, hiding the eyes I knew would be full of pain and sympathy. For me this time.

"From the Fellowship of Lions?" she asked carefully.

I nodded. Three years ago, I'd been recruited when I was barely sixteen by an organisation calling themselves the International Fellowship of Lions. They owned a private resort in Grand Cayman which catered to wealthy club members… with certain tastes. They persuaded young girls like me to work at the resort as 'company' for the members, in exchange for a lot of money, a new identity, and a fresh start after one year of service. We were diligently trained and placed in an isolated environment where they taught us what we were being asked to do was perfectly natural.

It was a sham. After our year was up, the resort owners conveniently disposed of the girls, whom no one would miss. We'd all been recruited from the streets of the Caribbean. Runaways, orphans, and all young, pretty girls existing on the fringes of society. In most people's eyes we were already lost, so when we disappeared completely, no one even noticed.

The body of my best friend, Carlina Arias, was found floating in the open ocean after we'd been told her year was up and she was starting her new life. AJ happened to be the one who found her body. I was lucky. Between AJ and Detective Whittaker, they'd uncovered the true nature of the resort and rescued me, along with many other girls. One of them being Hallie Bodden, a distant cousin of Thomas. She now lived with Thomas's family and I considered her the little sister I'd never had.

If my fellow constables knew of my past, they were kind enough not to mention it, but I suspected few knew. I ran away again after the resort was closed and spent a year sailing, which is when I met Ridley in the British Virgin Islands. It was with him I returned to Grand Cayman and decided to stay. After Ridley was murdered by a Mexican cartel, AJ and Whittaker were the ones who kept my broken heart beating. But now, once again, my past was resurfacing.

"What are you going to do?" AJ asked as I parked outside Fosters supermarket.

I turned the ignition off and sat still.

"I don't know what I can do," I replied honestly. The same question had been pinballing around my head all night. "He obviously avoided scrutiny after the place was closed down."

Most of the members were never prosecuted in any way. Unless it was proven they'd abused one of the girls or had sex with one under the age of sixteen – the legal age of consent in the islands – there were no grounds to charge them. A few had been tried in the press, but the membership list was protected under confidentiality laws, so most were never named in public.

"You could tell his wife," AJ said, looking over at me.

I scoffed, "What makes you think she'd care?"

"I'm sure she'd be pretty upset to know her husband was screwing around with underage girls," AJ asserted, "and paying a hefty membership for the privilege."

"It looks to me like Estelle Cosgrove is doing just fine," I countered. "Of course, she might like an excuse to divorce him and take half of everything. Believe me, they have plenty to go around. The diamond on her finger must be worth more than most locals make in a decade, maybe a lifetime."

"I know I haven't met her," AJ said softly. "But I can't help feeling sorry for her. Imagine your spouse having a dark secret of this magnitude. You'd feel so disgusted and stupid when you found out."

"Well, she must be stupid to not know," I said defiantly, and got out of the Jeep. "We'd better get the coffee and breakfast or you'll be late."

AJ got out of the passenger side and followed me towards the building.

"Well, you know if I can do anything to help, I will," she said. "Just ask."

"I know," I mumbled, stomping into the market. I hated AJ's optimistic view of everything. She was sensibly wary of strangers, but in general, she'd go out of her way to help anybody. I preferred to be sure of someone before I allowed myself to be involved in their lives, or them mine. Her annoyingly admirable empathy for others pissed me off. Especially when she was probably right.

5

STIRRING UP THE PAST

The office for the security company who'd supplied and fitted the alarm system at the Cosgroves' house opened at 8:30am. I sat outside in my Jeep, waiting for them to unlock the front door. I'd gone by the station in West Bay, changed into my uniform, then driven to the central police station in George Town and spoken with Detective Whittaker. As I had time before the case briefing with all departments at 10am, I'd offered to visit Caribbean Security Systems. Their name suggested ambitions to expand, but I only knew of their one office here on Grand Cayman.

A dark-skinned lady in professional office attire unlocked the door and eyed me curiously. Her eyes got wider when I stepped from the Jeep and she saw my uniform. She held the door open as I approached.

"I'm Constable Sommer. I'm here for the security camera footage we requested last night."

The woman's eyes got bigger still. "Something happen at one of our customers' premises?" she asked in a soft local accent. I liked the way the Cayman Islands' people spoke. It was almost musical how the sound of the words rolled smoothly up and down.

"A house on North West Point Road. Burglary around 9:30pm." I said as we walked inside.

"Oh my goodness," she mumbled, and guided me through their small showroom to an office in the back.

I gave her the address, and she tapped away on her computer for a few moments. I noticed a nameplate on her desk read Patti Weaver, and I took a business card from the stack in a fancy little holder.

"What time frame would you like the footage from, and which cameras?" she asked, peering over the triple monitors.

"How many cameras do they have?"

"Twelve inside the home and second building," she said, reading from her screen, "and ten more external cameras."

"*Dritt*," I said, louder than I'd intended.

"I'm sorry?" Patti asked, but I chose not to translate my Norwegian swearing.

"That must be a lot of data to store," I said instead.

"They're on our platinum plan. We keep all the footage on a local server and a cloud back-up for thirty days," she explained. "After that, we have software which edits the data down to motion-sensed footage only. We keep that for six months. It is then wiped and replaced with the new footage. But yes, it's a lot of server space."

I pulled a thumb drive from my pocket. "I brought this."

Patti gave me a sympathetic look and a smirk. "Yeah, that won't cut it." She reached behind her desk and took a small box from a stack on a shelf. "I'll put everything on an external hard drive and invoice the RCIPS. We've done this before."

I put my meagre thumb drive back in my pocket. "7:30pm until 10:30pm, please. And I'll need the sensor logs for the same period."

Patti nodded. "No problem."

"Is it easy for you to see the times when the system was armed?"

"Sure," she said, and looked at me for more information.

"When was it set after, let's say, 2:00pm?"

"It wasn't," she immediately replied.

"Thanks," I said, unable to hide a smile.

Patti looked like she wanted to ask me a question, but I turned away and she went to work on transferring the data to the hard drive.

Thirty minutes later, I stood next to Detective Whittaker, who was sitting at his desk. He'd connected the external hard drive to his computer, and had the video from one of the living room cameras on fast forward as we watched for activity.

"There he is," the detective said, as a figure moved across the room, looking like Charlie Chaplin in the sped-up film.

Whittaker scrolled the video back and let it play at normal speed. The figure entered the frame from the kitchen side of the huge living space, and moved towards one of the staircases.

"Looks like he came in through the side entrance," I commented as I noted the time and camera number in my notebook.

Whittaker checked a camera map he'd printed from the hard drive, then brought up the boot room view, starting two minutes before the footage we'd just watched. We waited and, after a while, the side door opened and the figure entered.

"Moves like a male," Whittaker commented as we watched the man close the door before crouching down, removing shoe covers from his rucksack and placing them over his feet. "And he didn't touch the alarm pad after coming inside."

"The log confirmed the alarm was never set," I said.

"Why on earth would Mrs Cosgrove lie to us about that when she knows they have a sophisticated system which monitors everything?" he asked, shaking his head.

"Probably panicked when she realised she'd screwed up," I countered, wondering why I was making an excuse for Estelle. AJ and her bullshit sympathies, that's why, I thought.

The camera's night vision was grainy and the burglar's all-black outfit hid most of the details anyway, but then he looked up at the camera and shone his torch directly at the lens. The camera instantly became confused, and the screen went black with flashes of light from the torch as it moved around the room. By the time the camera had returned to its night vision mode, the boot room was empty.

Whittaker selected the dressing room camera and again we watched an empty room in the dark for a while until the door opened and a light beam shone across the floor. We continued in silence as the burglar went straight to the framed picture and swung it away from the wall to reveal the safe.

"Well, that's the best way to break into a safe," Whittaker said as we watched the man quickly open the thick steel door. "It either wasn't locked, or he knew the combination."

"He does a good job of shielding what he's doing from the camera," I noted. "Scroll back to before he opens the safe door."

The detective did so, and I realised I'd just given my superior officer an order. "Sorry, sir. Would you mind scrolling back the video?"

Whittaker laughed and played the footage again.

"There," I blurted. "Look at his shoulder. You can see it moving."

"I think you're right," the detective responded. "He's putting in the code."

He stopped the video and sat back, looking up at me. "So what do we know so far, constable?"

Here we go again with the testing shit. "The perp is an average height and build male, with light-coloured skin. He's right-handed, between the ages of seventeen and fifty, and has access to either the homeowner's personal information, or the security company's. More likely the homeowner as the security company wouldn't know the safe code since it's not connected to the system. He entered through the side door, which was either left unlocked or he picked without damaging anything." I took a breath and thought if there was anything else. "I assume he left the same way, but we'll verify that in a minute from the film."

Whittaker nodded slowly as he processed what I'd said. "Explain how you determined skin colour and age, please."

"There's enough contrast around the eyes against the balaclava to say he's not dark skinned, so Caucasian or mixed race. He has no discernible limp and moves nimbly, crouching down without issue, but his movements aren't juvenile. He's more likely between twenty-five and thirty-five, but we can't rule out both sides of that yet."

"Okay, good," he responded and returned to the video footage. Using the sensor log as a guide, he found the moment when Mrs Cosgrove entered the house. Running the living room footage, we watched and waited for what we'd both concluded would happen. Sure enough, when Estelle walked over to the bar, the burglar came down the stairs and hid behind the couch. All I could think about were AJ's words about someone being inside your home.

Estelle walked across the room, passing within six feet of the couch, and before she reached the front door, the figure ran across the living area to the side entrance.

"That takes some steady nerve," Whittaker said, letting out a soft whistle.

"He knew a lot about this house," I commented. "Beyond the codes and access, he knew exactly where the safe was. Could it be an inside job? Insurance fraud."

"Then why not set the alarm, and why come home while the perp was still inside the home?" Whittaker countered.

"For the reason you just asked those questions," I replied.

The detective smiled. "Perhaps. But did Mrs Cosgrove strike you as someone acting?"

I thought for a moment. The woman had seemed genuinely shaken. Then an idea hit me and my mouth was open before I'd had time to think it through. "Maybe she didn't know? What if it was her husband?"

"He was the thief?"

"No, but he could have arranged it."

Whittaker considered the idea, and by his prolonged silence, I guessed he was having a hard time finding a reason my theory shouldn't be pursued. But what would that mean? If the husband became a suspect, his background would be investigated and it might come to light that he was a former member of the International Fellowship of Lions. The police already had that list and had legally been unable to do anything with it. It still didn't provide direct proof of any wrongdoing.

When the resort's computers had been seized, the activity records of the members and personnel files on the girls were found to be heavily encrypted. When an expert attempted to crack the coding, the files self-deleted. With the girls repatriated, the police struggled to get any testimony or identification of who they had escorted. I didn't help matters by going missing for a year.

I wondered what else was in that safe besides the jewellery the burglar stole. He'd been oddly attentive to the contents, and keen to hide exactly what he took from the camera. We only had Estelle's word on what went missing.

"It's time for the briefing," Whittaker said, rising from his chair. "We'll give the footage to SOCO for their analysis. They should be able to give us an accurate height and weight of the man from the video." He walked towards his office door before pausing a moment. "We should take a look into the Cosgroves' financial situation and background too. Maybe you're right about the husband."

I nodded my assent, but the gears in my mind spun at a terrifying speed. Right about what? The man's a piece of shit I'd like to see buried under a mountain of shame? Of course, Whittaker meant we should pursue him as a suspect, but I couldn't help wondering what kind of mess I'd just set in motion. If the man was innocent of burgling his own home, stirring up the past would do nothing but that: stir up the past. I could end up the victim once again.

6

OLIVE BRANCH

The briefing took an hour. I sat quietly in the back of the room, watching and listening, while Detective Whittaker explained the case and directed the different departments. When he suggested Randall Cosgrove should be a suspect, I scanned the room for reactions. I don't know why. Mention of the man's name made my skin crawl, but no one else in the room associated Cosgrove with the International Fellowship of Lions. Yet. The background check would soon reveal his name on the membership list, and then I'd see if anyone tied me to the case. The thought made me feel sick.

"Come with me," Whittaker said after the briefing. "We have an 11:30 appointment with Mrs Cosgrove."

I jumped at the chance to revisit the house. As much as it felt like I was sticking my head in the lion's mouth, I realised my drive for justice was dominating the fear of my past being exposed. Justice? I suspect humans have hidden their revenge behind the word since time began. Whittaker looked at me strangely from the driver's seat of his Range Rover SUV as we drove north towards West Bay. I guess I must have grunted or scoffed at my own thought.

What are you thinking? That was a question I absolutely hated.

In most situations, no one would appreciate hearing what I was really thinking.

"What's our approach with Mrs Cosgrove?" I asked quickly, deflecting the opportunity to be asked the dreaded question.

"I'm hoping she's figured out exactly what he took from the safe," he replied. "It'll be interesting to see her demeanour and mood, given time to think about the robbery."

"You think she'll own up to not setting the alarm?"

Whittaker raised an eyebrow. "We'll see. She's an intelligent woman. If she's kept away from the bar, I imagine she's figured out we would know from the security company's logs."

It dawned on me, as the detective described her as intelligent, that I hadn't paid enough attention to Estelle's background. I'd assumed she was a trophy wife. One day into my detective training and I was already letting emotions get in the way of the investigation.

I took out my mobile and Googled her name. A character on an American TV show called *Criminal Minds* popped up in the top few spots, then the usual social media returns for anyone with that name. Next up were a string of articles about an English dotcom company selling for 45 million euros five years ago. I clicked on one report, scrolled to a picture, and there was the woman I'd met last night.

"*Fy faen*," I mumbled. "She's no regular gold digger."

Whittaker's mouth curled into a slight grin, but he didn't say anything. I was certain he'd already gone through this process and knew I hadn't. Clicking to the second page of search results, I found an article from the *Cayman Compass* newspaper about Estelle donating money and supporting various environmental concerns. I remembered the Wyland painting covering the safe. I closed my eyes and visualised walking through the living room. A 36-inch version of Simon Morris's Amphitrite bronze statue was a centrepiece between built-in bookshelves. A Guy Harvey painting graced one wall of the foyer. Probably an original, if I had to guess.

I searched again on my mobile, this time putting in her name along with the artists I'd noticed. They had purchased each art piece at a charity fundraising auction, Estelle and her shithead husband proudly photographed next to their new acquisition, along with the artist. I felt bad for the artists, unknowingly committing their association to history with someone they'd run a mile from if they knew.

"Looks like she supports some worthy causes," I said, ignoring the bitter taste in my mouth.

"I'd say their marriage is on fairly equal footing when it comes to finances," Whittaker said. "But our background checks should reveal any troubles if there are any."

We turned off North West Point Road between the white walls into the courtyard of the Cosgroves' home. I noticed the big SUV was gone, and the house hadn't got any smaller in daylight. Whittaker parked, and we knocked on the front door. After a few moments, Estelle greeted us.

"Good morning," she said in a friendly, but businesslike tone. "Come inside."

She was dressed in black leggings and a casual blouse that no doubt carried a designer tag. The entrance and living area appeared even larger with sunlight pouring through the tall windows. I paid more attention to the art with a touch more appreciation, knowing at least the money had gone to worthy causes. Plus, I liked the sculpture and paintings.

Estelle offered us a seat at the kitchen island before putting glasses of iced water in front of us both. She seemed comfortable and at ease, but she avoided eye contact with me. Probably my fault. I'm sure she thinks I was curt with her last night and doesn't realise I'm that way with everyone. People are too sensitive. It's not always about them. Although, last night, my first impression of Estelle wasn't spectacular, so it *was* about her.

"Have you had an opportunity to inventory what's missing from the safe?" Whittaker asked after exchanging a few pleasantries.

Estelle slid a piece of paper across the counter to the detective. It was a neatly typed list printed from a computer.

"This should be accurate," she said confidently. "The values are purchase prices, not current market value, which in most cases will be quite a lot more."

Whittaker looked up from the list and his eyes betrayed his astonishment, although someone who didn't know the man would likely miss the minuscule reaction.

"And nothing else apart from the jewellery was taken, Mrs Cosgrove?"

"I don't believe so," she replied. "There was quite a lot of paperwork in there, so I'm not certain. But I can't imagine any of that would be of value to a thief. Insurance papers, titles, etcetera."

Whittaker's mobile rang in his pocket and he took it out, looked at the screen, and declined the call.

"My apologies," he said, moving the switch to silence the device. "I asked about anything else, as the burglar appears to sort through the contents."

I noticed the detective carefully watching the woman before him, studying her for a reaction. He did this with a relaxed expression, his voice even and professional, yet reassuring. If this was the mark of a good detective, I was going to suck at the job.

"You've seen the security camera footage?" Estelle asked.

He nodded. "Thieves generally want to be in and out of a home in the shortest possible time. It was odd that this man took the time to sort through the papers when the jewellery boxes were obvious."

His mobile vibrated on the table. Estelle and I couldn't help but stare at the phone, but Whittaker kept his eyes on the woman before him. When she looked back up from the mobile dancing on the countertop, she looked genuinely perplexed.

"I'm sorry, Detective, but I have no idea. It's possible he took some papers too, but it wasn't the deed to the house, the cars, or the yacht, and it wasn't the valuation paperwork on the jewellery he stole."

Whittaker smiled and glanced at his mobile screen. "My apologies again, Mrs Cosgrove, but it appears there's an issue that requires my immediate attention. I'll step outside to call the office. I'm sure this won't take long."

As the detective turned to leave, he gave me a subtle nod, then dialled a number on his phone and left the house through the front door. I had no clue what his nod meant. Don't talk to the woman? Continue the interview? *Faen!*

"I'm guessing you're not a Cayman Islands native," Estelle said, surprising me. Her tone was pleasant, and she smiled before taking a sip from her coffee cup.

"I'm from Norway," I offered, attempting to appear equally relaxed and non-confrontational. It felt awkward. I was sure she saw through me, although I was feeling less aggravated by the woman today. "I've lived here for a few years."

Estelle smiled again briefly before returning her attention to the coffee. Her olive branch had been extended and now it was up to me whether I swatted it aside or accepted the offer. I let Whittaker's words and manner play back in my mind for a few moments, but all that did was remind me of how shit I would be at this. Usually, silence was perfectly comfortable for me, but now, in this situation, it felt ridiculously awkward.

"When did you have this house built?" I asked for something to ask.

"We finished it three years ago," she replied. "We owned a condo on Seven Mile Beach, but once it became clear we would be spending more time here, we bought the land and hired an architect. It took eighteen months to complete and then we sold the condo. I live here most of the time, but my husband spends half his time in London on business. We kept our flat there."

Every muscle in my body tensed at the mention of her spouse, and a knot formed in my stomach. Did the woman who was looking at me with amiable eyes have any idea what her *gris* of a husband liked to do behind her back?

I unclenched my teeth to ask the next question. "Can you think of anyone here on the island who might wish you or your husband any harm, Mrs Cosgrove?"

7

GATHERING MOMENTUM

Estelle didn't appear to be surprised or distressed by my question. She thought for a few moments. "That's a difficult question to answer, isn't it?"

I shrugged my shoulders. I stopped myself before telling her, 'Not really.' That would certainly get this interview off on the wrong foot. "Think of it in these terms," I continued. "Have you had a disagreement with anyone recently? Do you have a letter from someone's lawyer? Is there a dispute over property, or family tension?"

"Your English is very good," she said in way of reply, which threw me after thinking I'd strung together a Whittaker-like response.

"It's pretty much all I've spoken for the past three years."

Estelle smiled, then looked thoughtful once again. "Nothing comes to mind. When I say it's difficult to answer, I really mean it's often hard to know who has a grievance against you." She sipped her coffee again, and I gave her time to elaborate. People's annoying habit of filling gaps in conversation can work to an interviewer's advantage. "I understand if a neighbour shouted at you about a tree overhanging their land or a noisy party, you'd know they're not happy with you. Or the person on the wrong end of a lawsuit. But what about the oddball who didn't agree with something you said at a charity function? Do they feel aggrieved to the point of breaking into your home?"

She had a point. A nutjob you inadvertently bumped into in line at the supermarket might be as pissed off as a former employee who you'd sacked. It also hit me there was a fine line between keeping an interview conversational and letting it wander off track. This was quickly getting lost in the woods and I'd only just started.

"Besides, surely this was someone targeting a nice home which undoubtedly had items worth stealing," Estelle said.

"As Detective Whittaker mentioned, the thief seemed to be particular about what he took," I retorted, guiding her back towards the path. "He didn't waste time looking through bedside drawers, yet he lingered on paperwork when the jewellery was easy to pick out. It's possible he was looking for something else."

Estelle frowned. "Like what?"

I smiled. "That's my question. What was in your safe that might be of interest? Either monetarily, valuable information, or leverage, perhaps?"

"You make it sound like espionage," Estelle replied with a brief laugh. "Everything in that safe is, or was, personal, not business related."

"You have other safes?" I asked.

"In London we do," Estelle replied, "and another…" She trailed off, but her eyes had already flitted over my shoulder.

"You keep business paperwork in London?" I asked, hoping she'd think I'd missed her slip.

"We do," she said, but the assuredness in her voice had softened. She knew she'd given something away she'd prefer remained unknown. The question was why a second safe on the property was a secret. I decided to leave that bruise alone for a while and make another spot sore.

I smiled as warmly as I could muster. "The burglar didn't have much trouble with the safe code," I said, and Estelle rolled her eyes.

"I'm always telling Randall, my husband, we need to change our passwords and codes on a regular basis, but he gets frustrated when he can't remember them. Honestly, he picks the most obvious four numbers."

"Last four of your mobile number, year born, year married, that sort of thing?" I asked and watched her response carefully.

"Exactly," she replied with a laugh, but her brow had knitted for a moment on 'year married', so I now knew her safe code. And her tell. I was starting to enjoy this. It was a good job I was wearing my police uniform to remind me of which side of the line I resided these days. Not that I'd ever been a burglar, as such. But I had broken into a place or two in my time.

I wrote a few lines in my pocket-sized notebook, knowing Whittaker would expect me to have done so. And he was right. It was easy to forget details after a lengthy conversation.

"And the house alarm was easy," I said, figuring it was time to really knock Mrs Cosgrove off balance.

Estelle looked down at the countertop and drew in a long breath. For a moment I thought I'd got carried away and played that card too soon, but she picked her chin up and shook her head.

"I'm sorry about that," she said. "Bloody panicked a bit, to be honest. I knew Randall would tell me what a stupid bugger I was, and I felt bad enough without him getting on my case. I am sorry."

"Being burgled is traumatic," I said, letting her off the hook. "It's partly why we come back the next day and chat some more. Things tend to be clearer."

That was pretty much bullshit, but I wanted her to trust me. Very few details gain clarity with time. If anything, it's the opposite. Our brains try to fill in the missing information, often creating elements driven by our subconscious biases and opinions. Like my own desire for Estelle to realise her husband was a scumbag.

"When is your husband returning?"

"He was going to take the next flight, which would have been this morning," she explained. "But he has an incredibly important meeting in a few days, so I told him nothing would change between now and then. I'm fine, and he should come after the meeting."

"At the weekend then?"

"Yes, Saturday."

I added the date to my notes and took a drink of water. My blood pressure had risen with the discussion of her husband and I didn't want my tension to come across in my next question.

"So, Mrs Cosgrove, what's kept in the other safe?"

"The one in London?" she asked with a look of confusion. "Just copies of corporate agreements and such."

"No," I responded, keeping my expression as unassuming as possible. "The other one here."

Estelle's eyes narrowed, and her brow knitted again. She went to speak, but thought better of saying whatever her first answer was going to be. A denial, I was certain.

"I don't know, it's Randall's," she admitted. "That's his office above the garage. He works up there while he's on the island. That's how he's able to spend half his time here."

"But you have no idea what he keeps in the safe?" I queried.

Estelle shook her head, and a look of concern washed over her. "I don't even know the combination."

"Is it the same wall-mounted model as the one upstairs?"

She nodded.

"Well, we could probably guess the code with a few tries," I replied, and grinned.

Estelle stared at me in surprise for a second before she burst out laughing. "I can't believe I'm finding anything funny the day after I've had a fortune in jewellery stolen from under my nose."

"I'm sorry," I said, but I didn't manage to wipe the grin from my face.

She waved a hand at me. "That's okay. I needed something to make me feel better. Maybe I'll have a go at safe cracking and find out what he keeps in there," she said, laughing again.

Perhaps it was seeing the woman's tensions release, or because the words were hovering just below the surface ready to burst free at any moment, but I was about to ask her if she knew her husband was a paedophile when the front door opened.

Whittaker strode across the foyer. "I do apologise for the interruption, Mrs Cosgrove, and I must further apologise that we have to leave. But if I may, I'll come back later today to finish our conversation?"

Estelle stood up straight and shrugged her shoulders. "That's fine if there's more you need to ask me, but your constable has covered everything, I believe."

The detective looked at me, then back at Estelle. His expression was full of concern, so I guessed his earlier nod meant 'be quiet and don't screw anything up'.

"In that case, I'll debrief with Constable Sommer on the way back to the station, and I'll contact you if I have any further questions. Thank you for your time, and again my apologies for the disruption."

Estelle walked us to the door and placed a hand on my arm before we stepped outside.

"Thank you," she said, smiling at me.

I nodded and smiled back. Her association with Randall Cosgrove prevented me from liking the woman, but my animosity had disappeared. I felt something along the lines of sympathy, and perhaps a hint of respect and admiration. She wouldn't be the first spouse to be duped by their partner. I wasn't sure if I was glad we'd been interrupted, or disappointed. Her husband's secret would undoubtedly crush the woman, or at least their marriage, and I welcomed anything causing him pain. But at what cost? Both she and I would be collateral damage, our lives turned inside out by the press, and subsequently public opinion. My disregard for people's opinion of me had its limits.

Detective Whittaker stayed quiet until we were clear of the house and heading south towards George Town. Returning to my usual space, I didn't mind or notice the silence as my mind churned through the mechanics of the case and my precarious association with it. When his mobile buzzed with a text message, it dawned on me he hadn't mentioned why he'd been called away.

"What was so urgent?" I inquired.

He read the text in short glances, keeping his eye on the road. "Missing person case," he said absentmindedly, putting his mobile down. "But first, what did you learn?" Whittaker asked, turning his attention to me.

I flipped through pages of my notebook while I focused my thoughts. "She admitted not setting the alarm, and apparently her husband used predictable codes and passwords," I began. "So it's possible the perp started running through obvious options and got lucky."

"Do you believe that?" Whittaker asked pointedly.

I pondered the question for a moment. "I believe her when she said her husband insists on easy-to-remember passwords, but I don't believe our thief stumbled across the right code to the safe."

Whittaker nodded. "Most people have so many logins, passwords and security codes, they can't remember them all. Even if they keep them simple, some websites make you change them periodically, and they vary on password length and content requirements." He glanced over at me. "He probably keeps them in a notebook or in what he thinks is a secure file on his mobile or computer."

"So, more likely he was hacked by the thief?"

"Probably," Whittaker confirmed.

"What about a contact at the alarm company, or hacking their system?" I asked. "Maybe he had a master override code." I groaned before the detective could respond. "The safe wasn't linked to the security company. That would only get him through the alarm, which, as it turned out, he didn't need."

"Exactly," Whittaker said as he took the first exit off the roundabout and joined Esterly Tibbetts Highway, the bypass along the back of Seven Mile Beach. "There's only a few security companies here on the island and they're all diligent about their background checks. But we'll still look at their staff records to be sure. Did Mrs Cosgrove suggest we investigate the alarm company?"

"Not at all," I responded. "She seems to be blaming herself more than anything. Well, and her husband's juvenile passwords."

"Okay, what else did you learn?"

I turned another page in my notebook and paused. A thought was forming in the back of my mind, gathering momentum, and I needed time to think it through clearly. But holding back information I'd learnt would bite me in my skinny arse.

"They keep most of their business paperwork in London, but she let slip there is a second safe in the house here."

"Really? And the thief didn't touch it? What's in it?"

I knew the second safe would get the detective's attention, as it had mine. Probably for different reasons.

"Estelle claims she doesn't know what's in it. The safe is in her husband's office above the garage, and no, the thief didn't find it."

"Or ignored it," Whittaker suggested.

"Or ran out of time," I added. "Estelle interrupted him."

"True," Whittaker agreed.

"From the security footage I'd say he was looking for something other than jewellery," I continued, my police mind overtaking my own agenda. "But Estelle says she has no idea what that might be, and couldn't give me any enemies that might be targeting her or her husband. He returns Saturday."

Whittaker pondered the information for a minute while he continued south towards central station on Elgin Road. Finally, he broke the silence.

"Sounds like you conducted a good interview," he said. "The contents of the second safe might give us a clue as to what the thief was actually looking for, if your theory is correct."

"Do you think it is?" I asked.

Whittaker grinned. "I agree it is strange for the thief to sort through his loot, especially when the easy pickings were so obvious. Could be he was hoping for something with cash value amongst the papers."

I held my breath and asked the next question. "Can we get a subpoena to open the second safe?"

Whittaker shook his head. "I wouldn't ask for one at this stage and I'd be surprised if a judge would grant one based on nothing more than a hunch. But we could ask Mrs Cosgrove to open it."

"She doesn't know the code," I shot back.

"That's right," he said, nodding slowly. "Then we'll keep that in our back pocket and see where the evidence takes us."

I breathed again. The crazy thought bouncing around my mind was based solely on two things. The fact that the thief appeared to be looking for something amongst the paperwork, and my knowledge that Randall Cosgrove had been a member of the International Fellowship of Lions. What if the burglar's intention was to expose Cosgrove? He just looked in the wrong safe.

If that was true, I had even more incentive to find the burglar – but I'd be thanking him instead of making an arrest.

8

STEVIE WONDER PAINT JOB

Jacob sighed for the umpteenth time in the past hour. He was bored. We were parked by the side of West Bay Road with the Christopher Columbus Condominiums in plain sight. Our obvious presence slowed passing cars to the speed limit, as I'd planned. I needed time to look through the files I'd brought with me.

"Can we take a loop around North West Point?" Jacob begged. "If da Sarge sees us sitting 'ere like dis, he'll have us on graveyard for a month."

"No."

He sighed again.

The paperwork I had was the employee files from Caribbean Security Systems with our own background checks included. They had twenty-two owners and employees. I had six more to go through. As expected, the background checks and police records revealed nothing. They wouldn't be employed at a security company if they had a rap sheet. I was learning more by searching their profiles on LinkedIn and social media.

"Where's that licence plate we s'posed to be looking for?" Jacob mumbled, flipping through his notebook. "Dat's it, just went by," he said excitedly, putting the car in drive and looking for a clear spot in the traffic.

I reached over and put the car back in park.

"Come on, Nora," he complained. "Dat guy got a warrant for a bunch o' parkin' tickets. We can still catch him."

"No."

I ignored Jacob's groan from the driver's seat and scrolled through the social media page of Patti Weaver, the woman who'd greeted me that morning. Most of her posts were kids doing shit that kids do, but a shared article caught my attention. The *Cayman Compass* reported 'Home ownership: A distant dream for young Caymanians'.

In the past few years, property prices had soared on the island, putting the most desirable locations well out of reach of the average local family. Foreign expats, corporations, and the wealthy Caymanians were buying up everything and anything with a view of the Caribbean Sea, driving prices through the roof. Two generations ago, islanders could live along the shoreline as they had for centuries, but now they were being pushed inland or eastwards in search of affordable homes.

In most cases, this meant a commute to the west end of the island, where the majority of jobs existed. Traffic had become a major problem as the workforce packed the one road leading into town.

Sharing an article didn't make Patti a suspect, but as I continued scrolling, I found more shared posts, comments and groups she was following which all expressed the need for change. The main focus was restricting property purchases by foreign nationals, as many Caribbean islands enforced. That horse had not only bolted but disappeared over the horizon, in my opinion, but I sympathised with their cause. Simply restricting foreign buyers would only serve to further increase prices. It would take a government-sponsored housing program to help the local families, but that was all out of my control, and current curiosity.

My interest was finding out how passionate Patti Weaver felt about the cause, and whether she was willing to do something radical about it.

Loud, thumping music assaulted my ears through my open window. I looked up and saw a decrepit Japanese import still a hundred metres away. It was lowered, with aftermarket wheels worth more than the rest of the vehicle, and some kind of blue light glowed underneath. The patchy flat black paint appeared to have been applied by Stevie Wonder, and the driver had his seat tilted back so he could barely reach the steering wheel or see over the dashboard.

"Haha!" Jacob yelped and looked at me.

I nodded. Why these *drittsekker* thought the rest of the island wanted to listen to their shitty music was beyond me. The fact that the idiot didn't think to turn it down while he passed a police car served to further prove his decision-making abilities. Jacob pulled the car around and followed one car behind the bass-reverberating rust bucket.

I was only nineteen, so I was supposed to relate to the youth, and I respected individuality, but why people chose to express themselves to the annoyance of others baffled me. Put some headphones on and blow your own eardrums out. At least wind up your windows.

The idiot turned right on Cemetery Road without using his indicator, and that was the final straw. I flicked on the siren and lights, and watched his head jerk up as he finally looked in his rearview mirror. I was slightly disappointed when he pulled over right away. It was the first decent decision he'd made, but a chase would have been more fun. I put the files down and got out once Jacob came to a stop.

I was almost to the driver's side door before the kid turned down the music and tilted his seat up.

"Licence," I demanded and watched the kid's eyes get bigger when he realised he'd been pulled over by a blonde-haired white chick. He was probably hoping for a distant cousin he could talk into letting him off.

He pulled a wallet from his back pocket and rummaged amongst scraps of paper to find his identification. I wondered if the notes were girls' phone numbers. It equally baffled me how some women were attracted to this ridiculous display.

I looked at his licence. He was seventeen years old. The picture was so recent it actually looked like him.

"Why you pickin' on me, man?" he grumbled.

"Because you broke the law," I replied, looking through the rear side window where the back seats had been replaced by a wooden box containing a pair of huge speakers.

"I ain't doin' nuttin' wrong, man."

"Did you indicate when you made the turn?" I asked.

"What?"

"Did you use your turn signal at the junction back here?" I repeated, pointing to the corner.

"Are you serious, man?" he replied. "Sure, I used it."

"Okay, I'll write you up for a fix-it ticket."

"Fix what, man?" he complained.

"Your indicator," I said. "If you used it, the bulb must be out."

"Shit, man. Maybe I forget dis once."

"Okay," I said pleasantly. "Do you normally wear glasses to drive?"

The young man lifted his mirrored sunglasses and rested them on his head. "No, man. I got perfect eyesight."

"It seems like you're having trouble seeing, sir," I continued, grinning to myself.

"No, man," he said, getting more agitated. "I see great."

"Then perhaps you'll notice I'm not a man."

The kid looked at me in confusion. I watched the penny slowly and finally drop. "Dis is bullshit, ma... miss. You pickin' on me 'cos I'm black."

I stared at him. "We pulled you over for disturbing the peace and failing to indicate for a turn. Do you know what indicate means?"

"Course I do."

"What does it mean?"

He rolled his eyes. "Indicate, like use da turn signal."

"Indicate means to point something out or show intention, which is a courtesy to other drivers, a safety measure, as well as the law."

My words appeared to bounce off his forehead and ricochet around West Bay.

"We didn't pull you over because you're black, pink or polka dotted. We pulled you over because you're an idiot playing your music too loudly. I don't give a shit what you listen to, but I didn't ask to hear it and neither did anyone else on the island. So, turn it down."

I shook my head. "Anyway, now I have probable cause: I could search your car and I'm sure I'll find a dozen more infractions."

He frowned as he processed my rant. "You don't got probable cause to search da car," he finally retorted defiantly.

"I can smell the weed from here."

His expression switched from annoyance to the realisation he could be in deep shit.

"You don't need to be worrying none, ma'am," he hurriedly blurted. "I'll keep da music down and indicate the shit outta my turns."

I tore the ticket from my pad and handed it to him. He read the citation and looked up at me with a frown.

"Dis is just for da indicator broken, which ain't broken."

"Should be easy to show you've fixed it then," I replied, and leaned a little closer. "But if I catch you blasting that shitty music again, I'll tear this piece of crap car apart and write you up for everything I can find, including the weed."

"Yes ma'am," he responded, and forced a smile. "Tank you ma'am."

I walked back to our police car, where Jacob was grinning at me.

"You have fun?" he asked as I got in.

"A little bit," I replied, picking my files back up. "He'll behave for a few weeks at least."

We watched the kid pull away. "Now can we make a patrol?" Jacob asked.

"No," I replied. "Not yet. Give me a few more minutes and then you can drive around wherever you want."

Jacob sighed again, while I returned to my mobile, and Patti Weaver's social media account. If campaigning for locals' rights was a sign of criminal activity, we'd have half the population as suspects. And be in North Korea instead of a beautiful Caribbean island democracy. I remained objective and searched for anything that would indicate a direct tie to the Cosgroves, or more aggressive activity towards foreigners.

Rather than scroll through years of posts, I began searching subjects, starting with the word 'protest'. I learnt Patti was an animal lover and believed in equal rights for the gay community. Next, I searched 'illegal', 'unlawful', and 'unjust', coming up with nothing pertinent.

It always struck me as curious and weird how thoughts and ideas fall into our conscious mind. I don't know why I searched for 'International Fellowship of Lions', but I did. Maybe because the subject had been forced back into my brain over the past thirty-six hours. A brief article I was all too familiar with from a time I tried my best to forget showed up in the search. I began looking through the fifty-something comments on Patti's reposting.

I didn't have or follow social media for a reason. My business was my business. The opinions of people who didn't know me or care about me were meaningless. As I read through the comments of strangers making their statements about shit they had no understanding of, my blood boiled. People slamming the girls for allowing themselves to be treated this way.

"*Faen ta deg,*" I muttered a loud without realising it.

"Are you okay?" Jacob asked. "I know dat's a really bad word you just said."

I nodded. "Yeah, sorry. I'm fine."

Jacob made me teach him a Norwegian word every day. I probably should have started with 'please' and 'thank you' instead of swear words. Of course I said I was fine, but I wasn't on many levels. I now had a further dilemma. Patti Weaver was vehemently defending the girls from the resort, which made me appreciate her. But if my theory about the burglary targeting Cosgrove because of his ties to the resort was correct, I may have just found the insider who provided the necessary intel to get the thief as far as the safe. A connection I wasn't sure I wanted to reveal.

9

DECISIONS

The green sea turtle didn't care who knew about my past. He didn't even care that I swam alongside him as he foraged for his breakfast. His powerful beak crunched on an orange sponge and smaller fish swarmed in to collect the tiny splinters which scattered all around.

I left the busy microcosm, returning to the surface 25 feet above for a breath of air. As I refilled my lungs, I squinted towards the shore where the sun was rising over the island beyond Barker's National Park. Turning to stare across the open ocean, the light sparkled on the sparse ripples disturbing the glassy surface. It wouldn't be long before boat wakes and the steady breeze would steal the serenity from the water.

Sleep had come in fits and starts, and nightmares I thought I'd finally suppressed returned. It was bound to happen with feelings stirred up about the resort. Some memories soften events with time, shaving the rough edges away and recalling more positive emotions. Others do the opposite. When you look back and realise how damaging and hurtful a circumstance truly was, the situation you took in your stride at the time becomes jarringly painful in recollection.

Drawing in a long gentle breath to fill my lungs, I dropped

below the surface and kicked down at an angle, starting my underwater swim towards shore. As I silently glided through the marine world, which lived in oblivious bliss to the turmoil above, clarity seemed to envelop my thoughts. Patti Weaver seemed like a lovely lady who supported the issues a good human being should be concerned with. She didn't deserve the scrutiny of the police, or the doubts that would inevitably arise from her employers regardless of whether she was innocent.

Returning to my shack, I washed the salt away under the outdoor shower and towelled myself dry on the deck before going inside to dress. I'd worn my uniform home, which cut out a stop at the West Bay station on my way to George Town. I filled a travel mug with coffee – a new addiction for me courtesy of AJ – and tried to keep my white shirt clean as I walked through the woods to my Jeep.

On the drive into town, my decision felt right and by the time I had parked and taken the files with me as I entered the main station, I was firm in keeping my suspicions to myself. Twenty minutes later, sitting across the desk from Detective Whittaker, I'd changed my mind.

I'd attended the morning briefing, where a few details had been discussed regarding the robbery, but the primary focus had been the missing person case. A fifteen-year-old girl, to be precise. Marissa Chandler. Adding a name always made it more urgent and personal somehow. Broken home, mother with alcohol and drug problems, patchy school attendance despite outstanding grades, and worst of all, she was a pretty kid with an innocent, childlike face.

"It might be happening again," I blurted, forcing the words from my lips so I couldn't turn back.

Whittaker looked at me with a confused expression. I stood and closed his office door, then leaned on the back of the chair, giving my hands something to grip in an effort to stop them from shaking. I had his undivided attention.

"There might be a connection between this girl and the

robbery," I said, scrambling to straighten my thoughts. I'd been keeping the evidence of the two cases separate in my mind, and now I needed to merge them to make any sense.

"How so?" he asked.

"Randall Cosgrove was a member at the International Fellowship of Lions."

"I know," he replied softly, to my surprise. It was bound to surface in the background checks, but he hadn't said a word or brought up the point in the briefing. In fact, he'd stated both Randall and Estelle had come up clean in the background checks so far. Perhaps for my sake. Or because Cosgrove's resort membership appeared to have no bearing on the robbery. Regardless, my own connection would now force him to boot me off the case, but the girl's safety was more important than my ego. Or the humiliation I would face when this detail was revealed.

"But I haven't seen a connection between Cosgrove and Marissa," he added.

"It's thin, but I found a link," I said, feeling bad for dragging someone into the case who I figured was trying to do a good deed. "Patti Weaver works for Caribbean Security Systems. She was very vocal about the resort when it was booked, and she's an advocate for locals' rights to island property."

Whittaker thought for a moment. "But even if this woman leaked information to aid the thief, that still doesn't connect either of them to Cosgrove's former affiliation with the resort."

His use of the word 'former' might be accurate, but for me, and I was sure the other girls too, past tense didn't make the nightmares go away.

"The thief was looking for something else in the safe," I explained. "You said yourself it made no sense to sort the contents. I believe he was looking for evidence against Cosgrove – he just looked in the wrong safe. I think they're working together to expose former members who got away with being paedophiles."

My own use of plurals was subconscious, but it did raise the question of whether the thief would strike again. If my theory held any water, of course.

Whittaker's eyes narrowed, and he studied me for a moment. "There's a bunch of assumptions tying all that together, Nora," he said softly, "and not a shred of hard evidence."

"I hadn't planned on saying anything until I had something more concrete," I admitted. "But when I heard the details about the girl, I had to speak up. She's the exact match of a girl they would target."

"Except she's local," he replied. "The resort's downfall was recruiting Hallie Bodden. You'd think they'd learnt that lesson."

"*They* would have, but *they're* all in prison," I retorted. "The members didn't recruit anyone. They're the end user. My guess is someone else has recognised the demand and is now supplying girls again."

"Maybe this wasn't the best case for you to gain experience after all," Whittaker said sympathetically. "You're in danger of making the evidence fit your theory, Nora."

"Yeah, yeah, I know it sounds like that," I said more impatiently than I'd intended. "But if there's even a chance this girl, or others, are being trafficked, we have to investigate."

The detective could be right. I had an emotional investment that might be skewing my judgement, but the potential downside of ignoring my hunch was too great.

"What do you suggest we do?" he asked pointedly.

"You interview Patti Weaver and see what you think," I quickly replied, "and let's look for any other missing person cases that fit the MO."

"I can tell you there's no other missing persons which fit the profile," Whittaker said. "We've had a couple of runaways in the past nine months, but they were both found and returned home."

"Then talk to Patti," I persisted. "If you think she's in the clear, then I'll drop it. If she's suspicious at all, then we can approach her boss and see about a forensic IT examination of her computer."

The detective sat back in his chair and pivoted back and forth on the swivel, drumming his fingers on the desk. "Okay, we'll stop by on the way to visit Marissa Chandler's mother. I'll talk to Weaver, but don't get your hopes up."

"I only have one hope," I replied as he stood. "I hope Marissa is another runaway and we find she's safe somewhere. Everything else will be what it will be."

10

HIDING SOMETHING

The drive to Caribbean Security Systems only took a few minutes. The previous day, I'd met Patti Weaver when the office opened, and no one else had been there. Today, it was mid-morning, and the place was bustling with people, making it hard to be discreet about a chat with the Caymanian woman. We asked to see Patti, and a young receptionist called her office. A moment later, Patti came to the front and greeted us. I could already see the concern on her face.

She led us to her office, and I closed the door as she offered us a seat.

"We just have a few follow-up questions regarding the Cosgrove break-in, if you can spare a minute?" Whittaker asked.

"Of course," Patti replied. "Anything I can do to help."

It takes a very arrogant individual not to be nervous when being questioned by the police, regardless of their innocence. It's unsettling, and most people wonder whether their involvement in a situation, however small, may have adversely contributed to the crime. Not to mention almost everyone has something in their lives, present or past, they'd rather not have known. For all she knew, we were here to ask routine questions about alarms. Yet Patti's hands were shaking.

"What is your role with the company, Miss Weaver?" Whittaker asked.

"It's Mrs," she replied. "And I'm what we call a security specialist. I help home and business owners plan their systems to suit their needs and budget."

"I see," the detective said with a pleasant smile. "So you met the Cosgroves when they purchased a system?"

"I advised them on their security during their house build," Patti replied. "But I haven't seen them in person since then."

I noted she was quick to distance herself from the victims. Or was I doing what Whittaker suggested? Shoving puzzle pieces into spaces they didn't fit. The line between emotional bias and following the evidence was about as grey as it gets. Especially to the individual whose emotions were involved. I was a black and white person and liked to think I was a logical thinker, but this crap had me second-guessing myself at every turn.

"Were they amenable during your interaction?" the detective asked. "Did they follow your advice?"

"They were very pleasant, as I recall," Patti replied, her shoulders noticeably relaxing. "Money wasn't really an issue, so they were happy to get the best of almost everything."

Pretty clever, I thought, Whittaker making the conversation about the Cosgroves. I learnt something new every day I spent with the man. I was happy to observe and listen.

"Almost everything?" the detective asked, picking up on her caveat.

Patti hesitated a moment before replying, a good indication she was managing and filtering her words.

"Just the safes really," she finally said. "They went with good quality pieces, but didn't integrate them into the main alarm system."

"Did they say why?"

"If they did, I don't recall," she replied. "It was a few years ago."

"Was that an unusual choice, based on the elaborate system they chose?"

Patti shrugged her shoulders. "Perhaps. Some folks think if the thief gets as far as the safe, then they've outsmarted the alarms, so nothing will stop them."

"Makes it easier when they're not set in the first place," Whittaker commented with a wry smile.

"Very true," Patti responded with a chuckle. He had her nicely relaxed now.

"Do your customers ever seek your advice on passcodes?" Whittaker asked nonchalantly. "Seems like an important part of the process."

"We offer a guideline in the paperwork we supply," she replied. "It contains general dos and don'ts. Most of the alarm keypads only have numbers and use a four-digit PIN code, which means 10,000 variations. So, picking a sequence of numbers that aren't obviously connected to you, but you can remember, is the key."

"Does the company keep a record of those codes?" Whittaker asked.

"We don't," Patti replied. "The client sets them on their own unit and they're retained internally."

"But every system has a master override, correct?"

"That is correct," she responded with a slight crease in her brow. "The customer sets up a verbal password with us, and if the alarm goes off, they're called and we'll only turn off the alarm and stand down emergency services if we're given the correct verbal password associated with the individual."

"But that verbal password is only used in the case of an accidental alarm. It can't be used to disarm the system at the house?"

"That's right. If we're given the correct password, we use our master override to turn the alarm off," she confirmed.

Whittaker smiled again. "Perfect. Thank you for explaining

everything so clearly. It helps us understand not only what happened but also what is possible."

Patti smiled in return and shuffled some papers on her desk. She was ready to be done. "Like I said, anything I can do to help." She slid a business card across the table. "Please call me if you think of anything else."

"We won't keep you much longer, Mrs Weaver," the detective said amiably. "Just a couple more questions if you'd indulge me while we're here."

Patti looked deflated, but she nodded.

"Has anyone contacted you recently with regard to alarm passcodes? Anyone suspicious, or who asked suspicious questions?" Whittaker asked, maintaining a friendly tone.

Patti's whole body tensed. "As I said, we don't have the alarm codes, Detective."

"Yes, you explained that," he continued. "But that's not what I asked."

The woman's mind was frantically scrambling, but was this guilt, or just the suggestion from Whittaker?

"No," she responded. "I can't think of anyone or anything suspicious."

"Because the master code would work on the keypad, wouldn't it?" he asked, unrelenting. "A thief wouldn't need the homeowner's code."

Patti took a deep breath and gathered her wits. "A thief doesn't need any code if the system isn't set, Detective," she responded firmly. "And I assure you the master codes are not something we make available to anyone except our monitoring staff who, as you know, are thoroughly background checked."

Whittaker stood and extended a hand. Patti got up from her chair and shook the offered hand.

"Thank you, Mrs Weaver. We'll be in touch if we have any further questions. I appreciate the time you've given us."

Patti looked relieved to see the detective open the door to leave.

"One more question," I said as I stood. "When you talk about the monitoring staff, they're not watching camera feeds from the properties, are they?"

Patti shook her head. "That would take a staff of a hundred and be cost prohibitive. If a company has that need, they usually employ their own onsite security. Our monitoring personnel have a computer workstation which alerts them when an alarm is triggered. We don't even have live access to all the residential cameras unless the client pays an additional fee and signs a waiver. We discourage the service as there are too many issues with privacy. The feed is recorded on our servers, but isn't viewed by our staff."

I thanked her and followed Whittaker out of the building. As we drove away to our next interview, he looked over at me. "What do you think now, after meeting her a second time?"

I considered his question for a few moments. What I thought was Patti Weaver was a nice lady who may or may not have helped a burglar break in to the Cosgroves' house. If she did, it was for honourable although perhaps misguided reasons. But Whittaker was digging for my opinion on next steps, which ultimately didn't matter. It would be his decision as to whether we'd further pursue Patti as a suspect, and I knew he wouldn't at this point. She'd revealed nothing that incriminated herself or justified turning her life upside down.

"She's hiding something," I replied. "But we have nothing beyond a suspicion."

"Everybody's hiding something," he said with a grin.

"Sure, but she squirmed when you asked about anyone suspicious," I added, replaying the conversation in my head.

"I'd be uncomfortable if a police detective suggested I may have leaked secret passcodes. Wouldn't you?"

I wasn't the best example on which to judge people's reactions to anything, but his point was valid.

"She didn't push back or get offended," I pointed out. "Most people's reaction would be to defend themselves, but she became evasive."

"There you go," he said, nodding approvingly. "So what's our next move with Patti Weaver?"

Usually, I'd think this through to myself before answering, but like those stupid maths tests in school, he wanted to see how I came by my solution. So I talked more than I liked to, sharing my thoughts. "We don't have enough evidence to justify a warrant to search her computer, and it would be a waste of time anyway, now she's been warned we're interested in her. Same with her bank account and mobile records, except with those she couldn't delete any suspicious transactions. I'd start with family and known contacts. Look for anyone with a criminal record and especially ties to the causes she's campaigned for. If we discover more evidence, then get a warrant for the bank and mobile."

"Where would you start on finding her contacts?"

"Go back over her social media," I responded. "Look at her friends list and see who she tags in posts, and who tags her."

"Good," he said, sounding like a proud teacher. "I can have someone at the station start searching."

"I already went through her social yesterday, so I'm familiar," I offered. "I can handle it during my shift this afternoon."

"Okay," he said with a hint of concern in his tone, and I felt him looking at me again.

"I'm fine," I said, deflecting what I guessed was coming. I didn't want to get pulled from either set of duties, for different reasons. Gaining respect amongst the local constables had taken a lot of effort, so I wasn't throwing that away by leaving them hanging if I missed my shifts. On the investigation side, I had career and personal reasons to see this through.

Whittaker slowed the SUV, and I realised we were in the worst part of George Town. It was amazing how quickly we could go from idyllic island paradise to office buildings for one of the banking capitals of the world, to a small area known locally as Dog City. Poverty has a way of assembling and taking over entire streets or sections of a town. I wondered if anyone ever moved into Dog City or if the dilapidated homes were simply passed down amongst family members who could never rise out of their circumstances.

Whittaker pulled me from my thoughts. "I'm curious about the question you asked."

Instead of responding, I looked out of the side window as he stopped in front of several small shacks crammed into what appeared to be one parcel of land. A few battered toys were scattered across the front yard and vehicles in various states of disrepair rested on jack stands. I got out of the car and waited for Whittaker to point out which building belonged to Marissa Chandler's mother. I'd deliberately dodged his inquiry. He should know better than to make a statement when he intended to ask a question. I don't do idle chit-chat. And everybody's hiding something.

11

DOG CITY

Stepping inside the tiny home was like entering a room of rejects. Every piece of furniture must have been pulled from the dump. The carpet was stained and filthy, rags hung instead of curtains, and a wall-mounted air conditioner hung loosely in its fixture, idle. The woman staring at us was certainly an outcast from society. Dressed in cotton shorts and a faded orange crop top, neither of which had seen the wash in a long time, her body was thin and emaciated. Her hands jittered and her eyes constantly searched the room.

"You find my girl?" she growled, struggling to light a cigarette.

"Not as yet, Mrs Chandler," Whittaker replied.

Elise Chandler dropped into a threadbare upholstered chair, but we chose to continue standing. I wanted no part of my body to contact anything in the shack and figured I might need to throw my boots away once we left. The heat in the room was unbearable, and the stench was like sticking your head in a rubbish bin. None of which Elise appeared to notice or care about.

"Then why you 'ere?" she asked, her eyes flickering our way before shakily moving on to whatever she thought she was seeing in the rest of her home.

"We had a few questions for you that might help us locate Marissa," Whittaker said.

"If I knew where she at, don't you tink I already bring her arse home?" the woman mumbled. "Now she gonna lose dat job."

"Where did Marissa work, Mrs Chandler?"

"I ain't no Mrs, damn it. Call me Ell if you call me someting," Elise replied, then seemed to lose her train of thought.

"Her work, Ell?" Whittaker tried again.

"She do accountin' books for da garage down da way," she said, waving a hand in a direction which may have made sense to her but seemed to indicate the southern hemisphere to me.

"And she works there after school or on weekends?" the detective asked.

Elise frowned as though it was the dumbest question in the world. "She had enough schooling. Dat place just put ideas in da girl's head."

"If Marissa wanted to get away for a few days, any friends or relatives she might stay with?" Whittaker asked, remaining patient and polite, which was beyond my capabilities with this woman. I was glad he was doing all the talking. I'd have her in handcuffs.

We received the same look as the previous question. "She don't have no time for friends, we strugglin' just gettin' by. Dat ain't obvious to you?" she complained, gesticulating at the refuse dump she called home. "Anyway, da copper already ask all dis crap. Why I gotta say dis again? You should be out dere lookin' for her."

Whittaker and I both looked up as we heard footsteps in the back of the shack and the sound of a cap being released from a bottle. A tall, thin, dark-skinned man strode into the front room and stopped in his tracks when he saw us. A scowl instantly crossed his face, contorting the wrinkles around his eyes as he glared specifically at me.

"Who da hell dis?" he bellowed, and Elise turned in her chair, finally noticing the man.

"Police, again," she grumbled. "Dey ain't done nuttin' yet. She still gone."

"Hello DeWayne," Whittaker said with a smile.

The man squinted, finally looking away from me and seeing the detective. His chin lifted in defiance. "What you want?"

"We'd like to find Marissa Chandler," Whittaker responded firmly. "Perhaps you can give us some idea where she might be. Or why she left."

"I don't know nuttin' 'bout dat kid, 'cept she ain't pullin' her weight round 'ere," DeWayne answered.

Whittaker smiled. "While I have you here, how about I check in with the station and see if you have any outstanding paperwork we may need to address," he said, taking his mobile from his pocket.

DeWayne's eyes gave away his intention, and I moved in unison with him. He had to turn to run, which gained me a step or two across the living room, but the beer bottle flung behind him took away any gain as I ducked to avoid being smashed in the face. He burst out of the back door, which hung loosely from one hinge, and shot between a dead car and a pile of unidentifiable junk. I almost twisted my ankle on a minefield of rubbish and objects scattered across the dirt, and was glad I was wearing boots instead of trainers.

DeWayne vaulted a broken-down waist-high fence, which I hurdled and gained back a step. He was nimble for a worn-out old druggie and knew the terrain, but I followed his moves and was slowly gaining. I considered pulling my Taser. I was probably close enough to hit him, but I might lose ground by taking it from my belt and setting up the shot. Besides, I was enjoying the adrenaline rush of the chase.

He leapt another fence and landed awkwardly on a tree root jutting from the dusty dirt of another backyard. I changed my angle as I left the ground and cleared the root, gaining another step. Ahead, he was either going through a house, or jumping another fence, but this one was higher and would require scrambling over. He angled towards the fence and I knew I had him. Until the dog appeared.

Leaving the back door of the run-down house in a full sprint, the Cayman brown hound had his jaw open, emitting a low growl as he anticipated the leg he intended to bite. Veering left, I put DeWayne between me and the dog, and focused on the fence. I heard a clattering as the man I was chasing lunged at the old metal and chain-link barrier. I reached the fence a moment later and leapt into the air, aiming to catch the top rail with both hands and hopefully one foot.

From my right, I heard the dog snarling, and a yelp, which I assumed was from DeWayne. My hands found the top rail and pain shot through me as sharp ends of the poorly cut chain-link scratched into my palms. My right foot hit the rail as well and my forward momentum, along with a solid push, flung me over into the next yard. I landed on all fours and looked up, panting for breath.

DeWayne hung over the fence, clinging to the chain-link on my side with his hands, while the excited dog retained one of his legs on the far side, a mixture of ankle and trouser leg clamped in its vicelike jaw. I stood and dusted myself off while the dog snarled and shook its head violently. DeWayne screamed like a man having the flesh chewed from his leg.

Deputy Dog seemed to have the perp successfully restrained, so I took the opportunity to read DeWayne his rights.

"You do not have to say anything, but it may harm your defence if you do not mention when questioned something which you later rely on in court. Anything you do say may be given in evidence," I said calmly, while the man thrashed and attempted to kick the dog with his free leg. "I know you're a little distracted right now, so just nod if you understand your rights, sir."

"Get da fuckin' dog off me!" DeWayne screamed.

"What goin' on out 'ere?" a woman shouted from the doorway of the home. "I can't hear da telly over all dis noise!"

"Sorry for the disturbance, ma'am," I said, smiling from the safe side of the fence. "Perhaps you could call your dog off, and we'll be on our way."

"Dat DeWayne?" she said, walking towards us.

"Yes, ma'am," I replied, as DeWayne was having trouble assembling coherent sentences.

"What da hell you up to now, DeWayne?" she scolded. "Here, Dug."

The dog stopped writhing around but didn't let go of his pound of flesh, his eyes trying to look behind him to see if his owner was serious.

"Did you name him after the dog in that animated movie?" I asked.

"Dat's da one," the lady replied. "Up it called, I tink."

"That's it," I said loudly over DeWayne's moans. "I don't watch TV, but my friend made me watch that movie with her. I liked it."

"Get him da fuck off me, whatever his name is!" DeWayne screamed.

"Dug, here!" the woman said firmly, and the dog reluctantly released his prey.

DeWayne slumped over the fence, landing in a heap in the dirt on my side. His ankle was a bloody mess and his shirt was ripped from the chain-link. I guessed his stomach was torn up from the wire, too.

"Nice meeting you, ma'am," I said with a wave. "And thank you Dug for your assistance."

"Take care now," the lady replied as she walked back to the house, shooing Dug in front of her. "You too, DeWayne."

I pulled his hand from clutching his bloody ankle and slapped a cuff around his wrist. With a knee in his back, I pulled his other arm behind him and cuffed the other wrist.

"Alright, get up, let's go."

"I need an ambulance," DeWayne moaned.

"I need a holiday in Bali, but neither of us is getting what we want, so pick your arse up."

"Dis is police brutality, man," he complained as I hauled on his arm.

"Yeah, I get that a lot. But you're the silly bugger who ran into that yard," I told him. "Not my fault Dug took a liking to you."

DeWayne finally got to his feet, or his foot as he couldn't put any weight on the dog chew which doubled as a limb. Sirens wailed, and I rolled my eyes. Typical Whittaker. We could have rolled out of Dog City nice and quietly with DeWayne bleeding in the back of his SUV, but now every house would empty out in a community that doesn't usually support RCIPS fundraisers.

I dragged the hobbling DeWayne down the side of the shack we'd ended up behind, to a sea of flashing lights and constables. Whittaker ran down the road to meet me.

"What on earth happened?" he asked, looking at DeWayne's bloody shirt and leg.

"He didn't run fast enough," I replied, shoving our perp towards a couple of constables.

"I figured you'd catch him," Whittaker said.

"Somebody beat me to it," I replied.

Whittaker looked around at the other constables, wondering who may have assisted. "Who caught him?"

"Dug did."

"Doug did?"

"Yeah, Dug," I said, grinning.

"Who's Doug?" Whittaker asked, not recalling a constable named Doug.

"This place is called Dog City for a reason, sir," I chuckled, walking away towards the detective's SUV.

12

GOING NOWHERE

Whittaker parked his SUV at the central police station, but left the engine running. I gave him a moment to gather his thoughts.

"I don't wish to discount your theory about young Marissa Chandler, but I'd say it's likely she's run away," he said.

"Why would anyone stay in that hell?" I agreed. "But she fits the profile, sir. A girl raised in that environment is prime for tempting. I wouldn't be surprised if she was abused at home. Certainly emotionally, if not physically. Being rewarded or promised a better life might feel like progress, even if it meant sacrifices."

He considered my words as he usually did. The detective was one of the most even-keeled people I'd ever met. It was an amazing feat considering how much he cared about the island and its inhabitants. He was steered by logic and evidence. I was often accused of being unemotional, but that wasn't true. I'm inexpressive. There's a vast difference.

"We could pursue the garage where she was working for hiring underage workers, but I'd say that will hurt Marissa more than the garage owner," Whittaker said. "We have probable cause to search the mother's house, where we're likely to find crack cocaine, or traces of it, as I doubt she has a stockpile. I'm guessing she smokes every ounce she can get her hands on."

"Maybe we do that once we've found Marissa," I suggested. "If she wants out of that house badly enough, she may prefer the foster system." I thought about the questions he'd asked at the house. In the morning briefing, one constable had mentioned Marissa didn't have other family here, but Whittaker had still raised the point in the interview. "Are we sure she doesn't have relatives on the island?"

Whittaker shook his head. "I asked Elise in case we'd missed something, but our records show Elise came here from Jamaica after Hurricane Ivan. Her husband at the time worked construction. She divorced him and he went back, but she stayed and married a local man. That didn't last long, but he gave Elise residency paperwork, and a daughter. Marissa's father hasn't been in the picture since she was a baby."

"But could Marissa have run to the father for help? Maybe she thought he'd take her in." I wondered aloud.

"He's in Miami as best we know. He left the island ten years ago," he replied. "And unless she found a boat to sneak off the island, Marissa is still here. She doesn't even have a passport."

I couldn't think of any other ideas and sighed. "Let's hope the constables asking around at her old school turn up something."

"That's our best chance at the moment," Whittaker agreed. "She hasn't attended for a while, but perhaps she made a friend whose family would take her in."

"All that is based on the idea she ran away," I pointed out.

"Maybe we can pry or trade something from DeWayne," he suggested. "He's a frequent flyer in the system, giving us plenty of bargaining chips. But we'll have to wait until he's released from the hospital. That should be this evening, so we'll question him in the morning. Beyond that, the two interviews gave us background and information, but nothing immediately actionable."

He was right. Both cases had stalled until we could dig up more evidence, and my theory of them being connected was just that, a theory. With nothing to substantiate what I was more and more convinced was true.

"I'll see what I can find in Patti's social this afternoon," I replied, with nothing more to offer.

He nodded and opened his car door. "Why don't you take a break and get some lunch before your shift?"

Part of me wanted to head into the office, start my online search, and pick up food on the way to West Bay before two o'clock. If Marissa was in trouble, every minute counted. But the idea of clearing my head for an hour and a half before my official job started also sounded appealing. Not to mention my hands stung like hell.

"Okay," I said and headed for my Jeep.

The midday sun beat down on my floppy hat, which looked silly with my police uniform, but I didn't care. Three bags of hot sandwiches from Heritage Kitchen sat next to me, and the smell was making my mouth water. My legs swung back and forth in rhythm with a classic rock tune that Reg was playing in the hut. The ocean breeze brushed across my face and I closed my eyes, letting the current world withdraw and allow me temporary respite from my demons.

The scene took me back to my childhood in Norway, sitting on a pier on the island of Hovedøya in the Inner Oslo Fjord. My father casting a fishing line with skilled precision. He softly spoke about the history of the islands, the fish he'd caught, and the wind patterns around the islands. Our sailboat bobbed in a mooring close by, where my mother sunned herself on deck, sipping a glass of wine and swaying gently to a song on the radio.

I felt myself beginning to wish for that simpler time before my life unravelled, and I quickly opened my eyes. Wishing was pointless. I looked across the beautiful turquoise water, admiring the paradise I was now fortunate to call home. With it came a cargo hold of baggage, but everyone has their shit to bear. I reminded myself that Marissa Chandler was likely accumulating an unfair portion of that shit as I sat here daydreaming.

I watched AJ pilot her Newton towards the dock and stood up to catch the bowline which Thomas was ready to throw my way. Ten minutes later, *Hazel's Odyssey* bobbed idly tethered to the jetty, AJ's customers were gone, and the three of us sat under the shade of the fly-bridge eating lunch. AJ and Thomas both chatted away about their morning and preparations for their afternoon customers. I knew my friend was waiting for an opportunity to ask me about my case, and Thomas sensed the same.

"I'll get da fill line from da hut," he said, hopping off the boat, taking his sandwich with him.

I loved Thomas, but I shouldn't be talking about police cases with anyone, and he respected AJ and I enough to acknowledge when we needed time to speak privately.

"Have you figured anything more out?" AJ asked right away.

I shook my head. "We're nowhere. And now a kid is missing who we think might be connected." The 'we' wasn't strictly accurate, but I needed an ally.

"I saw a news alert on my mobile about the girl," AJ said. "She's related to the robbery?"

"Indirectly. She fits the sex trafficking profile and with Cosgrove being the target, there's a link."

"So, are you questioning Cosgrove or searching his property?" she asked. "You think he has the girl?"

"Neither," I replied. "He's out of the country and the Cosgroves were the victim of a robbery, so we have no grounds for a warrant. I doubt he has the girl, but is probably dealing with the people who do."

"Blimey," AJ said, letting out a long breath. "It's incredible all that nasty stuff happened once here on the island. It's hard to believe it could happen again."

"There are sick fucks everywhere," I mumbled, and she looked at me sympathetically.

"What can you do now?" AJ asked.

Undoubtedly, that was the question, and I didn't have a brilliant answer. What could the police do next? Keep kicking over rocks and see what crawls out. We were hanging our hopes on Patti Weaver's connection to the robbery, and DeWayne providing a lead on Marissa. But I realised that wasn't what AJ asked. She asked 'what can you do now', as in me.

"I need to take a look inside Cosgrove's house," I said.

"How can you do that without a warrant or whatever it's called?"

I peeked out from below the brim of my hat and looked at my friend.

"Oh no," she whispered, looking around us for anyone within earshot. "You'll lose your bloody job, Nora. Probably end up in jail yourself. Besides, any evidence you find won't be admissible. I've watched all those shows on the telly. They're always throwing out stuff that's gained illegally."

"I don't plan on taking anything," I replied as matter-of-factly as I could, despite the adrenaline surging through my system as the idea formed in my crazy brain. "I just need to know if it's there."

"What evidence do you think is there?" she asked, looking at me as though I was mad. But that wasn't unusual. She looked at me that way a lot.

"There's a second safe which the thief missed. It's in the office over the garage," I explained. "We're sure the thief was looking for something he didn't appear to find in the paperwork, so it's likely to be in the other safe."

"Or not kept there at all."

That was true. This whole theory stacked a bunch of wobbly assumptions on top of each other and hoped they built something solid. The odds were they'd all fall down and come to nothing. But I wanted Randall Cosgrove to pay, whether he was involved in Marissa's disappearance or not. Maybe he'd been a boy scout since the resort was taken down, but it didn't matter. Some things were unforgivable. There was no statute of limitations.

"I'm confident there's damning evidence in that safe," I said with a certainty I didn't possess. "I need to see what it is before Cosgrove gets back to the island. Then I'll figure out a way to get a warrant."

AJ looked at me blankly. "Why are you telling me?" she said cautiously.

I smiled.

"I knew it!" she gasped. "You want me to share a bloody jail cell with you!"

"No, I want you to drive the boat."

"Huh?"

"All you have to do is drop me off at the shore and pick me up again," I said, as though I was asking her to pick me up eggs at the supermarket. "If alarms go off, you simply motor away and go back to bed."

She shook her head. "You're bonkers. I'm not helping you break the law. You're a bloody copper. Why are we even having this conversation?"

"Because young girls are being used as sex slaves and I can't live with that," I growled, laying on the guilt trip pretty thick.

"Might be," AJ retorted, with little conviction.

Thomas walked up with the whip hose and manifold in his hands, ready to refill the air tanks on the boat. He made enough noise to let us know to stop talking about anything he shouldn't hear.

"I'm sure Thomas will help me if I ask," I said loudly.

"Help wit what?" he asked.

"Nothing!" AJ shouted, giving me the evil eye, and I wondered if I'd pushed my friend too far.

"When?" she asked under her breath.

"Tonight," I replied, then hugged her and left before she could change her mind.

13

CARTS AND HORSES

The evening shift was dragging on. I had things to do. Jacob was extra chatty, asking a million questions about the two cases, but all I could think about was planning tonight. In English, there's a fitting phrase about putting the cart before the horse. My cart was in front, missing a wheel, and my horse was facing the wrong way. The idea of taking a look in the second safe had hit me as I'd been talking to AJ, and now I couldn't back out. Cosgrove was arriving on the island Saturday. I had to know what was in there tonight, which still only gave me Friday and part of Saturday to drum up a reason to officially open the safe. One step at a time, I reminded myself.

We'd made a sweep of our patrol area in West Bay, tossing a coin to see which direction we took. Jacob and I had devised a system. Well, I'd come up with a system, and he'd agreed to it. We'd mapped out three versions of our route, each covering the same areas, but in a unique pattern. We both flipped a coin at the same time to decide which one to take – two coins having three potential outcomes. One of us then flipped our coin to see which direction: heads meant clockwise, tails anticlockwise. With the time of day of our shift changing regularly, there was no way anyone could predict our patrol route or exact timing.

By 4:30pm things were quiet over the police radio and the commuter traffic was getting heavy, so we parked off to the side on the Esterly Tibbetts Highway near the last roundabout into West Bay. Our presence was enough to slow down the speeders and pretty soon the roads would be too busy for anyone to go fast anyway. I focused on my mobile while Jacob kept an eye out of the window.

Using my notebook, I jotted down names of people who commented and sympathised with Patti Weaver's posts on her social media. If they interacted on her personal pictures and family posts, I noted them in one column. Political and activist posts in another. If the names appeared in both, I assumed they were relatives or close friends.

After an hour, the traffic was thinning and moving more freely, so Jacob was anxious to change locations, and my eyes were getting tired from staring at the small screen. I'd gone back in her timeline for almost a year and decided that would be a good place to stop. Jacob put the car in drive and was preparing to pull out into a gap in traffic when I told him to stop.

'PM me,' a comment by Cayman MY Island said. That name hadn't appeared on her timeline before. The article was a follow-up in the *Cayman Compass* about the International Fellowship of Lions, and how after nearly a year, no one else had been prosecuted.

"What did you find?" Jacob asked.

"Gimme a minute," I muttered in response.

I clicked over to Cayman MY Island's page and scrolled through their posts. That didn't take long. There were none. A member since 2018, they'd set their banner picture to a nice shot of the ocean at sunset, and their profile picture was the Cayman Islands flag. The timeline showed the two pictures had been chosen back in 2018, but the person had posted nothing more. Yet their friends list showed 96 people. No bio information, age, contact email, nothing.

I don't use social media because I consider it a waste of time and I don't care what someone had for dinner last night, or how cute their cat looks. It's odd to me. People would never let a complete stranger wander around inside their home, meet their children, pets, and see all their stuff, yet they do it willingly on an Internet site where millions of people they don't know can see.

They especially let the world know when they're not in their house for a week. Travel pictures are most popular. It's a guided tour and availability notification for thieves. Regardless, I didn't use it, but I was becoming very familiar with the different platforms.

"Okay, we can go," I told Jacob, and he looked for another gap in the traffic. "Maybe a lead, but it's a long shot," I added to fend off more questions. "I'll send it to Whittaker and he can have someone dig deeper."

I texted the details to the detective and my thoughts immediately returned to what lay ahead tonight. If I'd read Estelle Cosgrove incorrectly, I wouldn't even get past the alarm. Assuming I guessed the code, the next problem was the cameras. I knew no one would be watching live, but if anything tipped off the security company, or the Cosgroves, I'd be seen on the recording.

A smile inadvertently crept across my face as the idea came to me. I needed to look like the thief. For once I was glad I had small breasts, but now I needed to find black trousers, a long-sleeved shirt, and hardest of all, a balaclava. Ski masks weren't exactly big sellers on the tropical island. The shops in West Bay would all be closed, except for Fosters supermarket, so unless I wanted to wrap myself in fresh fruit or frozen pizzas, I was going to be improvising.

"Hello?" I heard Jacob say.

"What?" I responded sharply.

"Woh dere!" he said. "I was just askin' if you want some coffee."

"Sorry. I was thinking of... stuff." It was a lame reply, but all this deceit was frazzling my brain. "Coffee sounds good."

I might need a bucket of coffee to get me through the night, I decided. I was feeling sleepy, and it wasn't even dark yet. Although that was probably nerves. Before swim meets and sailing races in school, I used to feel tired right before the start. It was my brain's way of keeping the nerves at bay by hiding in a calm, dreamy state. Although at that moment, it could also be the fact that I was working double shifts and not getting enough sleep.

Jacob parked the car outside Fosters and we both got out. As we walked to the entrance, I opened texts on my mobile. Whittaker had replied: 'Will look into them tomorrow.' I started typing a new message, this one to AJ, but stopped before I hit send. Regular texts are traceable and recoverable, even if you delete them. I kept the message – 'Need tender and dive hood' – but changed the recipient to AJ's phone number at her cell service provider email address. It would send the text to her mobile by bouncing it off the cell provider's server, which couldn't be tracked. We were walking back out with coffee and a pastry before she replied with 'WTF?'

My first reaction was annoyance, but then I chuckled, which garnered a strange look from Jacob as we got back in the car.

"Everyting okay?" he asked.

"Yeah, Whittaker said he'll look into it."

The concerned expression didn't leave Jacob's face, and I couldn't blame him. My responses didn't match my body language, but I didn't want to mention AJ's name or tell him I was chatting with her. There was no point in associating her with me today if things went badly wrong. I replied to AJ's message: 'Tender harder to see and doesn't have name on side. Dive hood cos I need one!'

I knew AJ had a variety of wetsuits for all conditions, but I didn't know how thick her dive hood was. I hoped it wasn't a seven-millimetre cold weather hood, or I'd be sweating my hair out tonight. A dive hood with a dark scarf around my nose and mouth was the best solution for a balaclava I could come up with on short notice. I had black jeans and a dark blue long-sleeved shirt that would have to do.

'You're nuts,' came AJ's response.

Tough to argue that point. I had a habit of charging into situations without a plan and relying on my wits. I think this qualified, but I did feel like my cart and horse were both facing the same direction now. Albeit in the wrong order.

'I know. Get a dinghy,' I sent back.

She replied with an emoji of a middle finger. But I knew she'd have both items ready to go.

14

10,000 COMBINATIONS

It was almost 11:00pm when I parked the Jeep by the dock and AJ and I walked down the pier to where she'd tied Reg's dinghy to a pair of cleats. I'd insisted she leave her van at her cottage so it wouldn't be seen in the vicinity. It meant she'd be walking home if the shit hit the fan and she came back without me, but her place wasn't far away. I was feeling more and more guilty about coercing my friend into this madness, but I needed someone to handle the boat.

The spotlight for our pier was off, but a bright light next door on West Bay Public Dock illuminated more than I would have liked. We quickly dropped into the dinghy, fired up the little outboard, and cast off the lines. AJ put the running lights on until we reached her Newton, moored a hundred yards offshore. She piloted the little inflatable around the far side of her dive boat, then killed the running lights and we waited five minutes. If anyone had seen us leave the dock, we hoped they'd lose interest when all we did was trundle out to her boat.

The moon was setting over the island to the north-west, and as we motored slowly along the coast, the lights on shore were the only glow keeping us from total darkness.

"It's not too late to turn around, Nora," AJ said quietly from behind the tiny helm station.

"If it was just about this *drittsekk*, I'd find another way to make him pay," I replied without turning back. "But I'm convinced this kid, Marissa, is in trouble, so I have to do everything possible."

AJ didn't say anything more, so I presumed she agreed on some level. Or accepted I was doing this with or without her. My little speech sounded noble, but I knew the act would only be noble if it worked out. If it went pear shaped, I'd be an idiot in deep shit. The risk didn't seem worth it when I spelled it out that way, but we were nearly there already.

The first and final parts of the scheme were why I needed AJ at the helm. The coastline was rugged ironshore, and even if I could tie the boat to something, the waves would keep bashing it against the rocks. She skilfully nosed the little dinghy into the shore until it bumped against the ironshore, where I could jump from the bow to dry land. We'd dropped me in front of the neighbour's behemoth house to the right of the Cosgroves' place. They appeared to be out of town and their landscaped waterfront had low-voltage accent lights which didn't illuminate the ocean. AJ was able to slip away and disappeared into the darkness.

The Cosgroves' house had far more lighting, including floods which bathed their pool area and coastline. I slipped a black cotton bandana over my head so it covered the lower part of my face and then put AJ's black hood on. The snug neoprene pulled the bandana down with it, and I cursed to myself as I struggled with the two items for several minutes until they were somewhat in place. Without a mirror, I had no idea, but they felt okay by touch and I could see where I was going.

I blew out a deep breath. I hadn't moved a step yet, and I was already sucking air and sweating. Moving along the edge of the ironshore, I found the boundary between the two properties and, staying low, I moved inland. A floodlight suddenly flicked on and I lunged forward into a stand of shrubs dividing the lots. I lay still, wincing from the scratches on my palms from earlier in the day.

Landing on dry dirt and twigs had broken the freshly formed scabs.

At least the security light I'd tripped was from the neighbour's house. They must have a motion sensor to the side of the building. I could now stay in cover of the shrubs and crawl along the Cosgroves' lawn to the office building. Nobody has grass in the Cayman Islands except the golf course and the filthy rich. It took tons of imported fertile soil and a gazillion litres of water sprinkled daily to keep it alive. Most people made their gardens look neat with crushed limestone and a few plant beds. But the grass was much nicer to crawl along.

The east side of the main house was on my left, and I knew Estelle's bedroom was above me on the first floor. If she looked out of her window, she might not be able to see me on the grass in the dark, but when I reached the door to the garages and office, there was a porch light, which was on. It was likely I'd already been picked up on the exterior cameras with night vision. I wondered if my arse looked good wiggling across the garden on my hands and knees. My skinny backside probably didn't appear very masculine, which screwed up my disguise.

At the door, I pulled on a pair of nitrile gloves and tried the handle, which was locked as expected. I took my pick kit from my back pocket and within a minute had it open. As a sixteen-year-old runaway, I'd learnt a trick or two. I stood, entered the hallway, and quickly closed the door behind me. On the wall, the alarm panel beeped, and I flipped the little plastic door down to access the number pad. If I'd misread Estelle, she'd changed the code, or they used a different code for the second building, there was about to be a lot of noise and one panicked Norwegian sprinting for the ocean and a long swim.

The Cosgroves were married on the 9th of June, 2001. The code was four digits. The key question was whether their code was day and month, or month and year. I entered 0-9-0-6, and the panel beeped louder and flashed at me.

"*Fy faen!*" I groaned.

In thirty seconds, the alarm would go off. Right now, an alert was pinging at Caribbean Security Systems, and they'd be calling Estelle Cosgrove and asking whether she'd punched in the wrong code. I needed to run. But I didn't. I punched in 0-6-0-1 and breathed again when the beeping stopped.

I had no way of knowing if the employee monitoring for alerts at the security company had called right away, or had waited to see if the owner had fat fingered the code. Either way, they'd see which keypad was used and may well be checking the cameras. I resisted looking up at the camera, which I knew was mounted above the door to the garage. Behind me were the stairs up to the office, and in the dim light cast by the keypad, I could see two more doors.

I opened the first mystery door and quickly stepped inside the darkened room, closed the door behind me, and waited. A trickle of light from a small, high window showed I'd chosen the bathroom as I'd hoped. There wouldn't be a camera in here. Well, there'd better not be, but Randall Cosgrove was a sick fuck, so I checked for the telltale little red LED light. There wasn't one.

I peeked out of the window which faced the ocean and looked to my right at the main house. No new lights were on. I'd presumed Estelle was home, but I had no way of knowing for sure. She could be out, or staying with a friend if she was freaked out after being burgled. What were the chances of being broken into twice within days? Pretty good as it turns out for the Cosgroves. If the alarm company contacted her on her mobile and she told them she wasn't home, the police would be called right away, and I wouldn't know until my co-workers showed up in the driveway. *Dritt!*

I couldn't stay in the bathroom forever. Five minutes, I decided, I'd give them five minutes. I hadn't worn a watch as watches, jewellery and tattoos were classic giveaways on a camera, so I had to count in my head. I made it to around twenty a bunch of times. Thoughts kept jumping into my adrenaline-infused brain and I'd forget to keep counting. The pit in my stomach said it had been at least five minutes, but I knew it hadn't. Regardless, I was done sitting around. No lights had come on outside, or in the house, and I couldn't hear sirens. I also reminded myself that the cameras weren't accessed live by the security company.

Opening the bathroom door, I moved across the entryway to the stairwell and made my way up. At the top, I met another door, which of course was locked. By the time I'd picked that lock, I was sure it had now been five minutes or more and I didn't see any movement outside through the landing window.

The office was big, but not as huge as I'd expected based on the building's footprint. A wall at the far end housed a pair of doors, both closed, and I wondered what they could lead to. Maybe Estelle and Randall both had an office?

Large windows down three sides leaked in enough light that I didn't need my torch to move about the room. A large wooden desk occupied the ocean view end of the office with a fancy leather desk chair. Bookshelves lined the east wall, and a pillowy leather couch and matching armchairs surrounded a glass coffee table. Little red LED lights in opposing corners gave away the two cameras covering the space. What was in short supply was a suitable picture frame on a wall.

I'd expected the safe's location to be obvious, but most of the art was framed photographs, too small to hide a safe like the one in the main house. I moved further into the room, around the furniture to the far wall. Between the door and the outer wall on the left side was a framed painting of a swordfish flying out of the water. Hung symmetrically on the right side was a similar painting of a marlin. Out of curiosity, I tried the door on the left. It opened into a full bathroom, complete with a large jacuzzi tub and a separate shower. These people obviously didn't like walking too far to take a shit. They had more toilets than beds.

I closed the door and tried the one on the right. It was locked. That really piqued my curiosity, and I desperately wanted to pick the lock, but I'd already been in the building much longer than I'd hoped. Choosing the picture frame on the right, I gave it a tug. It unlatched and swung away from the wall, revealing the safe. I walked over to the other frame on the left and tried it too. It was solidly mounted to the wall. At least there was only one, as Estelle had said.

Now came the biggest hurdle. Unlike the thief, I had no idea what the safe code was. I'd checked on the Internet, and the model of safe didn't have a maximum number of tries before it locked down, like an ATM or some online logins. But I didn't have a couple of days to try 10,000 different combinations. I was betting on Randall Cosgrove being as predictable as his wife suggested. I positioned my body to block the camera's view as best I could, mimicking the thief.

I started with 0601, but nothing in my life is ever that easy. I tried 0906. It wasn't that either. So I pulled a piece of paper from my pocket and held it close to the illuminated keypad, reading the short list of numbers I'd jotted down. I tried day–month and month–year for both of their birthdays with no luck. I tried the last four digits of their mobile numbers. That was all I had on my list. This is when the horse really needed to be in front of the cart and mine was off chewing grass in a meadow somewhere.

I tried to think of some other combination to try. According to our records, they didn't have children, so no useful dates there. I tried 1-2-3-4, then 4 of every digit from 0 to 9. I stared at the paper again. They were married on the 9th of June, 2001. I tried 2-0-0-1. *Dritt!* I'd come this far and risked so much to get nothing out of it. I looked at the locked door and was about to get my pick kit back out when I thought of one more number to try. 9-6-0-1. The safe opened.

I stopped myself short of jumping around like a five-year-old on Christmas morning, but it took a lot of willpower. I turned on the small torch I'd brought along and shone the beam into the safe.

"*Fy faen!*" I muttered out loud.

15

NOWHERE TO HIDE

Manila envelopes of papers were stuffed under and beside tall stacks of cash wedged inside the safe, leaving no room for anything else. Unless these were dollar bills, which I guessed they were not, I was staring at a lot of money.

The cash didn't matter. I was looking for something else. What that was, I still had no clue, but my gut told me there was something important to the case here. But now I needed to look through the contents and replace them in the same order I found them. I pulled out the top layer of bound bills and set them on the floor, confirming they were all stacks of $100 US notes. Wiggling and tugging, I wrenched three thick envelopes from the right side of the remaining money, which freed everything up.

One by one, I ran my torch over the envelopes. All three were from a company in the UK. Shoving two under my arm and holding the torch in my mouth, I opened the flap of the third and slid a wad of papers half out. It was a contract with the firm. I resisted the urge to thumb through and find Randall's salary. I was sure it would piss me off. Pushing the papers back inside, I placed the three envelopes on the floor to the right of the money.

A single, thick envelope now slid easily out from the left side of the cash, and I examined the return address label. It was from an attorney's office in the UK. I checked the papers inside and found they covered a lawsuit over some copyright. Nothing but pages and pages of legalese crap. I placed the envelope to the left of the cash on the floor.

I was glad I didn't have a watch with me. Everything had taken so much longer than I'd envisioned, and two hands reiterating that fact would have made me more anxious than I already was. It felt like a furnace under the dive hood. Occasional beads of sweat escaped the seal across my forehead, each one seemingly finding my eyes, which I constantly wiped. I glanced up at the window overlooking the ocean, although all I could see was the dark night sky. I was sure AJ would have left for the dock by now, figuring something had gone sideways.

I realised I'd moved my body out of position with all the bending down and looking through papers, so I adjusted my feet to block the cameras again. Anyone who studied the video would recognise my movements differed completely from the thief's, and I'd certainly supplied ample video, but it was part of my thin plan, so I stuck with it.

I grabbed all the papers under the cash and pulled them from the safe. There were more envelopes, loose papers, and documents. I dropped to the carpeted floor and sat cross-legged with the pile in front of me. The thief never did this, but he had a couch to set everything on. I put the torch back in my mouth, trying not to dribble DNA on the floor, and began searching through the stack.

As I discarded page after page of letters, printed emails and other work-related bullshit, I laid them face down to the side, forming a new stack in the same order. Beyond the cash, everything in the safe was business related as Estelle had suggested. I was getting angry. Randall Cosgrove's image kept shoving itself into my mind. The memory of his breath on my face as he told me how beautiful I was, and the chills running through my body from his touch. I closed my eyes, as I had done at the resort, desperate to shut out the living nightmare, but my brain wouldn't let me hide this time. I felt nauseous and filthy.

I growled like an animal through gritted teeth, directing my shame and disgust into more anger, mainly at myself. The fresh surge of adrenaline brought me back into focus on the task I was risking so much for. I continued ploughing through the papers, resisting the urge to fling the legal documents across the room. Randall had to be one of those wasteful arse-wipes who had his secretary print every email he received.

I slapped another useless sheet down on the floor and went to grab the next one. Instead of a piece of A4 paper, there was a small, 5-inch by 3-inch spiral-bound notepad, similar to the kind I use. Flipping over the cover revealed a name and a number on the first page. 'The Haitian 345 471 9935'. I turned the page and found a list of dates and times, one on each of the fifteen lines. I turned another page to find the dates continuing for three more lines. The rest of the notebook was blank. Hardly a smoking gun, but the notebook felt like the first potential clue I'd found. It could be his poker club schedule. It could be his bookie. But I had a hunch it was something else.

I put the notebook aside and quickly flicked through the remaining documents and envelopes. Nothing stood out as suspicious. They were all legal business papers of some sort. I looked at the notebook again and realised I didn't have any method of recording the data. I hadn't brought my phone as it could be tracked, and I figured I might get wet at some point in the night. The idea of bringing a pen and paper never crossed my mind.

I stood and hurried over to the desk. It was irritatingly spotless and neat, with nothing but twin computer screens, a keyboard, and a mouse perfectly arranged on the surface. I opened a drawer on the right and my torch revealed a tray holding a variety of pens and other office supplies. I took a pen. Looking around the room, I saw a large printer-copier thing on a wood and glass credenza which matched the desk. I wrestled with the paper drawer for a moment until it finally relinquished a sheet.

After making sure I'd reset everything, I went back to my piles and sat on the floor to copy over the details from the notebook. Once done, I began packing everything back inside the safe, as close to how I found it as I could manage.

I looked at all the cash. Every ounce of me wanted to take it all and drop it on the doorstep of the Cayman Islands Crisis Centre, a non-profit which helped women and children get away from abusive environments. But as soon as the safe was opened next, which I hoped would be by the Royal Cayman Islands Police Service, the Cosgroves would know someone had been in there. The security tapes would be reviewed, and the evidence would be thrown out, regardless of whether I was recognised or not. Any lawyer worth his salt would claim the notebook was planted.

I closed the safe and clicked the picture frame into place. Dropping the pen back into its drawer at the desk, I moved to the door, where I glanced out of the side window. Headlights swept across the front of the main house as a car pulled into the driveway. Under my feet, the building vibrated, and a groan emanated from the garage door as it opened. The lights swung around to face the garage building and I stepped away from the window. It was Estelle's Porsche.

I assumed she'd been home and had set the alarm for the night, but apparently she'd been out somewhere. Now she was home and about to walk into the hallway downstairs, expecting to disarm the alarm so she could enter the house. I moved without consciously thinking it through. I didn't have time.

Twisting the lock on the interior handle, I rushed out the door and pulled it closed. I scampered down the stairs, hoping the noise of the garage door hid my footsteps. Jumping the final few stairs, I landed in the hallway, punched the alarm code into the keypad, then hit the arm button. The now annoyingly slow 30-second arming beeps seemed to echo around in the darkness. Yanking the back door open, I twisted the lock on its lever and pulled the door closed behind me as I rushed out into the humid night air. I ran across the lawn to the row of shrubs and hurled myself behind them, hearing the alarm beeps fading behind me.

I twisted around behind the shrubs to watch the garage building just as a light came on inside the hallway. Estelle was about to be mightily confused by the alarm midway through setting itself, beeping loudly. I waited, panting and now sweating from head to toe. The stupid dive hood felt like hands crushing my head with a hot blanket.

The light inside the hallway went off as the door opened and Estelle stepped outside, casually closing the door behind her. She had a clutch purse in one hand, along with her car keys, and by the way she was walking, I guessed she'd had a few cocktails. She followed the path to the front door, her hips swaying in her short black skirt, then fumbled for a moment with the key to the door. As soon as she stepped inside the house, I bolted for the shoreline, staying closer to the Cosgroves' side to avoid the neighbour's motion sensor.

I considered diving straight into the water and beginning my long swim home, but stopped short when I remembered the piece of paper in my pocket. My notes wouldn't survive immersion in salt water for an hour. I crouched down and stumbled along the ironshore to the neighbour's side and sat down. Pointing my torch out to sea, I flicked it on and off three times, waited ten seconds, then repeated the three flashes. I continued the sequence until, much to my surprise, the faint sound of an outboard wafted my way. I couldn't help but smile.

AJ bumped the nose of the tender against the ironshore. "Where the bloody hell have you been?" she hissed, as I stepped into the bow of the dinghy.

"I was hungry, so I stopped to make a sandwich," I replied casually.

"Huh?" she grunted, staring at me.

"Will you please get us out of here!" I growled, and AJ eased us away from the shoreline, fading into the clutches of the night.

16

BLOWN TO SMITHEREENS

The wind whisking around my face helped wake me up. Cheap sunglasses did their best to fend off the early morning sun, but I still had to squint as I drove east. I was operating my Jeep on autopilot, and felt like I'd barely slept. That was because I'd barely slept. Amped up from the break-in and a head full of swirling thoughts hadn't led to a restful night.

I pulled into the tiny car park at Reg's dock and left the Jeep running as I walked down the jetty. AJ was heaving Nitrox tanks from the pier to the gunwale of *Hazel's Odyssey*, where Thomas lifted them over the rail and dropped them into the racks. She paused and looked up as I approached. She looked tired too.

By most of the Western world's standards, I'm not good with words. Part of that is a Scandinavian thing. We don't gush and blabber over every detail in life. You had a baby? Congratulations. 7.9 billion people currently living on the planet say that's not ground-breaking territory. You bought a new car? Great, you now have transportation. It's an SUV with three rows of seats, fancy wheels and every new electronic gismo available? Well done. You paid a shit-ton too much money to impress your neighbour.

Part of it is also me. I learned too young how precarious the knife edge is between life and death. We're all constantly one wrong move away from drawing our last breath. The unseen swinging boom of a sailboat. A blow to the head from a man you'd trusted. Revenge from an unforgiving cartel. When you've looked into the lifeless eyes of someone you love, the trivial day-to-day bullshit becomes irrelevant. And significant deeds stand out even more.

I put my arms around AJ and squeezed my friend. I could tell she was surprised, but AJ is a hugger, and her embrace reminded me of being held by my parents. That feeling of safety as though nothing in the world could hurt you as long as mum and dad were with you.

"*Takk*," I whispered and released her.

"You're welcome," she said as I turned away.

"Morning, Thomas," I said, walking up the jetty. I caught his beaming smile as he waved.

"Nora," AJ called out.

I paused and looked over my shoulder.

"Be careful."

I nodded and continued to my Jeep.

The rest of my drive to the central police station on Elgin Road in George Town was consumed by thoughts of how to revisit Cosgrove's second safe. Legally. Estelle didn't know how to get into the safe, so the contents were locked away until her husband returned tomorrow. Flights from the UK landed in the afternoon, so I had 32 hours.

There was no guarantee Randall would head straight for the safe. In theory, he had no reason to be concerned, but the chance existed, and Whittaker opening the safe with the notebook gone would be a disaster, all my eggs being in the basket which said the notebook contained damning evidence. Top of my priority list was tracing the mobile number. Next was searching police records for any reference to 'The Haitian' or a man from Haiti with a rap sheet.

I parked the Jeep and walked inside the station. Coffee and the drive over had roused me into a facsimile of functioning consciousness, and now I was on a mission. Right away, I sensed something had happened. Grand Cayman is a quiet island, and while the police are kept busy, we're usually dealing with trivial matters. Speeding tickets, the odd bar fight, serving warrants for unpaid child support. When something bigger goes down, it's big news in our little corner of the world.

"Briefing at nine," the constable at the front desk told me as I crossed the lobby.

"Which case?" I asked.

"Da robbery," she replied. "Dere been another one."

I concentrated on keeping my facial muscles relaxed, while inside my heart stopped beating and I thought I might vomit in the police station lobby.

"Really?" I managed to squeeze past my lips. "Where?"

"West Bay, best I know," she replied, shuffling paperwork and typing away on her keyboard. "Same MO I heard."

I forced my feet to move across the room and down the hall to the women's locker room. Sitting down on a bench before my knees buckled, I took several long breaths as though I was preparing for a freedive. If the alarm had been raised, the camera footage would be reviewed, and they would quickly see the figure last night wasn't the same thief. I'd cobbled together an outfit to mimic the burglar, but my movements would be different enough to raise suspicion. A closer inspection and they'd conclude it was two different people.

Estelle couldn't check what was missing as she couldn't access the safe, which meant they'd have to wait for Randall. He'd open it, say nothing's missing, and close the safe. The police had no grounds to question the cash or search the other contents. Forensics would pull every fibre and hair from wherever I stepped, and the odds were, despite the hood, a strand of my hair would have been left behind. My DNA, like all members of the Royal Cayman Islands Police Service, is on medical file.

However I looked at this, I was done. I couldn't see a way out.

Unless I ran. I probably had an hour before they realised there was a second thief, and 48 hours before my DNA at the scene would tell them it was me. In two days, I could be a long way from Grand Cayman, hidden in plain view on a vast ocean. I'd 'borrowed' a sailboat before and disappeared. I could do it again. Although this time there'd be no coming back. I'd be stealing the boat and adding my face and name to Interpol's wanted list. Running and hiding would be my way of life again. Forever.

I looked at my watch. It was almost 9:00am. Logic told me they had no way of knowing it was me yet, so I might as well attend the briefing and find out what Whittaker planned to do. *Dritt!* Whittaker. The detective had put his faith in me, and this is how I repaid him. By screwing up in the biggest possible way. I'd let my emotions get the best of me.

I slinked into the back of the briefing room and leaned against the wall, as far out of sight of the front as I could get. Detective Roy Whittaker, my mentor and perhaps the sharpest guy I knew, walked into the room and my eyes shot to the floor. I couldn't face him.

"Let's make this quick," Whittaker began, broadcasting his usually soft voice across the room. "We've had another break-in. It appears to match the one in West Bay on Tuesday night. The victim's name is Rosemary Chesterton-Clark, and the house is on Boggy Sand Road."

I practically melted down the wall. How I remained standing, I have no idea. My arms and legs were quivering. I should have been elated, but the relief was almost unbearable. I would continue carrying the burden of my impetuous deed and wondering if and when the hammer would fall. Finding the meaning behind the notebook and getting Whittaker into that safe just became even more crucial.

"Mrs Chesterton-Clark is a widow who lives alone," the detective read from his notes. "She only discovered items were missing first thing this morning when she looked in her safe for the first time in weeks. Her home is also secured by Caribbean Security

Systems." Whittaker searched the room with his eyes until he found me. I managed to hold his gaze, and we exchanged a subtle nod. "We have a person of interest at the alarm company, but it's early days and a frail connection at this point. Detective Weatherford has been at Caribbean Security since their office opened half an hour ago. He messaged me before I joined you, and on initial inspection of the alarm logs, it appears this break-in happened before the Cosgroves'."

Whittaker waited while everyone filed out of the room, pulling me aside when I reached him. "I have the pleasure of interviewing DeWayne at 9:30, if you'd like to sit in."

"Can I be bad cop?" I asked with a grin.

"I think you've established that status with the man," he replied. "But then again, no one in a uniform is on his good side. Best you observe and let me do the talking to start with."

I nodded. The fact that it wasn't me about to be interviewed at the station was still sinking in, and my legs had finally stopped shaking.

"9:30, interview room one," Whittaker said as he left the briefing room.

"Yes, sir," I mumbled as he departed. I was getting better at the 'sir' business, but it didn't come naturally. He didn't insist on it when we were alone, but it was required and expected in company.

I had less than fifteen minutes to put something in motion with the information from the notebook. Rushing down the hall, I found an available computer terminal at a shared desk. I had no idea how to track down a mobile number. Looking at the company directory on the wall in front of me, I dialled the extension for Rasha, the scene of crime officer I knew.

"SOCO office," came an English woman's voice I recognised.

"Hi Rasha, it's Nora Sommer."

"Hey, Nora. What's up?"

"If I needed to trace a phone number, how do I do that?"

"Well, you put a request in, listing the case number it's for, the detective or officer heading the case, and your name as the requesting constable," she explained. "It goes into the queue and I think it's TSU, our technical support unit, who handles it."

"*Faen,*" I muttered under my breath.

"I can tell you where to look in the system for the request," Rasha offered.

"Yeah, that's okay," I replied, trying to back out of the conversation. "I was hoping it was a quick search in a database. It's kind of a long shot thing."

"It is," she said, and I wondered how she knew it was a long shot. "The search is easy, but only certain people have access to the database."

"Oh, I see," I responded, realising my grasp of the English language and its idiosyncrasies still had some road to travel. "Do you have access?"

"Hmm," she said thoughtfully, and I heard the clicks of a keyboard. "I used to, but it's been a while since I traced a number. Let's see."

I kept quiet and hoped she had access, along with the inclination to help me out. We'd met during a couple of cases and also dived together a few times, so I had my fingers crossed.

"Looks like I do," she said brightly. "What's the number?"

"345 471 9935," I rattled off without needing to look at my notes.

"3-4-5-4-7-1-9-9-3-5," she repeated as she entered the numbers. "Yeah. Burner phone I'm afraid. Pay as you go, so we have no idea who it is."

My shoulders sank. "Well, that sucks. Does it say when it was activated or purchased?"

"Nope, nothing," she replied. "Do you have the mobile? If you do, we can run prints and try to pull DNA."

"I don't," I said, trying to hide the disappointment I felt. "Thank you for trying, though. We need to have a lionfish hunting day soon."

"I haven't been in the water for a month, so I'm ready," Rasha replied.

"I'll talk to AJ about it. Thanks again."

I hung up and slumped in the chair. This was becoming a roller-coaster ride of epic proportions. Except the lows were outnumbering the highs. I stood and started towards the interview room, still unsure where everything was located in the central station. And then I stopped. What was now considered the first break-in targeted an elderly widow. It hit me like a missile as it blew my theory to smithereens.

The thief wasn't robbing former resort members after all.

17

A FEW PONIES SHORT

"Good morning, DeWayne," Whittaker said cheerily as we entered the interview room. "I trust your overnight accommodation was satisfactory?"

From the chair where he was sitting with his hands cuffed, DeWayne scowled at the detective. The jail-issued jumpsuit was much cleaner than the clothes he'd been wearing yesterday, but a night in the cell hadn't fixed his wonky teeth or his lousy disposition.

"Keep dat bitch da hell away from me, man," he grumbled, glaring at me.

I stared back with a devious grin and gave him a wink I hoped Whittaker didn't see. DeWayne slapped his handcuffs on the metal table and cursed under his breath. Whittaker hit start on the room's digital recording system.

"I see you remember Constable Sommer from yesterday, and in case you've forgotten, I'm Detective Whittaker."

We both sat in chairs across the table, facing the prisoner. I began making a plan of action in case the guy took a lunge at us. Who knew what he was coming down from, but it was likely making him irrational and unpredictable. Not that DeWayne struck me as the stable type at the best of times.

"I'm told you've declined to have a lawyer present," Whittaker stated.

"Can't afford no lawyer," DeWayne mumbled.

"The court can provide you with a lawyer, which I'm sure they explained to you."

DeWayne shook his head. "Dey out ta get me."

"I assure you they're not, but for the record, the suspect has declined counsel," Whittaker said. "And you're aware this interview is being recorded?"

DeWayne nodded.

"I need a verbal confirmation, DeWayne. You know the routine better than I do at this point."

DeWayne looked up. "Yeah," he said with an irritated glare.

"Thank you. Now let's begin with, why did you run from us?" Whittaker asked.

"You threatened me, man."

"And how did I threaten you, DeWayne?"

"Sayin' I was wanted an' all," he replied, waving his restrained hands around.

"That wasn't a threat," the detective responded patiently. "I was simply pointing out it seemed like an excellent opportunity for us to check the current status of your various interactions with the Royal Cayman Islands Police Service and our fine court system."

DeWayne frowned. That was clearly too many words for him to process without pictures.

"Dat crazy bitch chased me, so I ran," he said, pointing at me.

I gave him another smirk, and he quickly looked away. This was kinda fun. I was bad cop without saying a word.

"Let's keep our discussion civil and respectful, DeWayne," Whittaker insisted. "There's no reason for name calling."

"Da piece missin' from my leg say dere is!" DeWayne complained.

I slid my lips back a little and bared my teeth. DeWayne flinched.

"She crazy!" he yelped.

Whittaker looked at me. "Constable Sommer? I assure you she's a fine police officer, and she pursued you *after* you made the decision to run."

A pang of guilt rushed through me. His compliment was very nice, but not exactly accurate based on my antics last night. DeWayne cursed and grumbled under his breath.

"Let's talk about Marissa," the detective continued.

DeWayne shrugged his shoulders and stared at the tabletop.

"Her mother, Elise, is your girlfriend?"

Another shrug of the shoulders. "Sometimes," he muttered.

"Okay, would it be accurate to say you have a relationship with Elise Chandler?"

"Sometimes," DeWayne replied again.

"And what about her daughter, Marissa? How would you describe your relationship with her?"

DeWayne frowned. "I don't have no relations wit dat bitch."

"So, you two don't get along?"

"We don't nuttin'!" DeWayne snapped back, getting agitated. "She keep outta my way, and ain't got nuttin' to do wit her."

"And you don't have any idea where she may have gone?"

DeWayne shook his head. "I tell you, she keep outta my way. I don't know what da bitch up to." He shuffled in his chair and Whittaker waited. "No doubt she just take off. Tired o' takin' care o' Ell." DeWayne looked up. "It her kid, not nuttin' to do wit me. You should be askin' Ell where her kid got to."

"In your opinion, Marissa has run away from home, then?"

"I don't have no opinion on da matter," DeWayne quickly responded. "I'm tellin' you, I got nuttin' to do wit her."

"Seems like you have pretty strong feelings about someone you have nothing to do with, DeWayne."

The skinny man practically writhed in his seat.

"A pretty young girl like Marissa. Quite a desirable young lady to some men, right?"

DeWayne's eyes darted around and he licked his dry lips.

"I'm not saying you have desires for the girl, but perhaps you know someone who does?" Whittaker said amiably.

I swear I could hear the gears grinding and turning in DeWayne's mind. It was painful to watch his drug- and alcohol-mired brain try to wade through the facts and fiction, which were undoubtedly a jumbled mess in his head.

"We just want to make sure Marissa is okay, DeWayne. Put us in touch with whoever she's involved with so we can confirm she's alright. Then we'll all move on with our lives."

Damn. Whittaker had me thinking he'd let DeWayne go if he gave us a lead. That's how good the man was at interviewing a suspect. DeWayne's merry-go-round might be a few ponies short, but the detective still had to know the right approach to take.

"DeWayne, should I list the cornucopia of charges currently against you?" Whittaker said. "An outstanding warrant for possession, resisting arrest, assaulting a police constable… let me think, what am I forgetting…"

"I didn't assault no one!"

"You threw a beer bottle at Constable Sommer, DeWayne. That's assault."

"I dropped da bottle, and she ran herself toward it."

I couldn't help myself. I tried to keep it in, but a bit of a laugh forced its way out. DeWayne scowled at me until I sneered his way, which made him flinch and look away.

"Do you realise you're not leaving our custody anytime soon?" Whittaker asked. "Bail will be well out of your reach and, adding these additional charges to your priors, the judge will dish out some serious jail time." The detective leaned forward, resting his elbows on the table. "We can talk about helping you on some of these charges, but not unless you give us something to work with. And right now, finding Marissa is our top priority."

DeWayne rocked in his chair, his face contorting into all sorts of odd expressions as he wrestled with the idea of spending a long time in jail. Or he may have been thinking about lunch. Or had to pee really badly. It was hard to know.

"Now's the time, DeWayne," Whittaker continued. "When I leave the room, I'm moving on, and you'll be at the mercy of our slow-moving judicial system. But I'm sure your trial will come up in three or four months, six at the outside. That time will fly by. Of course, when you're found guilty and we stack all these offences on top of each other, six months will seem like a blink of an eye compared to the years the judge will give you."

DeWayne's eyes searched the table and then the walls as he rocked back and forth. "I need to tink," he mumbled. "I ain't sayin' I know nuttin', but I need to tink about it a few minutes."

Whittaker sighed. "Okay. I'm going to fetch a coffee for me, and one for Constable Sommer. When I return, you tell me what you know. That'll give you a minute to think. But if you're just wasting more of our time, I'll make sure the judge knows you deliberately stalled our investigation. That clear?"

DeWayne cursed, and did a half nod, half head shake kind of thing, as Whittaker got up and walked out of the room. The suspect's eyes flicked in my direction repeatedly, as though he was paranoid about what I would do now the teacher had left the classroom. I had no idea why he was so afraid of me; all I did was run after him. Dug was the one who snacked on his leg. Regardless, afraid he was, and I wasn't about to let the advantage go to waste. I reached over and hit pause on the recording. DeWayne's mouth dropped slightly open and I'm pretty sure he stopped breathing.

"I know where you hang out," I whispered.

"I want da... da udder man back," DeWayne stuttered.

"I bet you do," I said, grinning. And then an idea hit me.

"He already knows it's The Haitian," I said, carefully watching the man. "All you have to do is tell him what he already knows and he'll help you out."

DeWayne stared blankly at me until his brow slowly knitted into a frown. He looked like he didn't have any idea what I was talking about. Now I'd really screwed things up. If this *dummenikk* started blabbing about *me* telling *him* about Haitians, my half-baked scheme would come unravelled. I had to back out of this if the name meant nothing to him.

And then DeWayne mumbled quietly, "I ain't givin' dat man up."

Talk about a blind squirrel finding a truffle. Or something like that. My heart thumped in my chest, but I stayed calm. "Okay. No help for you then."

"If you knew dis man…" DeWayne hissed. "I'd rather go to jail dan be dead."

I shrugged my shoulders. "Doesn't matter to me. We're about to nab him, anyway."

"Den you don't need no help from me!"

"Oh, you'll help us alright," I said, with a big smile. "You just won't get the benefit from him."

He looked at me, puzzled. I waited. "What da hell you mean?"

"I'm just saying, we'll tell him you're squealing away so he thinks he's up shit creek. It doesn't matter to us whether you help or not."

His face dropped, then slowly twisted into anger, before settling on panic. "He'll kill me, man!"

I shrugged my shoulders again. "Not if he's locked up here, or extradited back to Haiti."

DeWayne groaned.

"Like I say, your choice. Help Whittaker and he'll throw you a bone. Don't help and you'll probably be in the same prison area as The Haitian." I laughed. "Wouldn't that be a crazy coincidence?"

"You can't do dis bullshit, man."

"I'm not a man, and all I'm doing is chatting with you while the detective gets us coffee."

"You're a bitch."

"It's been said."

"Fuck!" he swore through gritted teeth, thumping the table with his hands.

I heard the door handle turn.

"Remember," I whispered, "This needs to come from you, or you won't get credit for helping."

I quickly hit the record button as Whittaker closed the door with his foot and put two coffees down on the table.

"You two get along okay while I was gone?" Whittaker asked as he sat down.

"Not a word out of him, sir," I lied. "I don't think he likes me."

DeWayne let out a big sigh.

"So, what's it to be?" Whittaker asked. "Are you going to help me, or are you wasting our time?"

DeWayne looked up. "I ain't never met dis guy, but everyone calls him Da Haitian."

18

NO MORE MOUNTAIN TO CLIMB

I stood behind Whittaker, who sat at his desk while he showed me how to request a phone number trace through the RCIPS system. I played suitably dumb and prayed that Rasha wouldn't see the request. When he was done showing me, he searched for the number himself, as he was one of the few people with direct access to the database.

"Here," he said, pointing to his screen. "It's a pay-as-you-go phone, which means we're out of luck on finding the owner."

"Shit," I groaned in my best disappointed voice. Acting required expression, and I was the opposite of expressive, but at least I was behind Whittaker, where he couldn't see my face.

DeWayne had given up the phone number, which matched the one I'd found in Cosgrove's notebook. Beyond that, he couldn't tell us anything useful. He'd never met The Haitian, only spoken to him over the phone, and he'd found the man through a stranger in a bar. The stranger had told him The Haitian was looking for pretty, young island girls to serve drinks at parties and hang out on rich guys' boats. He had Marissa call the number, and the next day an envelope was waiting for him at the same bar. There was $200 in the envelope, which he threw away. The envelope, not the cash. Although I expect he threw the money away as well in exchange for drink, drugs and dice games.

I believed everything apart from him not knowing the stranger. It was probably a friend who he didn't want to give up, or his drug dealer who he'd never cross. He also said The Haitian called him a day later saying the girl never showed up, so I guess there were two things I didn't believe. Selling your girlfriend's daughter to a sex-trafficking fiend wasn't a legacy most people would want left behind. If she didn't show up, DeWayne wasn't responsible. In DeWayne's peanut brain.

So, now we had the name and phone number in the ongoing report, almost certainly linked to some form of wrongdoing. But still no excuse to open Cosgrove's safe to find the matching information.

"What now, Constable Sommer?" Whittaker asked as I returned to the front side of his desk.

"Search our database for any references to The Haitian," I replied, having already thought about these steps all morning. "Have uniforms stop by the dodgy bars and ask if anyone knows or has heard of The Haitian. And have immigration check for work permit holders and resident aliens from Haiti."

"Good," he responded thoughtfully. "We can cross-reference the list of names from immigration against our system. If this fellow is indeed recruiting girls into sex trafficking, it won't be his first venture into criminal activity."

I leaned on the back of the chair and thought through the process of a man from Haiti moving to the Cayman Islands. The immigration service didn't hand out work permits like candy, and residency was almost impossible for anyone except the independently wealthy.

"He either grew up here, or he's applied for a work permit under a false name," I said, continuing my thought process aloud. "He would have been denied a work permit with a criminal record in the system here, or in Haiti. It's also unlikely he's skilled in a trade worthy of a permit. Far more likely, he used someone else's identity to enter the Cayman Islands."

"Unless he's recently adopted 'The Haitian' moniker, it's unlikely he grew up here," Whittaker said. "Based on our theory that he's likely to be a career criminal, we would have heard of him before."

"Especially if he's operating at the sex-trafficking level," I added.

Whittaker looked at me thoughtfully. "I'd say that puts him in the stepping-on-toes category."

"I don't follow."

"Who'd be the first to take notice if someone new encroaches on their turf?" he asked me.

"Whoever's turf it is," I replied, getting his point.

"We'll pay Brenda McGinnis a visit," Whittaker replied with a smirk. "She'd know of anyone flexing their muscles in town."

I'd heard AJ talk about Brenda McGinnis. They'd crossed paths at some point. According to AJ she was a mean, old Scottish woman who'd taken over the family business from her equally treacherous father. Brenda ran just about everything corrupt on the island, cleverly hidden behind her legitimate import business. According to her reputation, she didn't take kindly to competition.

"I'll have the team here work on tracking down The Haitian via computer," Whittaker continued, "and we'll drop by and visit McGinnis." He sat back and looked over at me. "In regard to the robbery case, we have a request in to the social media company with a warrant to seek the name and email address of 'Cayman MY Island'. They're notoriously slow in getting back to us, if we can't prove imminent threat to life. I also asked TSU to dig into it. They'll search the site for more interactions from the user. Maybe they made comments on someone else's posts that might help us identify the person."

"Has Detective Weatherford come up with anything more from

the second break-in...?" I said, pausing to correct myself. "Which is actually the first break-in."

"Is it?" Whittaker replied with a grin.

"I thought the camera footage was from before..." I stopped myself again. "Right, we don't know who else hasn't realised they've been burgled."

He nodded. "But yes, Weatherford says in his opinion it's the same perp. Same outfit, movement, MO."

I stood up straight, ready to leave, but Whittaker didn't move. He drummed his fingers on his desk and slowly swivelled from side to side in his chair. He had more to say, and was thinking about how to say it. Which worried me.

"You realise I'll have to pull you from both these cases," he said somewhat sympathetically.

"I presumed you would at some point," I admitted. "But I was hoping we'd get further along before that happened."

"It should have happened when you expressed your theory of them being connected," he responded. "Certainly from the robbery case, as you know the victim."

I cringed inside at the idea anyone would consider Randall Cosgrove a victim. Red hot spikes in the eyes would be too good for that *drittsekk*. Whittaker went to say something else, but held back. Maybe he realised what he'd said, or perhaps it was written on my face.

"Maybe I can focus on the Patti Weaver angle of the robbery," I offered, "and as far as Marissa goes, we still don't have a direct connection or enough evidence to say she's been taken under duress."

Whittaker was looking at me again, but he seemed more relaxed.

"Your English is impressive," he said, to my surprise.

I shrugged my shoulders. "Not much opportunity to speak Norwegian in the Cayman Islands," I replied. "I practise my Spanish occasionally, but otherwise all I speak is English."

"Did you learn Spanish in school?" he asked, sliding his chair back and standing.

"No, I learnt Spanish from Ridley," I replied, knowing the detective would feel bad for bringing up a subject tied to my dead boyfriend. But he'd asked, and that was the truth. "He grew up in Mexico."

Whittaker straightened his tie. "Of course. I should have pieced that together. Sorry."

"That's okay," I said with a smile. "Can I stay on the cases for now?"

He laughed as he walked around the desk. "Well played." Offering for me to lead, he followed me down the hall. "For now, yes. But there'll come a point you'll need to be disassociated with the Cosgrove case. We don't need a creative lawyer taking advantage of your connection. For many reasons."

For many reasons indeed, I thought. I was committed to seeing Cosgrove suffer for his sins, even if it meant my history would need to be revealed. But I wasn't prepared to go to jail in the process, and I'd foolishly stuck my neck on the line. I was one digital video rewind away from a cell. Maybe that was a bit dramatic as they still had to put me at the scene, but it felt like Wile E Coyote's anvil was waiting to drop. I did watch telly when I was a kid.

We walked across the car park towards Whittaker's SUV, and I checked my watch. It was 10:45am. Most of the morning had passed by and I was no closer to a police warrant to search the safe.

I remembered watching a documentary on mountaineers climbing the 8,000-metre peaks, some without using supplemental oxygen. Those people were remarkable athletes and adventurers, not the herds of mediocre climbers paying shitloads of money for someone talented to drag them up Everest. These men and women were the real deal.

One of them talked about two key elements for staying alive in the biggest mountains on earth. Put one foot in front of the other, he'd said. Then do it again, until there's no more mountain to climb. Make good decisions was his second point. Make decisions based on logic and experience, not dreams and hopes.

That's what I needed to do. Keep working on the investigation and not let my emotions lead me into poor decisions. Or at least any more poor decisions.

19

DIFFERENT RULES

Whittaker idled down a driveway towards the Caribbean Sea just outside George Town. I'd passed by this place a thousand times and often wondered what the story was. A single-level home stood on our right and a warehouse on the left, leaving an unobstructed view of the water between them.

The dated house had a discoloured tile roof and lapboard that hadn't been power-washed in decades. The warehouse was a newer structure and small by modern standards. No more than 50 metres long by 20 metres wide. Two large roll-up doors flanked an office door and window. An older model Mercedes was parked by the house and we pulled up alongside a small box truck by the warehouse.

As we got out of the SUV, Whittaker paused a moment.

"McGinnis can be..." he began saying, then thought a moment before continuing. "Obtuse. Do you know the word?"

"It's one of the angles in a triangle."

"That's true," he replied, "but it also means deliberately awkward or difficult."

I closed the door. "Why in English do your words not mean one thing?" I asked, somewhat rhetorically, although I was curious.

"Did someone say you were out of words at some point, so now you must double up on the ones you have?"

Whittaker looked at me across the bonnet of the SUV. "I'm guessing it has more to do with the language developing with so many dialects in different regions."

"That would be funny," I said.

Usually, I kept my whacky thoughts within the confines of my quirky mind, but I found myself saying more things out loud around the detective.

"What would be funny?" he asked, not moving.

See, that's why I keep things to myself. Now we had to have a conversation about a subject that was mildly amusing, but irrelevant in the big scheme of things.

"I just pictured two medieval English blokes running into each other, and one threatens to hit the other one over the head with a bat," I explained. "The second peasant says go ahead. A flying gerbil can't hurt too bad, then I'll hit you with my club. The first bloke looks around confused, because he's wondering where all the other members of this organisation are. See, you could go on for a while like that. I thought it was funny."

Whittaker grinned and shook his head. "You're an interesting human being, Nora Sommer."

"Thank you, sir," I replied as we walked to the office door.

As soon as Whittaker opened the glass-paned entry, we were practically bowled over by a rush of air conditioning and cigarette smoke. I followed him inside with my eyes watering and wondered if I could hold my breath for the duration of the interview.

"Shut the damn door," came a thick Scottish accent from behind a desk, slightly obscured through the haze.

"Hello, Miss McGinnis," Whittaker said politely.

"What the fuck do youse want?"

Brenda McGinnis was not a small woman, nor a good-looking woman, and clearly wasn't a friendly woman. Her desk was a disorganised pile of papers, overflowing ashtray and various filthy coffee cups. A bottle of whisky was half hidden behind her computer monitor. The temperature in the office was borderline arctic.

"I was hoping you could help me with a fellow we're trying to find," Whittaker ventured, ignoring her brusque greeting.

Brenda aimed her beady eyes my way, her irises and pupils indistinct from each other. The whites of her eyes were more of a murky cream colour, lined with tiny blood vessels running everywhere like streams feeding a pond.

"Who's yer new lapdog, Detective? One o' them mail-order lassies, is she?"

My muscles tensed and I glared back, but held my tongue. I finally needed to take a breath and immediately coughed and spluttered.

Brenda laughed. "Ooh, I like her. She's got the fire in her eyes. Better not turn my back on this one."

"Do you know a man who calls himself The Haitian?" Whittaker asked.

"Not personally, no," Brenda replied, shifting her eyes back to the detective.

"But you know *of* him?"

"O' course," she replied, and I could see a smirk beginning to take shape around her thin lips.

"Can you tell us where we might find him?"

"Sure I can," she said and could hold back her grin no longer. "Haiti. There's a million of the bastards to choose from."

Whittaker turned to me with an 'I told you so' look. I don't know if he intended for me to have a go, but I wanted to move this shitshow along, so I took the plunge.

"Do you traffic underage girls?"

Brenda laughed again and looked back and forth between me and the detective. "Yer catalogue lassie's got some balls, hasnae she?" She fixed her stare my way. "I run an import business – yer grandaddy here should know that by now. An' if I *were* to meddle in things frowned upon by the likes o' youse, it wouldn't involve underage gals."

"We have reason to believe The Haitian is doing just that," I said, forging ahead. "There's a girl missing, and we need to find this man."

"How should I know anything aboot this fella?" Brenda replied, but her voice had softened.

"You're a smart businesswoman with her ear to the ground," I said, hoping I didn't sound too patronising. "Not much happens in town without you knowing."

"If he disnae bother my business, I couldnae give a shit aboot him," she replied before lighting another cigarette.

I felt like I was getting lung cancer just standing in the office for five minutes. I had no idea how this woman was still alive if she'd spent her life chain smoking this way. Maybe the hard alcohol neutralised the tar, but I doubted that was a medically sound theory.

"But you said it yourself. You don't condone preying on young girls, so help us save this kid."

"Where the fuck are you from, lassie?" Brenda asked, leaning back and looking me up and down again. "Ye have an accent, but ye know all these fancy words."

"Norway," I replied.

She squinted at me through the cloud of smoke she'd just exhaled, deepening the wrinkles and creases around her eyes.

"I don't rat people out, is that clear? So dinnae think ye'll be dropping by for a wee little chat every time you cannae find granny's lost cat," she said firmly. I waited while she took another drag and leaned forward. "When a lass is eighteen, she's had enough chance to figure out this world," she continued, shaking a finger at me while ash spilled all over her desk from her cigarette. She didn't seem to notice. "If she cannae make the right choices after that, it isnae for me to give a shit. But, because I dinnae like sick fucks picking on kids, I'll give ye what I know. This wanker hangs oot at Coconut Joe's. There most nights, I'm told."

"What does he look like?" I asked.

"He looks like a fucking Haitian," Brenda whipped back. "Want me to do everything for ye?"

I grinned and shrugged my shoulders. "Sure."

Brenda lifted her chin and glared at me. Slowly, a smirk crossed her face, evolving into a laugh. "Shame ye chose to wear that monkey outfit, lassie, I reckon I couldae found some work for ye."

"Young, old, tall, short?" I asked, risking her wrath.

"Best I know, the little shit is a wee man halfway in years between the two o' yer," she said, stubbing out the cigarette butt and reaching for the pack. "Skedaddle aff, now. I've business to do, and yer costing me money."

Nodding my thanks, I marched outside. I had never been so relieved to draw in hot, humid air before. Mentally noting to undress on the porch before going inside my shack tonight, I didn't know whether I should burn my clothes or attempt to launder them.

We got into the SUV and Whittaker hit the button and lowered both front windows. He hadn't said a word since we'd walked out. I began thinking about how to say sorry for jumping into the interview. But I wasn't sorry. She'd given us a lead, and it hadn't appeared likely before I took a run at her.

"You did well," Whittaker said as he backed out and started up the driveway.

"I didn't know if it was okay or not," I said, surprised, but pleased by the compliment.

"The key to interviewing is reading the room," the detective said. "Every situation is unique, and often you have very little time to establish a path with a suspect. You read this situation correctly."

"You taught me that this morning," I responded.

He looked over and I could tell he was trying to recall if he'd explained the process to me earlier in the day.

"I watched what you did with DeWayne, sir. You showed him how he was screwed, and how you could help him out of it," I explained. "It was impressive." I left out the part about me putting

DeWayne's balls in a vice while the detective was out of the room, but I'd still been genuinely impressed by Whittaker's interview.

"Well, thank you. And good job for paying attention. Just remember, they're never the same twice, not even with the same perp. They learn too, especially if they've been through the system a time or two."

I added his words of wisdom to my expanding data bank. "It's weird, isn't it?" I said, as the thought hit me.

"What is?"

"That woman, Brenda McGinnis. She's a known criminal, right?" I asked.

Whittaker scoffed. "As our friend Reg would say, she's as bent as a nine-bob note."

I had no idea what that meant exactly, but I'd heard Reg say it and I took it to mean the detective agreed with my statement.

"So we know she is. She knows she is. And she knows that we know she is," I rambled. "But we just had a ten-minute conversation with her, and she'll carry on doing illegal things, and we'll carry on not arresting her."

"Different rules," Whittaker said in way of reply.

I looked over at him, unsure what he meant.

"We have a set of rules we must abide by," he explained. "They have a distinctly different set of rules, but they must play by them too. The difference is, we can never break our rules, and theirs move around based on their risk-versus-reward tolerance."

"Sneak a little contraband into the country and it's hard to discover, therefore hard to justify too much resource," I replied, hoping I followed his point. "Leave bodies floating in the harbour, and the whole force is on her arse."

"Something like that, yeah," he said, nudging his glasses up his nose and glancing my way.

"Believe me, I've been trying to put Brenda McGinnis away since I was a rookie constable like you. Better policemen than me have tried too, not to mention the effort that went into catching her father back in the day." Whittaker let out a long breath. "She's a wily one, but one day she'll slip up and we'll get her."

"We'd better hurry," I commented. "There's no way her lungs can last much longer."

"I think she's part cockroach," Whittaker said, letting a grin slip across his face. "She defies medical wisdom."

"That'll explain her dazzling looks," I mumbled.

We drove in silence for a minute before the detective spoke again. "Just remember, our rules aren't flexible. We have lines we don't cross."

I sat as still as I could in my seat and focused on breathing. "Gotcha," I finally responded.

20

NOD'S AS GOOD AS A WINK...

Coconut Joe's was in the middle of Seven Mile Beach on the inland side of West Bay Road. It had all the signage and stereotypical feel of an island tourist trap, but it actually served great food and was frequented by locals as well as visitors.

Whittaker pulled into the car park for the Seven Mile Beach Resort, directly across the road, and found an empty spot facing the restaurant. Blocked by palm trees, colourful signs and bright green wooden fencing around the front of the business, we couldn't see anything inside. It was all outdoor seating, but the space was partially shaded by a roof, and the rest by large trees and broad café-style umbrellas.

"I'll take a walk through and have a look," Whittaker said, and opened the door.

"Won't that be suspicious?" I asked. "What if you're recognised?"

He paused. "Hungry?"

I nodded. I was hungry.

"What would you like?" he asked.

"Whatever fish taco special they have."

He nodded and closed the door. Plenty of businesspeople

dropped in for lunch or picked up food to go, so he'd thought of the perfect cover. His suit didn't immediately give him away as law enforcement, but my uniform certainly did, so I understood why I had to stay put. I watched customers come and go while I waited in the SUV. I didn't see anyone remotely fitting the thin description Brenda had given us.

Whittaker returned after fifteen minutes, carrying a bag. He slid into the driver's seat and handed me the food. The aroma of the grill and spices quickly filled the vehicle.

"No luck," he said as I gave him a carton from the bag. "Mainly tourists, one table of locals, and no one at the bar."

"Did you ask anyone about him?"

Whittaker shook his head as he picked up a taco. "Couldn't risk one of the staff being a friend who might give us away. I know the owners, and they wouldn't stand for anything illegal operating from their restaurant. If they knew, that is. The guy must just hang out there, or keep his dealings well concealed. Even so, it doesn't guarantee a staff member isn't moonlighting as The Haitian's eyes and ears."

We sat and ate lunch for ten minutes, watching more people come and go from Coconut Joe's. The scene was very relaxed, the music not too loud, and the clientele was a mixed bag. I knew from driving past at night, once the dinner crowd thinned out, the place turned into more of a gathering place for the young and trendy. The music was louder, lights were flashy, and unattached locals and tourists alike were busy trying to become temporarily attached.

"I have an idea," Whittaker said as he wiped his lips with a paper napkin. "We'll set up surveillance on the bar this evening. I'll talk to West Bay Station and have you and Jacob assigned to me later in your shift. Bring a change of clothes with you."

"To go undercover?" I asked, barely hiding my enthusiasm.

"Dress like a tourist from Norway," he replied. "Sit at the bar and observe. See if you can spot The Haitian."

I wondered what a Norwegian tourist looked like in Whittaker's mind. Our traditional costume was called a *bunad*, which was an elaborate dress with intricate embroidery and silver jewellery. Some Europeans would recognise one. Most Americans couldn't even find Norway on a map, so I doubted any would know of a *bunad*. To them it would look like an Amish woman went nuts accessorising. I wouldn't be surprised if Whittaker had researched a little about my country, but I guessed our national costume was not what he had in mind.

He dropped me back at the station on Elgin in time for me to drive my Jeep north, grab clothes from home, then on to West Bay station for my regular shift. I had a jumbo cup of coffee with me and spent the first 30 minutes explaining what was happening to Jacob. My partner liked routine, normality, and predictability. Maybe that's why they put me with him, or perhaps it was just the way things worked out, but I was the antithesis of all those things.

Once Jacob was clear that his role in the evenings stakeout would be to hang out nearby and stay out of sight, he settled down. Jacob wasn't afraid of being involved in the fray – I trusted him with my life – but he needed to know the intimate details of all that was expected. He was a planner. I was a bull in every china shop I came across. According to AJ, at least.

We flipped our coins and ran our number one – two heads – route, anticlockwise, with nothing suspicious going on as usual. The radio was quiet, but it was early. The Friday evening action usually heated up around sunset, then settled down for an hour or two during dinnertime before business picked up from 9:00pm on. We only had to worry about our patch until just before 7:00pm, as that's when Whittaker had us meeting him and the team he was assembling.

I made Jacob pull into Fosters supermarket so I could get rid of my earlier coffee, and refill my travel mug. A coffee-flavoured energy drink called to me from a shelf as I made my way to the bathroom in the back, but I decided the triple dose of caffeine advertised on the can was a bit much. Actually, if I'd found one chilled, I'd have bought it, but it was probably good I didn't.

The sun was setting as Jacob pulled out of the car park and

waited at West Bay Road. Crossing the car park opening from the left, an elderly lady was leading her husband, whose left hand rested on her shoulder. We often saw the couple around town. He usually had the handles of a single cloth shopping bag in his right hand, as he did now, and they slowly made their way from the shops to home or vice versa. The lady waved in greeting and thanks as they waddled along.

"Dat's goin' to be me and my missus one day," Jacob said with a smile.

"You planning on going blind?" I asked, wondering who schedules the loss of their eyesight.

"No! I don't mean dat part," he retorted. "I'm just sayin', when da kids are all grown and goin' about der own business, that'll be me and her, just doin' our own ting together."

His statement had a strange effect on me. Part of me saw the beauty and simplicity in the love he clearly shared with his wife. Perhaps I was even envious. But part of me became defensive and almost angry. I'd thought I was in love once, as a sixteen-year-old girl in Norway, and then I discovered what love truly felt like with Ridley. But both men were dead. Either directly or indirectly because of me.

I'd resigned myself to a life without a partner, and for the most part, I'd come to terms with being alone. But Jacob gave me a glimpse of what I was truly missing, which opened a wound I went to great lengths to keep closed. I knew people wanted me to find somebody else. To be happy. Perfect examples of truly wonderful relationships surrounded me. Not just Jacob, but AJ and her boyfriend Jackson, Reg and Pearl, even Whittaker and his wife, Rosie. But the risk was too high.

Physical love I could manage on my own when needed. I'd already experienced the best sex I could possibly imagine, and the worst imaginable. For some women, being abused or raped destroyed their self-worth and sent them down a path of endless toxic relationships. Ridley saved me from that. Being with him was an overwhelming feeling of physical and emotional joy. I'd finally felt safe. Settling for anything less would be an insult to his memory and carve another slice of my soul away.

Tyres squealing brought me out of my thoughts and I looked around for the source. Jacob had been waiting for a seemingly endless line of commuter traffic to pass, but now all the cars had come to a halt. To our right, a car had stopped at a strange angle at the next entrance into the car park. I threw the door open and jogged that way.

As I approached, I could see the elderly lady bending over next to the car. The driver's window was rolled down, and a man was shouting loudly, but I couldn't make out what he was saying. My jog turned into a sprint, and I heard Jacob turn on the siren and reverse behind me. Sitting on the tarmac was the old man, with his wife trying to assist him to his feet. I rushed to their side.

"Are you hurt?" I asked, looking the man over.

"No worse than I were, I don't believe," he said, his face turning towards the source of the new voice.

"If you're ready, I'll help you up," I told him, and he nodded.

With a hand on his shoulder, I moved behind him, then crouched down and slid my hands under his arms. "Ready?"

"Best I'll be," he replied, and I lifted with all my strength.

I was stunned by how frail the man was. I was able to raise him to his feet on my own. His wife fussed and touched him, checking his arms for signs of trauma.

I noticed blood trickling down his hand. "You're bleeding, sir. I should call an ambulance."

He smiled. "It's nuttin', child. Don't take much ta make stuff fall outta dis old body dese days."

His wife took a handkerchief from her pocket and wiped his hand, wrapping the cloth around so he could hold it in place with his thumb. The man in the car had grown quiet after I arrived, but I heard him call out again, with less vigour than earlier.

"Looks like everyone fine. Can we clear the way?"

He spoke with an accent I placed as Eastern European, but I couldn't pinpoint the country. I glared at him and he looked away.

"Best we get along," the old lady said, picking up the shopping bag and slipping the handles into her husband's hand. "Don't mean to be holdin' up all dese folks."

"Wait a second," I said, putting a hand on her arm to slow her down. "What exactly happened here?"

"They didn't look where they were going, that's what happened," the man in the car shouted from his car.

Jacob walked up beside me, having parked our vehicle nearby with the lights still flashing.

"Move this guy out of the way," I told Jacob. "But make sure he doesn't leave."

I took a picture with my mobile of the car's precarious position in the entranceway before helping the two old people to the pavement.

"Now tell me what happened," I asked the lady again.

"We was walkin' across the driveway, and I checked both ways," she said nervously, still shaken from the incident. "Den dat fella come turnin' in all tyres screachin'. Took me by surprise. Guess he slammed on da brakes and skidded some. He caught Dell, and I couldn't hold him up, so he come a cropper." She shook her head. "I'm so sorry, Dell, I s'pose I shoulda seen da car comin'."

I looked over at the tyre marks on the road running across the tarmac of the car park entrance. "You didn't do anything wrong. If you were already walking across from pavement to pavement, you had the right of way."

"We don't want to cause no trouble," Dell said, and his wife patted his arm.

"Wait here a moment, please," I told them. "I'll be back."

I clicked a picture of the tyre marks as I walked towards where Jacob had pulled the guy over next to our patrol car. I took a few deep breaths before I reached them. Maybe I should have taken a few more.

"Can you tell me what happened?" I asked him through the driver's window.

"I was driving here, and the people, they not looking out for cars," he said, gesticulating with his hands. "I have to slam brakes to miss them."

"But you didn't," I replied calmly despite my blood boiling.

"I didn't what?"

"You didn't miss them. You hit the old man."

"No, no, maybe brush him little bit. It was nothing," he said with another wave of the hand. "He should see me coming," he added.

"He's blind," I pointed out.

"Why blind guy walking around in traffic when it is now dark outside!" he shouted, getting even more animated.

"Because it doesn't matter to him," I said in a mixture of disbelief and anger.

"What not matter?"

"He's blind, you dumb fuck. He has no idea whether it's dark or light, makes no difference to Dell."

He looked stumped for a moment. "Then she should be one to watch."

I could tell Jacob was getting concerned as he shuffled from one foot to the other next to me. He was probably worried about what I was going to do. He needn't have been. The driver, on the other hand, was too arrogant to be worried, but he should have been.

"Get out of the car, sir," I ordered. "Bring your licence, registration, and insurance."

"This is ridiculous. They are fine. I leave now."

He moved his hand towards the ignition, but before he reached the key, I had the door open and my Taser resting against his neck.

"What the fuck is this!" he yelped.

"Please get out of the car, sir," I ordered again.

"Nora!" Jacob groaned desperately beside me.

The man eased himself out of the car and stood.

I smiled at Jacob. "Why don't you search the car? He seemed in a hurry to leave. Maybe there's something he'd rather we didn't see."

Jacob still looked worried, but he nodded. I moved the Taser down to the base of the man's back. "Let's walk over there and take a look." I shoved him in the direction of the tyre marks he'd left.

"This is crazy. You can't threaten me like this."

"I haven't threatened you," I reminded him. "You already tried to flee the scene once. I'm making sure you don't try again."

I stopped him by the entranceway. "See the footpath to our left?"

"Of course."

"See the footpath on our right?"

"Yes," he mumbled.

"That means pedestrians have the right of way across this driveway."

"Not if I'm already here," he complained. "If they run out in front of car, is their fault."

I wanted to pull the trigger on my Taser so badly. "Your claim, which is different to what you said earlier, is that those two elderly people over there ran out in front of you while you were turning in? The old man was on the floor here," I pointed in front of us. "And your skid marks are over there to our left. You're claiming those two sprinted across like gazelles and almost made it before you hit him?"

"Barely touched him," the man said again.

"How do you feel about apologising to these lovely people you almost killed?"

"Not almost killed! Really? Small knock is all."

I shoved the Taser into his lower back again.

"Okay, okay, I say sorry."

We walked over to the couple. She still looked bewildered, but Dell had a slight smile on his face. I guessed his hearing was tuned in better than most people's, as he relied on it so heavily. He must have heard my conversation with the driver.

"I'm sorry for barely touching you in roadway," the man said, less than sincerely. "Glad you okay. I go now?"

I scoffed.

"It'll be one more minute, if you don't mind waiting," I said to the couple, who both nodded. I shoved the driver towards our cars with my free hand and holstered the Taser. "You can go," I said casually. "Once I've written you up for reckless endangerment, failure to give way to pedestrians and whatever else I can think up in the next few minutes."

"You're bitch!"

"That's not very original."

I pushed him again, begging for him to turn around on me, but he didn't. It was definitely a good thing I didn't buy the energy drink. I would have tasered his sorry arse before he ever got out of his car.

21

INGRID

I hated paperwork, but sometimes it was worth the hassle. Viktor Melnyk was from Croatia and working in the Cayman Islands on a work permit as an architect for a commercial developer. The icing on the cake would be if they voided his work permit for the legal issues he now had.

It was nearly 7:00pm when we pulled away from Fosters, so I told Jacob to keep his eyes on the road while I changed. Good thing it was dark outside or there would have been a few calls to the station asking why some blonde was writhing around in the passenger seat of a police car, struggling to put a summer dress over her bra and panties. I could almost feel the heat from Jacob's embarrassed red cheeks as he tried to watch the road without catching glimpses of me. He's such a gentleman.

I'd chosen a bright yellow dress with a bold floral pattern which hit just above my knees. Releasing my hair from the low bun I wore while on duty, I did my best to sort out a few of the tangles. I usually never wore make-up, but a dash of lipstick and eyeliner seemed appropriate for my cover. I'd argued with myself over footwear, and finally settled on a pair of white and light blue trainers with low socks. The pair of heeled sandals with straps that wound up my calf were really cool, but running in them would be an ankle twister, and who knew what the evening would bring?

Whittaker was waiting for us in the car park of the hospice building tucked in the woods one street over from Coconut Joe's. Maybe he figured there weren't too many people who'd come running out to see what all the fuss was about. Another unmarked police car was next to the detective's Range Rover, and a van used by the firearms unit.

I heard a wolf whistle when I stepped out of the car and looked over to see Williams laughing. The head of the firearms unit had given me a hard time when I'd first started with the force, but I'd earned his respect during my first major case. I flipped him off, and he laughed even harder.

Whittaker quickly gathered us for a briefing. The plan was simple. I would wander into the bar and hang out for a while, order a drink and some food to appear like a tourist, and see who showed up. We didn't have fancy crap like earpieces no one can see, or hidden microphones, so good old hand signals would have to do. Two plain clothes constables would sit in the restaurant, hopefully within visual contact of me. Whittaker would be across the road in his SUV, and the cavalry would be here in the hospice car park, ready to go. Jacob was to wait with Williams and his two men.

My signal was to rub my right ear if I believed The Haitian was there. If I rubbed the back of my neck, it meant I was sure and they should come in and grab him. The two policemen eating dinner would use texts on a mobile to communicate with Whittaker. If I rubbed my neck, they'd call in Williams's team. If The Haitian didn't show up, we'd quietly leave and try again tomorrow. I hoped the guy showed up. A lot could happen to Marissa in the next 24 hours. We needed to find her.

Whittaker sent the two constables on their way to get a dining table, and I waited for a text telling us they were seated. Jacob paced around nervously. I felt calm. But watching him made me wonder why he was so anxious. I was the one who had to make this work, by not giving myself away, and using the right signals.

When I chewed all that over, I felt my stomach tighten. I hated being the centre of attention.

The mobile in Whittaker's hand buzzed, and he gave me a nod. I began walking down the lane, then around the corner to Coconut Joe's as the detective rolled by in his SUV on his way to the resort car park.

By the time I approached the front entrance, the butterflies were gone and my mind was completely focused. A hostess greeted me and asked if I wanted a table, which I declined and headed through the patio towards the bar. Out of the corner of my eye, I saw the two constables who were smart enough to look me over. Two guys without dates would not ignore a 5-foot 9-inch blonde walking by.

The L-shaped bar wasn't busy. It was also quite small, with six chairs lining the front and two more around the side. The bartender, who looked like a local man in his late twenties, served a couple of tourists at the end of the front side, both sporting shiny new local dive shirts. A dark-skinned man sat alone on the short side. He watched me walk up as I chose a stool at the front, nearest the corner.

I looked at a laminated menu while I waited for the bartender to approach me. When he'd finished serving drinks to the tourist couple, he moved down and slid a beer mat across the resin topped bar in front of me.

"Wat would you like, miss?" he asked with a distinctly Cayman accent, which I was sure he could turn up or down based on who he was talking to.

"Can I have a fruity rum drink, please? And a glass of water. I've been in the sun all day," I said, laying on a heavy coating of my own accent.

"Fruity rum drink, no problem, mon. I'm Freeman an' I'm 'ere to get yer anyting you need," he said, now sounding more Jamaican than Caymanian. Most tourists didn't know the difference and expected the stereotypical jolly island barkeep. That was good. When he walked up, I could have been one of the many foreign workers on the island, especially in the dive industry, but now he'd decided I was a visitor.

The man to my right wasn't The Haitian. He might well be from Haiti, but he didn't fit the description we had. This guy was taller than me and in his twenties. I needed to hear him speak to narrow down his nationality. I looked his way and smiled. He had his barstool tipped back on two legs with his shoulders against the wall behind him. He was facing the restaurant, but glanced at me. I nodded a greeting.

"Dey put da cheap rum in da fruity drinks, ya know," he said casually. "Better ta order da good rum over ice. Your…" He patted his flat stomach while he searched for the word.

"Stomach?" I offered.

"Dat's it, yeah, da stomach. It tank you later," he finished with a laugh.

He was Haitian. English was his second or third language. His accent sounded ethnic French and was likely Haitian Creole.

"I'll try that next time, *takk*," I replied, and held up the chilled glass of colourful liquor Freeman had just set down. "*Skål*."

The stranger tipped his tumbler of rum in my direction, then took a sip. I tried the ridiculously sweet concoction I'd ordered and wasn't surprised to find my new buddy Freeman had not been shy with the cheap rum. Tipsy girls turning the bar into a party was always good for business, and for adding notches to his bedpost. He was going to be disappointed on both counts with me.

"Where you visitin' our beautiful island from?" Freeman asked, leaning against the counter along the back wall.

"I'm from Norway," I replied, keeping it simple. I wanted to engage them both, but not too keenly. My target wasn't here yet. There was a Haitian population on the island, but it was small, so the likelihood of the guy to my right being here to meet a friend was pretty high. I'd become more friendly if The Haitian arrived.

"Where you stayin'?" the stranger asked.

I rolled my eyes and gave him a smirk. "I don't make a habit of telling men I just met where I'm staying."

They both laughed.

"Probably a good idea," Freeman cackled. "How long you here? Dat okay to ask?"

"Depends how the evening goes," I replied and pretended to take a sip of my drink while they both cracked up laughing again.

"I hear tings about ya women from over der," the stranger said with a broad smile.

While they both laughed some more, I lowered my glass below the bar and tipped half of it out. "If you heard we Scandinavians are a little crazy, then you heard right," I said and followed it up with another fake swig before I sat the glass on the bar top. The two men fist-bumped. From the way they interacted, it was clear they knew each other.

Behind the bar, a muted TV aired a football game from England, which had to be a repeat based on the time difference. Freeman subtly tweaked the music up louder as he wandered down to check on the tourists. He was keen to get the atmosphere rolling.

I noticed the stranger's eyes move towards the restaurant entrance behind me, but I resisted turning around.

"What's your name?" I asked him instead.

"Didi," he replied and tipped his stool back onto four legs.

"I'm Ingrid," I told him, then glanced back up at the TV for somewhere to place my gaze and resist looking over my shoulder. It had switched, or been interrupted, by a news show. Marissa Chandler's picture was on the screen with 'Missing' in big letters. Two people at the bar had a reaction. I was one of them. I tried to keep my head facing the television while my eyes flicked to Didi. He was at the very edge of my peripheral vision and had a lousy angle to see the screen. He was still looking at whoever I assumed was approaching.

Freeman was looking up at the TV. He slowly turned and stared at me. His eyes narrowed, and he waggled a finger in my direction.

"You look like someone…" he said, but trailed off.

A man sat down next to Didi and the two greeted each other in Creole, pulling my attention their way as my heart started racing.

The new guy was a short man with a small frame and a shaved head.

"Dis is Ingrid," Didi said, introducing me to the man I believed to be The Haitian.

I held up my drink. "Nice to meet you. What's your name?"

I pretended to sip again, then placed the glass down while the man looked me over without replying. I smiled and rolled the small hoop earring in my right ear. The Haitian sat back without a word, the corner post blocking my view of him. Didi's mobile buzzed on the bar top. He casually picked it up and read the message. His body tensed.

I glanced to my left, where Freeman had moved to the far end, facing away. He turned slightly, and I saw the mobile in his hand. *Fy faen!* The news show must have triggered his memory from the old Skylar Briggs kidnapping case. I'd been all over the news and the Internet. So much for my undercover career. I quickly rubbed the back of my neck and stood up from my stool.

The Haitian was already gone. He must have slipped away when my back was turned. I went to step around the corner of the bar but managed to stop just in time. The barstool Didi was swinging slammed against the corner of the bar, splintering wood shards everywhere. The hefty seat of the broken stool slammed me in the ribs and knocked me off balance, sending me over my stool and tumbling to the ground.

By the time I'd picked myself up, Didi was gone as well. The two constables stopped to see if I was okay, but I shoved them in the only direction the Haitians could have run, which was through the kitchen.

"I'm fine. Go after them!"

I whipped around. The tourists were on their feet wondering what had just happened, and Freeman tried giving me an innocent look.

"Are you okay?" he asked.

My glare in return told him I wasn't falling for his bullshit, and he glanced around for options. Williams and Jacob were running through the restaurant, so his only escape was the door out the back of the bar into the building, which was down my end. I planted my hands on the bar top and leapt, tapping a foot on the bar to carry me over, and landing on the rubber mat, just as Freeman reached the door. On the wrong foot, I weakly swung my right arm, which was enough to send him crashing into the door frame and halting his progress. That gave me time to pounce.

Grabbing his right wrist, I kicked the back of his knee. As he crumpled, my own knee followed him down, landing in the small of his back. His shoulder and forehead took the brunt of the fall, then my weight knocked all the wind out of him. A sea of amazed faces stared at us from the kitchen, where the staff weren't sure what to do.

"Police," I said, in case anyone decided to help the bartender being attacked by a Scandinavian tourist.

Freeman gasped and spluttered, his left hand reaching for his mobile on the kitchen floor in front of him where he'd dropped it. I twisted his wrist a little harder as I snatched it up first.

"I don't think so, *drittsekk*! That text you sent makes you an accessory to a lot of shit. You're under arrest."

22

FIRST OUT OF THE LONGBOAT

I was going to have a colourful bruise on my ribs, but worse than that, my pride had taken a hit. Driving north in my Jeep, I ran through the events of the evening in my mind. I wasn't sure what I could have done differently, but it was my job to evaluate the players at the bar, and I'd failed with Freeman. Earlier in the day, Whittaker had even mentioned about not trusting the staff. The two Haitians had got away, and the bartender hadn't said a word apart from demanding his lawyer. Wherever Marissa was, she was spending another night there.

From the end of Esterly Tibbetts Highway, I turned left on Batabano and headed into West Bay. In town, instead of turning right towards home, I stayed straight and made my way to Northwest Point Road. I was dead tired and craving a shower, but it was Friday night, so Reg's wife Pearl would be playing at the Fox and Hare. And AJ would be there. No matter how worn out I felt, I knew sleep would elude me with so much on my mind, so I chose a glass of wine and some friendly faces.

Leaving the Jeep on the edge of the road as the car park was full, I made my way to the front door, letting my hair free of the ponytail I needed for driving the open top CJ-7. The place was packed. I pushed my way through the crowd with Pearl singing her heart out from the stage. I found my group at their usual table, and people shuffled seats to make room for me.

Before sitting down, I went to Hallie, Thomas's cousin and the teenager I considered my little sister. I gave her a long hug.

"You look gorgeous," she said, looking up at me. "But you look stressed out too."

I caressed her hair and kissed her forehead. "Long day is all." I was about to walk around to my seat, but I paused and spoke loudly into her ear so she could hear me over the music. "Be extra careful at the moment, okay? Don't go anywhere alone, especially at night."

She frowned. "Does this have something to do with Marissa?"

"Do you know her?"

Hallie nodded. "She goes to my school. Well, sometimes she does. She's super smart, but her mother is a mess."

Hallie Bodden knew all about lousy mothers. Her mother OD'd and left her alone on the streets at fifteen, easy pickings for a professional recruiter to dazzle her with money and opportunity. It was fortunate timing; the resort was taken down before Hallie's innocence was stolen, and I prayed we could do the same for Marissa. So many aspects of this case made me think of Hallie. It terrified me.

"Any ideas where she could be?" I asked.

"I checked with all my friends at school. Nobody's seen her in over a week," Hallie replied. "The police came by today and asked us all. I'm really worried, Nora. She's often talked about leaving her mum's, and she knows our door is open to her, but I think she would have come to me if she'd just run away. I wondered if she had a boyfriend, but she'd tell me. We're really close."

"We'll find her," I said, hoping I sounded more confident than I felt at this moment.

I sat down next to AJ, and the rest of my friends greeted me enthusiastically. Letting out a long breath, I tried to ease some of the tension away. I couldn't decide if this was a mistake, inserting myself into a room full of people having a great time. I felt like the one black cloud in a bright blue summer sky. Maybe I should have gone straight home and kept my lousy mood to myself.

AJ slid her Strongbow cider bottle my way. "You look like you could use this," she said, leaning close so I could hear her over the music.

I nodded and took a long swig. It was cold and refreshing.

"Want a cider, or something else?" AJ asked. "I'll go to the bar."

I was about to ask for my usual Chardonnay, but I didn't. "I'll have a Seven Fathoms rum over ice."

"You really did have a rough day!" she replied, before asking the others who needed a fresh drink. When she started towards the bar, I got up and followed her through the crowd.

As we leaned on the robust wooden bar rail, waiting for Frank the bartender to come our way, AJ spoke right next to my ear, so no one else could hear.

"Did you find her?"

I shook my head.

"What about the Cosgrove bloke?"

I shook my head again. "No closer."

Pearl was wrapping up her final set, so we joined in with the applause. No closer was right. I only had part of the day tomorrow to get Whittaker into the second safe at Cosgrove's. Meanwhile, finding Marissa had become the top priority. As it should be.

I would gladly throw away my new law enforcement career in exchange for seeing Cosgrove pay for his sins, but telling Whittaker what was in the safe would *only* throw away my career. Without affecting Cosgrove. He couldn't use my word as probable cause for a search warrant, and there was only one way I could know what was in that safe. I'd be the only one in trouble.

I had focused on the phone number from the notebook, but there was more information. The dates. I assumed they were a log of days Cosgrove had arranged to meet a girl, but I couldn't be sure. If only we'd arrested The Haitian, we could pressure him into giving up his clients in exchange for some form of leniency. He would be deported back to Haiti, so trading charges in the Cayman Islands' system wouldn't matter. But hopefully he wouldn't realise that.

Frank made his way to us, and we ordered our drinks. The house music was quieter than Pearl's playing, but the raucous chatter had built up, making conversation just as difficult. We returned to the table and distributed drinks before AJ nodded her head towards the door. As we walked outside into the balmy night air, the noise dropped to a background drone as the door swung closed. We sat down on a bench to the left.

"So, give me the scoop," AJ said as she leaned back and relaxed.

She wasn't looking for gossip; she was asking about me and my day. I wasn't supposed to discuss police business, but I trusted AJ and Reg completely, plus they did contract work for the RCIPS, so didn't fall under that rule in my book.

"We think this guy who calls himself 'The Haitian' might have something to do with Marissa's disappearance," I explained. "I did an undercover thing tonight, but I fucked it up and he got away."

"Bloody hell, you were undercover? What went wrong?"

"I didn't realise early enough that the arsehole bartender was working for him. He recognised me from the stupid TV and gave me up."

AJ looked incredulous. "You were on TV tonight?"

"No, from the mess with Skylar and Massey."

I couldn't be sure that's what happened, as Freeman wouldn't say a word, but it was the only explanation I could think of.

"Oh. Well, I guess when millions of people watch you on a live Internet stream for half a day, a few of them will remember your ugly mug," AJ said, and grinned at me.

She brought a smile to my face, and I was glad I'd gone to the Fox and Hare.

"But still nothing on that nasty bugger, Cosgrove?" she asked.

I shook my head. "If we'd caught The Haitian and got his mobile, maybe Cosgrove's number would be in there. That might be enough for a warrant," I explained. "But I screwed that up."

"Being recognised is hardly screwing up, Nora."

"I should have called in the guys when I first saw The Haitian, but I wanted to be certain," I replied. "Ten seconds later, everything went to hell, and he got away. Anyway, it looks like the thief isn't targeting former resort members like I thought. There was another break-in, and it was just this old lady's house."

AJ chewed that over for a minute. "But wait, wasn't your entire theory based on this burglar bloke looking for something he didn't find?" she asked sternly. "Isn't that why you had to…" she lowered her voice despite us being alone outside the building. "Go and look last night?"

"I found something, didn't I?" I answered defensively.

"But that's not the point, dunderhead," AJ said, clearly annoyed. "Your basis for risking everything, including me, was horribly flawed!"

I wasn't sure what a dunderhead was, but I guessed it didn't mean genius. The English have so many slang words and phrases I can't be expected to know every one I'm accused of being. Regardless, I knew she had a point. Which pissed me off. Maybe I should have gone straight home after all.

"I knew there was something in the safe, and there was," I said in a weak defence.

AJ stood up. "I'm going back inside."

I could handle her being angry, but she wasn't. Well, she was a bit, but more than that, her voice was full of disappointment, which hurt more. It was the same way with my father when I was young. Feeling like I'd let him down crushed me far worse than a slap on the backside or being yelled at. I reached out and took AJ's hand.

"Sit down. Please."

I heard her sigh, but she dropped back onto the bench.

"I'm sorry," I said, and squeezed her hand.

"Nora, you're like a bulldozer with everything. You rush in all half-cocked and crazy."

"I thought I was a bull? Now I'm a bulldozer too?" I said, and forced a grin.

"You're a herd of enormous animals plus a building site full of heavy, earth-moving equipment, all charging around looking for fragile household items to smash," she replied, her voice softening and a smile creeping across her face.

"I'm really sorry," I said again. "I shouldn't have dragged you into my crap."

"You shouldn't have..." she looked around again for any inquisitive ears, "done it at all."

I thought about her words for a few moments. Of course, she was right. I shouldn't have broken into the house. It was wrong in every conceivable way. But I had to do it, and I'd do it again under the same circumstances. There again, maybe I was only saying that because I didn't get caught. Yet.

"If I can do anything to stop young girls going through what happened to me, I have to do something," I said, looking at the ground. "But I shouldn't have involved anyone else."

"Be more careful, is all I'm saying, Nora. Think things through before you go bowling in."

"Like you?" I grinned. AJ wasn't known for holding back when push came to shove.

"I pussyfoot compared to you, Viking!" she said, looping her arm around mine. "You're out of the longboat, up the beach and swinging your axe around while the rest of us are still deciding whether the island's worth taking." She grinned at me. "But always come to me. Hopefully, I'll do a better job of talking you out of the mad shit, but I'll always drive the boat when you really need me."

We both stood, and I hugged my friend. She squeezed me back in the firm and comforting way she always hugged me.

"I'm going home," I said, when I let her go.

"Come back in and relax awhile. You didn't have a chance to chat with Pearl. You know she has to keep up with all her island daughters."

"Tell her I said hi," I replied. "I've had as much of this bleeding heart, hugging shit as I can take for one night."

AJ shook her head, and I walked across the dark car park to my Jeep.

Hiking in the gloom through the trail in the woods to my shack took nearly as long as the drive home from the pub. Sometimes I practised making my way without a light, in case the need ever arose, but I'd had enough excitement in the last 24 hours, so I used the torch on my mobile. Once I reached the shack, a faint yellow porch light illuminated the last few metres to the steps. I liked the yellow as it didn't attract the bugs and gave a softer glow.

I put my key in the door and glanced down to check the pebble I always left. I crouched down and searched the gap between the door and the jamb. Nothing. Standing back up, I tried to recall that morning. I'd been half-asleep when I'd left the house, but I couldn't picture myself placing the little rock as I usually did. I opened the door and berated myself for being complacent.

My silly precautions were important to me. I'd spent years watching my back, hiding, and being careful. I found comfort in my routine. Flicking on the lights, I made a cursory check of the shack, which took all of twenty seconds. There were only two doors to open; one to the bathroom and one to the small wardrobe. They were both clear, and nothing looked out of place. I drew the curtains and pondered whether to pour myself a glass of wine before going to bed. It was amazing how drained yet wide awake I could feel.

I opened the fridge door and reached for the box of cheap wine. Perched on the shelf above was a folded piece of paper, resting like a place card on a table. Neatly typed on the front were the words 'Good evening, Nora'.

23

LAUNDRY CHUTE

I stared at the note with the fridge door open while cool air escaped into the room. Whether I'd put my pebble in place or not, someone had been in my home. Someone who knew how to pick a lock. I stood up straight and realised I'd been holding my breath. Releasing the air from my lungs, I looked around the living area with adrenaline surging through my body. I was wide awake now.

It took a minute to convince myself that whoever left the note was long gone. But they were. Why leave a message if they were hanging around to smack me over the head? I pulled a pair of nitrile gloves from my rucksack and took the note from the fridge, closing the door. I unfolded it to reveal more type on the inside…

'Don't interfere. I know who you are.'

I dropped the piece of paper on the kitchen counter as though the note itself could harm me. My stomach was in knots. Don't interfere with what? Or who? As I discovered earlier in the evening, too many people know who I am, so although it sounded threatening, it wasn't nearly as worrisome as them knowing where I lived. I slipped the note inside a clear plastic evidence bag and sealed the top without writing the requisite information on the outside.

I ditched the gloves, opened the fridge again, and poured my overdue glass of wine. Sitting on the sofa, I gave myself a minute to settle down before running through the possibilities. There were only two obvious ones. The Haitian. But that meant he'd singled me out amongst a taskforce of police officers, discovered where I lived, typed up a neat note and placed it in my home. All in the last two and half hours, while evading the police, who now knew what he looked like.

The second option was the thief. He had time, and he had the skills. The typed note, neatly placed, was far more in keeping with his deliberate and careful approach. But I had the same question. Why me? I'm not the lead on any of these cases. If I went running into the station and told Whittaker to back off, he'd laugh at me. I had no influence or power over the detective's cases.

Which could only mean the thief knew I'd broken into Cosgrove's place. He'd either seen me do it, or had access to the security cameras. Had he planned to go back and look in the second safe? Maybe he saw the cash I pulled out on camera? Patti Weaver just shot to the top of the suspect list again. She had to be feeding him the information or showing him the video.

My theory about the thief targeting former Fellowship of Lions resort members was blown out of the water since we learnt he'd already robbed the old widow. But even if he wasn't looking for evidence about that, he was certainly looking for something beyond the jewellery he took. It wasn't the cash, as he wouldn't need to shuffle through reams of papers to find bundles of hundred-dollar bills. Regardless, I was being warned to stay out of it. I was stumped.

I sipped my wine and tried to think of anyone else who'd gain something from scaring me off. That idiot I ticketed for hitting the blind man this evening? No way he knew where I lived. I wasn't followed tonight – I'm paranoid, I always check – and I'd already interfered with his day. There wasn't any more interfering to be done, only prosecuting, which was out of my hands.

The idea that Marissa was being held somewhere kept returning to my thoughts, nudging its way into the logical path I was trying to follow. Marissa... what if it was her? Maybe my subconscious was poking a finger at me, trying to get my attention. Could she be involved in something of her own free will, something she wants the police to stay out of? She could be hiding with friends and doesn't want to be returned to her mother. Which I couldn't blame her for, but why go to the lengths of breaking into my place? Plus, according to Hallie, she'd be the friend Marissa would run to.

I'm not sure when I fell asleep, but I finally did, and woke up at dawn on the sofa with a stiff neck. Pale light seeped into the room around the edge of the curtains as I stretched and rubbed my aching muscles. I felt a sharp pain and lifted my shirt to reveal a technicolour bruise on my ribs. The events from yesterday dumped on me like a laundry chute of stinky underwear. I sank further into the sofa. Giving myself a mental kick up the arse, I decided there was no point moping about it. I went to the kitchen, aiming straight for the coffee maker.

On the counter sat the plastic evidence bag containing the note. My heart skipped all over again as I stared at the innocent slip of paper with a far from innocent message. It felt like the final few pieces of sweaty knickers had been stuck in the chute and now dropped on my head with a thud.

What the hell should I do with the note? The answer to that question lay entirely in the knowledge of who'd left it. If it was the thief, I had an overwhelming problem. Once we found him, he'd likely spill the beans on my visit to the Cosgroves'.

My first case in detective training and I might have a vested interest in not catching the culprit. Or at least refraining from handing him in until I knew where he stood. What a shitshow.

I shovelled grounds into a reusable pod, dumped water into the back of the little coffee machine I'd recently purchased, and hit the brew button. A red light blinked at me yet nothing happened.

"*Fy faen!* Stupid piece of crap." I moaned and thumped the top of the plastic contraption.

The red light continued to blink, and I realised I hadn't put a coffee mug underneath it. The stupid machine was saving me from pouring piping hot coffee all over the counter. I took a mug from the dish rack by the sink and slid it in place. The red light stopped blinking.

"Screw you," I mumbled. "No one likes a smart-arse first thing in the morning."

I peeled off the summer dress I'd slept in and threw it in the hamper on my way to the shower. I stood under the spray for a few minutes, letting the warm water wash away my fatigue, confusion, and doubt, leaving me centred. And pissed off. Anger was a tricky emotion. For most people, it clouded their judgement and logic, making them erratic and prone to making more mistakes. For me, it manifested in determination, and helped laser point my focus. That was good, because I was angry a lot.

Quickly dressing, I tipped the coffee into my travel mug, grabbing my keys and rucksack, before stepping outside. I carefully set two pebbles in the door jamb, then checked the back door before I left. The little stone was still in place from whenever I'd set it there ages ago. I never used the back door.

It was my day off, but I didn't care. Marissa couldn't afford for me to take days off. Not having to take my regular shift with Jacob meant I could stay on the cases all day. As long as Whittaker allowed me to. We were fast approaching a time when he'd have to pull me or risk compromising the cases, especially the robbery.

As I traipsed through the woods towards the road, I thought about an alarm system for the shack. I'd always considered it to be a waste of time, and the pebbles were for my sanity rather than a necessity. But not anymore. My treasured, private space had been violated, and with apparent ease. 'Don't interfere,' the note said. Well fuck you, I thought, as I threw my rucksack in the back of the Jeep. I have eight hours to figure out a way to get Whittaker into the second safe. My priorities hadn't changed. Find Marissa, and take down that bastard Cosgrove. Whatever happens after that, I'll deal with the consequences. Or go back on the run.

24

ACE IN THE HOLE

I reached the central station at five to eight and found Detective Whittaker already in full swing. He appeared to have been there a while. He walked with purpose towards me down the hallway as I approached his office.

"Freeman should be in the interview room now. Let's have a chat with him. Maybe's he's more cooperative after a night in a jail cell," he said, without breaking stride. I turned and followed him. Now would be the appropriate time to tell him about the note in my refrigerator. But I didn't. I didn't even have it with me. I'd hidden it at home.

Our suspect looked like he hadn't slept much, but his lawyer, Mansfield, was fresh as a daisy and ready to do battle. Whittaker made introductions and started the recording, which was Mansfield's cue to leap into action.

"From what I've seen and been told, my client has been wrongly accused and detained with no evidence whatsoever that he's been involved in anything elicit. Unless you have something you're yet to reveal, I don't see why we're not walking out of here right now."

"Why did your client try to run?" Whittaker responded calmly.

"He was scared for his safety," Mansfield retorted. "Bar stools were being thrown and men were charging through the restaurant. He was stepping into the building in fear of his life. Until your constable attacked him, that is. Who, by the way, did not identify herself as a police officer."

Whittaker turned to Freeman, who'd been staring at the table, his cuffed hands in his lap. "Is that true, Mr Freeman? You were scared of a 110-pound young woman?"

The suspect quickly looked up and scowled at the detective, shooting me a glance for good measure. Mansfield rested a hand on Freeman's shoulder to keep him quiet.

"Antagonising my client doesn't change the facts, Detective. Can we leave now?"

"Why did you warn the two men?" Whittaker asked, ignoring Mansfield.

"It wasn't a warning. He was simply stating a fact," the lawyer answered, keeping his hand on his client. "He recognised Constable Sommer from that awful kidnapping case, and was pointing it out to the gentleman at the bar."

"He's a friend of yours, then?" Whittaker shot back. "The man who identified himself as Didi. The man who assaulted my constable."

"She hadn't identified herself as a police officer," Mansfield chirped in.

"But your client had just informed him of that fact," Whittaker said firmly. "And Didi's reaction was to assault her with a bar stool."

"That has nothing to do with my client, Detective. He's not responsible for this Didi fellow."

"Correct," Whittaker snapped. "But Didi is a friend of your client's, and Didi and the man seated next to him at the bar are wanted in connection with a missing girl. That makes Mr Freeman here an accessory to kidnapping, and guilty of aiding and abetting."

"Whoa, whoa! That's a huge stretch, Detective," Mansfield responded, throwing his hands up. "Just because he recognises the constable and sends a text to a guy he knows from sitting at the bar he tends doesn't make him involved in anything. This is ridiculous."

"Is that how you know Didi, Freeman?" Whittaker asked, pointedly.

Freeman looked up, then turned to his lawyer, who nodded his assent to answer the question.

"He comes in da bar a lot, so dat's da only way I know da guy."

"What about his friend?" Whittaker quickly asked, jumping on the chance to engage the suspect directly.

"Same, man. Dey both come in da bar regular."

"What's the other guy's name?"

Freeman looked down at the table again.

"As my client says, he doesn't know these men outside of Coconut Joe's," the lawyer replied, inserting himself back into the conversation.

"Look," Whittaker said impatiently. "Right now, all I see is a guy who's impeding our investigation into a missing girl, which makes it very clear you're involved in some way. I don't know why else you'd be protecting these two men."

Freeman groaned and shook his head. "I can't, man."

"Fine," Whittaker said and stood up. "Back to the cell. I'm going ahead with charges of obstructing our investigation and aiding and abetting."

"Resisting arrest," I added before I could keep myself quiet.

"Indeed. Resisting arrest," Whittaker concurred.

Mansfield leaned over and whispered in Freeman's ear. He whispered something back, then the lawyer turned to face us.

"Could I have ten minutes alone with my client?"

"Ten minutes. That's it," Whittaker replied. "I can't have you wasting any more of my time with a young lady missing." He reached over and switched off the recording before heading for the door.

I stood and followed the detective out of the room.

"What do you think?" Whittaker asked me once we were outside the room.

"I think he's better friends with Didi than he says, and I wouldn't be surprised if he has The Haitian's number on his mobile," I replied, thinking how badly I wanted to see his list of contacts and the call log from his phone. There would be a number I was sure I'd recognise. Not that it did me any good, but somehow it seemed like progress. We still needed the Haitian, or his phone logs, to match up with Cosgrove.

If Cosgrove used his mobile and not a burner, that is. Shit, I hadn't considered that before. My feeling of progress didn't last long. I forced myself back to Whittaker's question.

"Is he helping them take underage girls? I doubt it. The age they're targeting wouldn't be in the bar at Coconut Joe's. If they look old enough that their fake IDs are believable, then they're not the girls these creeps are looking for. They want young."

"We have his mobile and the call logs, but if The Haitian is in there, he's not saved by that name," Whittaker replied. "We'll trace the numbers, but that will take time."

"No way a guy trafficking young girls has a traceable mobile," I said, not just because I already knew, but because it was a fact.

"True, but we'll run them in case," Whittaker said, scratching his stubbly chin.

"Do we have security camera footage of The Haitian from last night?" I asked hopefully.

Whittaker scoffed. "It's lousy resolution and the bar camera's been turned so it misses the two seats at the end."

"That's convenient," I commented.

"Exactly. The owner told me he'd set them up himself. I spoke to him last night. He made sure there was crossover between all the cameras."

"So Freeman moved it to avoid his friends," I said, and Whittaker nodded. But we both knew that would be impossible to prove.

"The camera pointing across the restaurant picks him up as he enters, but with the poor light and the way he keeps his head dipped, we can't grab a decent image for ID, or facial recognition," Whittaker explained.

So much for the police knowing who we were looking for. We were no closer than we'd been right after DeWayne had given us the name. The Haitian certainly wouldn't be showing up again at Coconut Joe's anytime soon. He was still just a name. He could be anywhere.

"After this interview, you'll need to sit down with our sketch artist," Whittaker added. "Best we can do for now."

Great, I thought. It's on me again, and I barely saw the man. "What about Didi's number? We know Freeman texted him."

"They're tracing it now, but I suspect you're right. It'll be a burner." Whittaker sighed and lost himself in thought for a moment. "I'm sure his lawyer is explaining to Freeman that he can give us The Haitian's mobile number without fear of retribution. The guy will have ditched the phone by now, or at least pulled the SIM. We'll try tracing and tracking it, but I'm not holding my breath."

"We need a name," I said quietly.

"Or another location," Whittaker pointed out.

"Freeman's scared of The Haitian. He won't give us anything he thinks might come back on him."

Whittaker nodded again. "Let's hope he's just as scared of going to jail for helping traffic young girls. He'll find they don't greet sex offenders kindly inside."

He walked back down the hall and shoved the door to the interview room open. "Time's up, let's talk," he said as he strode in, sat back down, and restarted the recording. I hurried along behind him.

"I'd like to start by restating my client is innocent of all these..." Mansfield began, but Whittaker held up a hand and interrupted.

"I gave you ten minutes to decide whether you're helping us, or going back to a cell," he barked surprisingly loudly. I even jumped a little. "Save your rhetoric. I need information to stop these scumbags from preying on young girls. Do you have something useful or not?"

Mansfield held out his hands to calm the detective down and Freeman looked terrified.

"Yes, yes, we do," the lawyer blathered. "It just needs to be clear that my client has nothing to do with these men except for serving them drinks."

Whittaker abruptly stood up, his metal chair skittering across the concrete floor behind him.

"Wait!" Freeman shouted. "Sit down. I'll tell you what I know."

Whittaker slowly lowered himself back into the chair, which he had to reach out to pull back to the table. "I'm listening."

"The one guy goes by Didi, and da udder one never say his name," Freeman began. "I call him sir, but I hear Didi on da phone one time talk about meeting wit Da Haitian, and dat's da man dat show up."

"We know all this, Mr Freeman," Whittaker said bluntly.

The suspect looked surprised. If he considered that slice of information to be his ace in the hole, he'd just slapped down a pair against a full house.

"I have his number on my mobile," Freeman said reluctantly. "It saved under da name 'Soda'."

"Soda?" Whittaker questioned.

"He always order just a soda," Freeman replied, shrugging his shoulders.

"You realise that doesn't help us either, right?" Whittaker replied.

Freeman's expression dropped again. "How come, man?"

"That pay-as-you-go phone is already in a canal somewhere. I said something I can use, Freeman. Where can I find these men?"

Freeman shook his head. "I have no idea! I only see dem in da bar, man. Dey tip me real good, so I bullshit wit dem and hang out when it ain't busy. I ain't never seen dem outside da bar."

"Yet you have their mobile numbers saved? That's hard to believe. Did they tip you well enough to move the security camera to avoid where they always sit?" Whittaker said, starting to rise once again.

Freeman now looked petrified. "Shit..."

Mansfield quickly grabbed his arm once more and Freeman clammed up. They exchanged a few more whispers as the detective dropped back into his seat and looked impatiently at his watch. If I didn't have so much other crap riding on the outcome of these cases, I'd be revelling in the interview masterclass I was privy to.

"There's a gym I hear Didi talk about," Freeman muttered, as though the walls would tell The Haitian he'd grassed on him. "Sharkey's. It's in West Bay."

Whittaker looked at me, and I nodded.

"Shitty place in a derelict building attached to an even shittier house on Watercourse Road," I confirmed.

Whittaker frowned at me. I guessed he was looking for different phrasing, but that's what the place was. He turned back to the suspect. "Once again, not much use, Freeman. Do you really think these two are heading to the gym for a good workout while we're looking for them?"

Freeman lifted his cuffed hands in frustration. "Dat's all I got, man. I tell you, I ain't got nuttin' to do wit dem outside da bar."

Whittaker stood up.

"Is my client free to go?" Mansfield asked.

"It's Saturday," the detective replied as he turned to leave the room. "The judge can see about bail on Monday. Until then, he's staying here. Maybe we can clear his involvement by then, in which case it'll just be the resisting arrest charge."

"She didn't announce she was police!" Mansfield complained. "It'll never stick, and you know it."

Whittaker paused at the door. "Guess we'll see on Monday. Have a good weekend, gentlemen."

25

NO STONE UNTURNED

The image on the screen didn't look like anyone I remembered seeing. Between the grainy video image and my brief view of the guy, I was confident he had two eyes, a nose and a mouth. Beyond that, everything was vague. That wasn't completely true, but the details I recalled didn't help provide the sketch artist with useful elements to construct a likeness.

My brain had checked off what little information Brenda McGinnis had given us. He was from Haiti, small framed, and in his thirties or forties. Throw in my observations that he had a shaved head and was dark-skinned – which was almost guaranteed as he was Haitian – and we had a generic picture of half the male population of the Caribbean nation.

We still used the term sketch artist, but these days it was a computer program instead of paper, and selections from a menu rather than strokes of a pencil. The operator was still incredibly talented as the options were endless and subtle adjustments infinite, but their main strength was patience. She was used to the lengthy process, whereas I was watching the minutes tick by into an hour, and going nuts.

When I finally joined Whittaker in his office, I still didn't recognise the face on the computer monitor I'd just left, but it wasn't going to get any better without some kind of psychic hypnosis regression, or seeing the bloke again.

"Anything new, sir?" I asked as I knocked on his open door.

He looked up from behind his monitor where he was making notes on a spiral-bound pad. "Not much on The Haitian, I'm afraid. How did the sketch go?"

"Pretty shit," I replied.

"Really? She's usually brilliant at tweaking that software," he said, raising an eyebrow.

"She is, but I was shit. I only saw the guy for a moment and I didn't register as many features as I should have."

"For both of them?"

"No, I think we got Didi close."

We'd worked on Didi first and that had gone okay, but the important one was The Haitian himself.

"We'll send both images over to Immigration and see if they can come up with a match," Whittaker said optimistically. "If we track down Didi, he'll take us to the other guy. The local news is waiting on the images as well. Having the entire island watching for them will help us."

"It'll also clog up our phone lines and tie up our people, won't it?" I asked, plonking myself down in one of the chairs in front of his desk.

"That's the downside," he admitted, "but it's usually worth it." He peered over his desk at me. "Don't get comfortable there, constable, we're heading out the door."

I realised I'd slouched in the chair without an invitation and jumped to my feet. I'd been lost in my own thoughts again. "Sorry, sir," I mumbled, and he grinned as he grabbed his jacket and notebook on the way out of his office.

"We do have something on the burglary, though," he said as he walked briskly down the hallway. "I'll explain in the car."

"What about the phone numbers from Freeman?" I asked, my mind unwilling to switch cases yet.

As we descended the stairs to the ground floor, he pulled out a folded piece of paper from inside his notebook. At the bottom of the steps, he handed it to me. "Here are all the numbers and the frequency he called, or was called, by each phone. If they were in his contacts, the name is on there."

I scanned the list, trying not to trip over myself or run into anything as we crossed the reception area. I found 'Soda'. 345 471 9935. It matched the number I'd found in the safe. I felt a surge of energy and hope. I didn't know why, as Cosgrove's notes had labelled the number as being The Haitian, but burner phones were too easy to replace and I had no idea when Randall Cosgrove had written the number down.

I looked at my watch as we hit the heat and humidity of mid-morning. It was 10:15am. Time felt like a big dog tugging on the end of its lead. I was being dragged along at a pace I desperately needed to slow down.

"Are we going to the gym?" I asked Whittaker as we climbed into his SUV.

"We are," he replied. "I have Williams watching the gym in case they show up there."

"Which they won't," I said, reminding him of his own point.

He smiled. "Correct, they won't. But criminals tend to rub elbows, and in this case lift weights, with other criminals. Williams is keeping a lookout for our two, but he's also watching who else frequents the place."

"Leverage?"

"Exactly," he responded, backing out of his parking spot. "Usually, no one in a place like that will help the police, but if we get lucky and stumble across one of them with an outstanding warrant, then maybe they'll talk."

Now I was truly pumped up and ready to taser some lowlife until he squealed. But West Bay was north, and the detective was driving us out of the car park, heading south.

"I thought we were going to Sharkey's?"

"We are," he replied. "But we're making a stop first."

"The burglary?"

He nodded as he pulled onto Elgin and blended with traffic. "We received an unusually fast response from the social media site. Our friend, Cayman MY Island, had his page suspended based on our inquiry. Apparently, once they took a look, they discovered his account is clearly under a bogus name, which is frowned upon for a personal page, but also the email associated with the account and all the account activity is from the IP address of a hotel's business centre computer."

"Untraceable to an actual human," I thought aloud.

"Precisely."

"What hotel is it? It could be an employee there." I suggested.

"The Grand Caymanian."

I thought for a moment. "I don't know that hotel. Where is it?"

"The Holiday Inn Resort on North Sound. Out back of Crystal Harbour."

"I know the Holiday Inn," I replied.

"It was called the Grand Caymanian from the day they built it, then Ramada branded it for a year or two, and now it's Holiday Inn," he replied. "You'll find the locals still refer to it as the Grand Caymanian. If a chain brand stays around for long enough, maybe we'll finally come around to using their name."

If we were heading to the hotel, we'd also be driving north. "So, where are we going?"

"We're dropping in to see our friend, Patti Weaver," Whittaker replied as he swung into the car park for Caribbean Security Systems. "I think it's time she came clean with us."

My heart skipped again.

"Another burglary?" the receptionist asked as we walked in.

"Not that I'm aware of," Whittaker replied. "We had some follow-up questions we hoped Mrs Weaver might help us with."

The receptionist dialled an extension. "Patti? Da police are here again. Dey need your help."

I would love to have seen the look on Patti Weaver's face when she heard that. It would take an incredibly stoic person not to show a guilty reaction. But we didn't, and in the minute or so it took her to come up front, she could easily have composed herself. My next curiosity was her reaction to seeing me again. If she had seen the video feed and somehow pieced together with the thief that it was me breaking into Cosgrove's, she'd have to be Meryl Streep not to react.

Patti greeted us warmly, and we followed her back to her office, where Whittaker made a point of closing the door behind us.

"How can I help?" she asked, seemingly unperturbed. Definitely calmer than the last time we spoke with her, and not a hint of a weird look in my direction.

"When we spoke before, I asked if anyone suspicious had approached you recently," Whittaker asked. "Have you had a chance to think that over some more?"

The question caught her attention, and she tensed in her seat.

"I can't say I've thought about it much more, Detective, but my response is still the same," she replied. "Nothing comes to mind."

"In that case," Whittaker continued, "I'd like to ask you about someone who approached you on social media. This person goes by 'Cayman MY Island', and they asked you to private message them."

Patti sat in stunned silence, her eyes unsure where to look while her mind whirred. "Who?" she asked, her brow furrowed.

"Cayman MY Island," Whittaker repeated. "They capitalise the M-Y as though they're middle initials, but clearly it's intended as 'my'."

"And this person messaged me?"

"They posted on your page for you to message them, Mrs Weaver," he responded.

"They did..?" she mumbled.

"Did you?" he asked.

"I'm sorry, Detective. Did I what?"

"Message them, Mrs Weaver."

She dithered and fussed while taking her time to respond. Maybe she *was* the Cayman Islands version of Meryl Streep. Or genuinely confused.

"I have no recollection of what you're talking about, I'm afraid," she finally said. "When was this?"

"Almost a year ago," I contributed.

Patti looked at us both and scoffed. "You're expecting me to remember a comment made by someone on my feed a year ago?"

"Bring up your page and scroll back twelve months, Mrs Weaver," Whittaker told her, pointing to her computer monitors. "Find the post in question. It was an article about the International Fellowship of Lions. It was a member-only resort closed down for illegal trafficking of young women."

She clicked away on her keyboard and began searching through her social media page. "I remember the resort, Detective. Awful what they were doing there. Thank God you figured it out." Her eyes flicked his way for a moment. "But a shame so many got away with it."

"How do you mean?" he asked. "We brought all the people operating the resort to trial."

She sat back from the computer. "I mean all the members. You didn't prosecute them."

I really wanted to thank this woman for her compassion, but I settled for smiling on the inside.

"Here's the post you're talking about," she said, focusing on the screen once more. "I see that comment, but I don't recall anything about it, and I certainly didn't respond to them."

"You're sure, Mrs Weaver? We have requested the messages by warrant, so we will see any interaction," Whittaker said.

Patti sat up again. "Detective, I assure you I didn't message this person back, and I've certainly not been involved in compromising this office in any way!"

Detective Whittaker spent the next five minutes calming Patti down and trying to convince her this was a normal avenue of inquiry, and she shouldn't be offended. She was still pretty offended when we left.

"She didn't crumble under pressure, did she?" I said as we drove away.

"Best defence is often offence," Whittaker replied.

"You think she's lying?"

The detective shook his head. "No, I don't think she's lying." He looked over at me. "One of the less glamorous parts of this job is treating good people as though they may be criminals."

I felt bad for Patti. But I was more relieved for myself. It appeared she wasn't involved. But why this 'Cayman MY Island' person had an interest in the resort still intrigued me.

"Do we still pursue the hotel lead?" I asked.

"Oh yes," Whittaker quickly replied. "Never leave a stone unturned."

26

ANDRE THE GIANT

Williams was sitting in the back of a rusty van with magnetic landscape services signs on the doors. The RCIPS owned a variety of such signs, all bogus company names. We arrived from the north and parked on Glidden, a side street off Watercourse Road. We weren't far from Benny's, the bar I'd dragged Jonty Gladstone out of.

The neighbourhood had gone downhill over the past decade or two, but was slowly bouncing back as the price of land skyrocketed. Most locals were selling out and moving farther away from the water, buying nicer homes, and still pocketing cash. Some were still holding out, and unfortunately, some were the riff-raff.

The gym was 50 metres beyond the van, so we easily stayed out of sight while we approached along the verge, then climbed in the passenger door. The windows were down, but leaving the engine and therefore the air conditioning running, may have drawn attention, so the old van was like a sauna inside. Williams sat on a wheel arch in the back, watching out of the rear windows. He wore a white sleeveless undershirt damp with sweat and knee-length baggy shorts. I couldn't help but notice the vest fit snugly over his well-toned physique.

"Nice uniform," I quipped as I sat across from him, leaving Whittaker up front.

"Thought I'd blend in, but dat's blown now your skinny white arse showed up," he retorted.

Whittaker loudly cleared his throat.

"Sorry, sir," Williams quickly apologised, and winked at me.

I looked at the run-down house with a hand-painted gym sign over the door of an attached outbuilding. Both were a matching colour of peeling pale blue, and the business side of the establishment looked just as ready to fall down as the home. It was the smallest gym I'd ever seen. The outbuilding was no larger than a single-car garage.

The shell of an old vehicle rested amongst overgrown weeds to the side of the house and a metal wire fence stood mostly upright, marking the front of the property. The gates to the gravel and dirt driveway were open, and by the look of the way they'd embedded themselves into the ground, they'd been that way for a while.

"Anyone we know?" Whittaker asked.

"I seen a couple o' younger lads go in," he replied, then turned to Whittaker. "Den Jumbo Flowers showed up not ten minutes ago."

Whittaker let out a long sigh and rubbed his forehead. "Great."

"Who's Jumbo Flowers?" I asked.

Williams chuckled.

"He's another frequent flyer," Whittaker said in a pained tone.

"Isn't that who we want?" I pointed out.

"Yeah, but we'd prefer it not be him," Williams said. "But I did check, and of course he has an outstanding warrant," he added, pointing to his laptop on the floor next to him. "Assault."

"Hm," Whittaker murmured.

We stayed quiet and let the detective think for a minute.

"I don't see underage girls being in Jumbo's wheelhouse," he finally said.

"No, sir," Williams agreed. "In fact, he got a younger sister in high school. I believe dey call her Lil' Jumbo."

"Poor kid," I said.

Williams shook his head. "Believe me, if she don't like da name, ain't nobody gonna call her dat. Reckon she came up wit da name herself."

"Doesn't sound like little sis is the ideal look for sex traffickers," I said.

"Don't mean Jumbo ain't protective o' her," Williams replied. He had a point.

"Alright," Whittaker said decisively. "I'm going in there alone. Constable Sommer can bring my SUV up to where we are now, and Williams, you move the van into Ebanks Road on the other side of the gym."

"You sure you want to go in alone, sir?" Williams questioned.

"Jumbo knows you and I'm guessing I know his reaction when he sees you," Whittaker explained. "He won't expect me to be armed, or be serving him a warrant, so I might have a chance at a conversation."

"Are you?" I asked.

"Armed? No," he replied. "Oh, and if Jumbo comes your way, you can try tasing him, but make sure you run afterwards."

"Huh?" I grunted. Anyone I'd seen hit with a Taser dropped like a stone.

"Dey stop him eventually, but he likely keep coming for a bit," Williams explained, climbing into the driver's seat as Whittaker stepped out of the van.

As I ran down the road towards the Range Rover, I contemplated a human being that was only delayed by a fully charged law enforcement Taser. I was curious to see this guy, and I didn't have long to wait.

I was just turning the SUV around in Glidden, when a mountain disguised as a man appeared, running through the back gardens of the neighbouring homes in my direction. He slowed to straddle a low fence before continuing his earth-pounding flight. I swear I could feel the ground shake with each step he took.

The man's running style was more of a series of lunges, each saved by thrusting a tree trunk-sized limb ahead to stop the fall. I could see he was already gasping for breath. I guessed he could bench-press the Range Rover, but cardio wasn't his forte.

I pulled the SUV forward to the stop sign at Watercourse, hoping he'd ignore the unmarked vehicle. I watched in the rear-view mirror as Jumbo reached the roadway five metres behind me. With Whittaker's vehicle already in reverse, I accelerated backwards just as Jumbo bent over with his hands on his knees to catch his breath.

The impact was incredible. The big Range Rover violently stopped and Jumbo staggered about three steps and stayed upright. I couldn't believe the airbags didn't go off, and was stunned that the human who'd been hit by 2500 kilograms of steel was still on his feet. I shoved the shifter into park, and leapt out of the SUV.

Jumbo's head was the size of a prize-winning pumpkin and the expression on his stone-like face was half dazed and half pissed off. I figured the pissed-off percentage was about to increase as the dazed part wore off. His body shuddered and shook as the barbs of the taser hit his barrel chest, yet he remained upright.

I heard tyres squealing behind me but I daren't take my eyes off the hulk before me. Just as I was convinced he was still coming after me, he attempted a step and crumpled to the ground. His massive body twitched and jolted as he lay on the road.

Williams came running up, with his gun drawn. "You okay?"

"Yup," I said, keeping my finger over the Taser trigger in case Jumbo needed a second burst.

"I'm surprised that stopped him," Williams remarked as he holstered his gun and took the handcuffs from my belt.

"The SUV stopped him," I explained. "The Taser put him down."

I flicked the safety on the Taser so I couldn't accidentally zap Williams as he dragged Jumbo's arms behind his back and tried to cuff him.

"I need another set," Williams said, laughing. "Dis guy's too big, his hands don't come together behind his back."

"You hit him with my car?" Whittaker asked, arriving out of breath. He handed Williams a second set of cuffs and stared at me.

"Can we just say he ran into it?" I replied.

Whittaker studied the back door of his shiny silver Range Rover. There were several dents. He ran his fingers across them, then glared at me. "Really?"

By the time Jumbo could be helped to his feet, we had two police cars on the scene and any chance at a quiet chat was out the window. Half of West Bay now knew the cops had busted Jumbo Flowers. Again. We manhandled him into the back of the Range Rover while Whittaker told all the other officers to leave the scene.

"You okay?" I asked the big man, who made the inside of the SUV seem like a Fiat 500. His shaved head brushed the roof lining and his knees were buried in the back of the passenger seat, which was slid all the way forward.

"Great," he replied in a deep voice which sounded like thunder rolling. "My mornin' bin perfect. You?"

He didn't look perfect. I'm pretty sure his head had caused one of the dents in Whittaker's tailgate, as a knot was forming. I wondered if he had a concussion. I wondered how anyone could tell if he had a concussion.

"Sorry to run you over," I told him.

He shrugged his shoulders and looked me over. "I ain't bin arrested dat way before."

Jumbo reminded me of André the Giant's character in *The Princess Bride*. That was another movie AJ had made me watch with her. I enjoyed it, but I'd told her it was just okay or she'd have gone into a frenzy of showing me more movies. Fezzik; that was the character's name. Jumbo reminded me of a cross between Fezzik and Shaquille O'Neal, the basketball player. Without the big smile. Both of those guys always seemed to be smiling. I hadn't seen Jumbo smile once since we'd met. Although that may have been circumstance related.

Whittaker climbed in the driver's seat and closed the door. He looked up at the rear-view mirror. "Hungry, Jumbo?"

"I could eat," his voice boomed from the back. He was actually soft spoken, but the bass tone seemed to vibrate everything around him like a subwoofer speaker.

Whittaker drove us to Heritage Kitchen, my favourite food shack. I walked up to the window and ordered our food while Whittaker extricated Jumbo from the back seat, and they sat on the sea wall overlooking Seven Mile Beach. The detective removed the handcuffs from the big man's wrists, which I considered brave, but maybe food was an anchoring force with Jumbo.

Whittaker sat on the wall chatting and asking him about his family, who apparently the detective knew down to cousins, aunts and uncles. I noticed Whittaker made a point of asking about his little sister. Once the food order was up, I fetched the sandwiches and we all ate in silence for a while. Finally, Whittaker put half his sandwich down and wrapped it back up.

"I need your help, Jumbo."

The big fellow frowned. He'd already eaten all of his own sandwich and he wiped sauce from around his lips with a paper napkin. "What help? I figured you just hungry yourself, stopped to eat on da way to da station."

"Where we go from here remains to be seen," Whittaker replied. "The warrant on you is for assault. Who was it you assaulted?"

"It weren't no assault," he replied, shaking his head. "Dat ol' fool just causin' trouble again. Come around drunk, fussin' at mama."

"Your papa?"

Jumbo nodded. I handed him the second half of my sandwich. I'd seen him eyeing it.

"Tanks," he said and smiled at me.

He was remarkably pleasant for someone I'd run over and tased.

"Was he hurt?" Whittaker asked.

"Nah," Jumbo replied with a mouthful of fish sandwich. "I just cuffed him upside da head. He were fine once he woke up."

I wondered about the size of the man who created the giant sitting next to me.

"You know you need to be careful, Jumbo. You're twice his size," Whittaker said.

Now I wondered what his mother must look like.

"Anyway, I dare say I can help you out on that warrant," Whittaker continued. "But only if you help us."

Jumbo frowned again. "I ain't no rat."

"You may feel differently about these gentlemen."

The sandwich I gave him had been inhaled, and he licked his lips. "Who?"

"I'm told there's a pair of Haitians who frequent the gym," Whittaker explained. "That's all I was coming to ask you about, but you took off."

"Yeah, sorry. I don't like your jail much."

"Well, it's not supposed to be a summer camp," Whittaker replied. "But anyway, these Haitians, do you know them?"

"Why you tink I tell you if I do?"

"They're suspected of trafficking young girls," Whittaker responded.

"No shit?"

"We believe Didi is involved, and the man who goes by 'The Haitian' is the ringleader," Whittaker replied.

I watched Jumbo's expression change. He didn't look happy. "Didi come by da gym most days, but da li'l one, not so much. Didi seemed like a good dude. Shit."

"There's a young girl missing," I weighed in. "We need to find these men."

"Young girls," Jumbo muttered like an earthquake. "Dat's fucked up."

"Well?" Whittaker asked. "I won't give up my source. They won't know it was you."

Jumbo looked at me, then looked at Whittaker. "I don't know

shit about da li'l guy. But Didi, he bin rentin' dis old place past da north end o' Watercourse."

I took out my mobile and brought up maps, clicking on satellite view. I handed Jumbo the phone, and he used his giant paw to scroll around until he found the place.

"Here," he said, but his finger took up half the screen so it didn't narrow down the location much.

Taking the mobile back, I pointed with my own finger. I felt like a tiny child next to him, but with a few directions, we narrowed down the house he was trying to show us. I nodded to Whittaker.

"Your warrant will disappear and you'll have a new hearing, but I need you to show up this time."

"What'll happen when I do?"

"If what you told me happened is true, your case will be dismissed."

"I'll be dere."

"Where can I drop you off?" Whittaker asked.

The big man looked up at the food shack. "Tink I'll stay here for lunch."

Whittaker peeled a ten-dollar Caymanian note from his wallet and handed it to Jumbo. "Thanks for your help. And like I say, your name won't be mentioned."

"Nice meeting you, miss," Jumbo said to me as he started towards his next meal. Then he stopped and turned around. "No," he said, wagging a finger at Whittaker. "Make sure you tell dat Didi it were me. He gotta problem wit dat, he can come see me."

27

KIMI WHO?

In short order, Whittaker organised a small tactical force to raid the house Jumbo had given us. We'd gone straight to West Bay Station where he had Williams bring in two of his officers, then contacted Ben with the Joint Marine Unit to cover the ocean side.

Looking at the satellite image, the small dwelling was buried in the woods, a hundred metres from a paved road and a hundred metres from the waterfront. A narrow dirt driveway curved towards the house from Duxies Lane, and an even narrower footpath led to the ironshore coast.

Somehow, Ben had to get a couple of his men ashore to approach from the path, and we'd try to sneak down the driveway using the woods as cover. If it was similar to most of the woods on the island, it would be a dense coverage of low trees and thick shrubs, but we'd do our best to stay out of sight.

I was saying we, but Whittaker made it clear in the briefing that I'd be waiting with him while the armed officers secured the building. I couldn't wait to go through firearms training so I could be on the front lines for situations like this, but Whittaker was more than a little hesitant to sign that request. It was smart on his part, as I saw no reason not to shoot people like Randall Cosgrove. While I understood the need for due process, I was a victim who knew his guilt all too well. Every breath he took was stealing oxygen from a planet better off without him.

We parked on the right-hand side of Duxies, just short of the driveway. We then waited for what felt like forever for Ben to get in position and let us know his men were ashore. He'd had to come up the coast from George Town and around Northwest Point to our location, then launch a RIB – a rigid inflatable boat – for his men to be dropped off. The patrol boat's draft was too deep for the shallow water.

His men, using call sign Team Bravo, radioed they were moving along the pathway, so Williams and his crew, dubbed Team Alpha, left the van. We all had our earpieces and lapel microphones, and with the code this and code that over the radio, it all felt very James Bond. AJ was obsessed with the new Bond movies, as well as the old ones with the Scottish bloke in them. She said the movies with all the other actors were all a load of crap. I'd been subjected to a marathon session of her favourites one stormy weekend. They were good, but I liked the Swedish dragon tattoo movie better. I related to that chick.

Whittaker drummed his fingers on the steering wheel, while I sat staring out the window towards the driveway. Something glinted in the trees on the far side of the dirt trail. I moved my head back and forth a few times, and each time, the sun caught a reflection.

"*Fy faen!*" I muttered, shoving the door open.

"Nora!" Whittaker shouted. "What is it?"

"Camera," I called back as I sprinted towards the trees. Sure enough, a small black security camera was mounted in a crook of the tallest tree. I pointed at the device and heard Whittaker calling over the radio.

"Teams Alpha and Bravo, be aware we've spotted a camera at the entrance. Suspect may be aware of our presence. Over."

Trotting back from the driveway, I spotted a car speeding up towards me from the end of the cul-de-sac. I leapt inside the van just as the vehicle smashed the van door closed, trapping my ponytail. I cursed myself for not putting my hair in a bun that morning. Whittaker whisked the police van around and took off in pursuit. I clung to the grab handle with my left hand and keyed my mic with the other.

"Suspect in a blue left-hand drive saloon leaving Duxies Lane. We're in pursuit. Over."

I hung on as Whittaker slammed on the brakes at the T-junction with North West Point Road. He looked both ways, searching for which direction the car had gone. I took the opportunity to open the door and retrieve my hair. Whittaker turned left, then immediately right onto Watercourse. I presumed he hadn't seen any sign of Didi in either direction of North West Point and chosen the only other option.

The detective was right. Up ahead, the rear end of the speeding car was getting smaller in the distance. I called the direction in over the radio as I struggled into my seat belt. Watercourse had a ton of small streets leading off each side before meeting up with North West Point Road again, cutting off a corner of the island. Hell Road was the only other option that led anywhere. To my knowledge, everything else was small housing estates. Yet I watched the brake lights glow on the car up ahead as it slowed and disappeared to the right.

"Where is he going? These side streets don't go anywhere," I thought aloud.

"West on Hillandale Close," I radioed in as Whittaker braked hard, making the tyres screech. We were still travelling at a speed I didn't think we could make the turn. The front tyres shuddered, then finally bit enough to redirect the hefty vehicle, and thankfully no one was coming the other way.

Hillandale was lined on both sides with brightly painted single-storey homes, set back from neatly maintained front gardens. The road curved left, then kinked left twice more until we were travelling south. With the turns close together, we could no longer see the blue car, so I kept watch on either side in case he'd dived into someone's driveway. Up ahead, the road became a dirt driveway, continuing towards several more homes. Just before the tarmac ended, there was a paved road on the right.

Whittaker launched the van into the ninety-degree turn and I caught the street sign as we flashed by. "West… I think, on Windstart Drive," I called in over the radio, losing track of my internal compass.

Windstart turned another hard right after only 100 metres, but a dirt trail continued straight, curving slightly left. A dust plume hung in the air and Whittaker didn't hesitate, steering us onto the rough, unpaved street. I bounced in the seat as we hit pothole after pothole, but the detective didn't back off. This was a side of the man I hadn't seen. He was laser focused ahead and wheeling the van like a expert.

"You're quite the Kimi Räikkönen," I grunted between bouts of air being jarred from my lungs.

"Who?" he muttered as the van slid around a turn on the loose dirt and gravel.

Kimi's Finnish, but Norway doesn't have any famous race car drivers, so I'd settled for a Scandinavian Formula One driver. It was a compliment, if Whittaker had known the reference.

"Dirt road heading… heading generally west," I spluttered into the radio.

Out of the dust cloud ahead, the rear bumper of the car appeared. Whittaker had caught him. The car swung right, and as we followed, the van jolted one more time before the roadway smoothed out. We were back on tarmac, but I didn't have a clue where, and there was no time to bring maps up on my mobile. As the hazy cloud cleared, I could see the road ended at a T-junction, and on the right was the Fox and Hare pub. We were on Bonaventure Road, which I'd considered a cul-de-sac until now. Apparently, it could be a through road if you didn't mind a bit of off-road driving.

The car slowed as it reached the intersection, but I could tell the driver wasn't planning to stop and look. Turning hard left, the blue saloon skidded onto North West Point Road and disappeared from our view. Whittaker braked hard and brought the van to a stop at the junction just as we heard an almighty crash. Edging forward, we peeked around the turn and saw Didi's car sideways in the road, steam billowing from the engine bay. Smashed into the left front corner was a police patrol car.

Whittaker pulled the van across the middle of the road, blocking any oncoming traffic, and we both leapt out.

"Send all available units to an MVA at the corner of Bonaventure and North West Point Road. Two ambulances, asap. Possible injuries. The road is blocked," I called into the radio as we ran to the vehicles.

Both cars were destroyed. It was my first serious car accident, and the scene felt like something from a war zone. A sense of violence and destruction hung in the air, and I could smell petrol, antifreeze, and hot rubber. The front ends of both cars were crushed, shortening and crumpling their bonnets considerably. Pieces of wreckage and glass were strewn around, and fluids ran across the road.

"Secure the suspect," Whittaker ordered, as he continued to the police car.

I glanced inside the car I presumed Didi had stolen. Blood ran down the driver's side window, but I could see the airbag had deployed and hung limply from the steering wheel. I pulled on the handle, but the door barely budged. Metal creaked and groaned, but the buckled A-post wouldn't allow the door to open. I ran around the other side, slipping on the antifreeze and oil slicks, just managing to stay on my feet. I pulled on the passenger door handle, which opened easily.

I bent down and looked inside. The first thing I realised was Didi hadn't been wearing his seat belt. His body was slumped in the seat, but above him, blood streaked across the headliner. The airbag had done its job and halted his forward progress on impact, but the energy had launched his unrestrained body upward into the roof. Didi's head sat at an odd angle on his shoulder and I didn't need to look any further to know his neck was broken.

One less *drittsekk* in the world, which was fine with me, but we needed information to find The Haitian. Didi was all out of information.

28

NO DO OVERS

The two police constables were both beaten and banged up. One had a broken nose, but fortunately they'd both been wearing their seat belts and the patrol car had front and side airbags. While the coroner took care of Didi, and tow trucks cleared the scene, we convened at the West Bay Station.

It was now a little after 2:00pm. Cosgrove would be landing sometime soon and I still had nothing to justify an official search of his second safe, where I knew evidence sat waiting for us. A nagging urgency kept pushing me to the edge of telling Whittaker what I knew, and leaving it in his hands to figure out how to make the search happen. Which, of course, would end my career in a jail cell for breaking and entering.

Whittaker was standing across the room, sipping a paper cup of crappy station coffee. We were the only two there. I took a step towards the door to push it closed when his mobile rang.

"Whittaker," he answered.

Rather than stand there waiting, with my thumb up my backside, I left the room in search of coffee. Maybe caffeine would bring me to my senses. A few minutes later, with a paper cup in hand, I met Williams in the reception area, and walked with him towards the briefing room. He'd left his two men at the house, searching through Didi's things.

"That was Estelle Cosgrove," Whittaker directed at me when we entered the room. "Looking for an update. Her husband arrives shortly."

I detected sympathy in the look he gave me, and I guessed it meant my time on that case was going to be over, although he didn't say so yet. He turned to Williams. "What do you have?"

"A name," he replied, flipping open a notebook. "Didi is actually David Derrick Antoine. We have his passport and we found utility bills and a copy of the lease."

"Any documentation or notes tying him to anybody else?" Whittaker immediately asked.

"No, sir, afraid not. But da house has two bedrooms, and both da beds have recently been slept in. One bathroom wit two toothbrushes, but only da one set of toiletries. Maybe De Haitian been staying dere too."

"Clothes?" Whittaker asked.

"None in da second bedroom, only in da udder room, and dey's Didi's size."

"Maybe The Haitian crashes there sometimes," I suggested.

"Could be," Whittaker replied thoughtfully. "The mobile recovered from the wrecked car is at Central Station and I've ruined Eileen from TSU's Saturday by calling her in," Whittaker continued. "She'll try to crack his password, or access the data on the SIM."

"Does it have a fingerprint lock?" I asked, aware of the grisly task of using a dead man's digit to unlock the device.

"Burner phone," Whittaker replied. "Cheap, so it doesn't have any bells or whistles."

"I emailed da name over to immigration as soon as we found it, sir," Williams said.

Whittaker nodded. "Good. Now we hope he entered the country with his friend, or at least sometime close to when The Haitian did. If we get a match on the description we gave them, they'll send us the picture from their visa for us to look at."

"My shitty description," I muttered.

"I told them to send us anything even close," Whittaker added. "We don't have huge numbers of people from Haiti on work permits here, so I'm hoping we'll narrow this down quickly."

"But that only gives us a name," I pointed out. "Not a location."

"Correct, but we'll have a good photograph to distribute. He has to be living somewhere, just like Didi. Maybe his landlord will see the news and reach out."

"Unless he was living with Didi and cleared out after last night," I said.

"Possible," Whittaker replied with a sigh. "But he would have had to leave by boat. The airport was on high alert for anyone fitting his description, especially on a Haitian passport."

"I guess we're on hold until we hear from TSU or immigration," I said, not doing a good job of hiding my frustration.

"Then we have time to drop by the Grand Caymanian," Whittaker replied, getting to his feet.

"Holiday Inn Resort," I corrected. "Sir."

The detective ignored me, so I shut up and quickly followed him, especially as this was connected to the burglary case, and he was still including me. I'd noticed he'd been very subdued since the car chase, and I couldn't tell which part of the event was troubling him. Usually, I'd leave someone alone as it wasn't my business what they were working through. If they wanted my input, they could ask. But I was curious, so when we reached the bypass without him uttering a word, I inquired.

"Sir, what's on your mind? Did I screw up?"

He looked over at me, and I could see his surprise.

"What makes you ask that?"

"You seem upset or mad about something," I replied.

"No, I mean the screwed-up part," he said. "Do you feel you screwed something up?"

"I'll pay for the dents, if that's it."

He managed a smile. "The department will pay for the damage. It was in the line of duty. Unorthodox and not recommended, but in the line of duty, nonetheless." He took a few moments before he continued. "Truth be known, I'm mad at myself."

For a second, I thought he was going to say something about bringing me along on cases too soon, or he shouldn't have asked me to drive his SUV. Then he spoke again.

"I could have avoided the accident. I was pursuing too aggressively."

It was my turn to be surprised. I thought he'd done an incredible job catching Didi. He couldn't know the guy would do what he did. "Didi killed himself, sir."

Whittaker slowly shook his head. "He did. But I pushed him into a situation in which the scenario could happen."

"You can't control his actions."

"No, but I should predict his reactions," he replied solemnly. "Once he'd bolted in the car, it was clear he was desperate to evade us. My actions put a series of events in motion. I chose to pursue him at high speed. I should have known he would do everything he could to outrun us, which meant taking the risks he took."

"We couldn't let him get away," I pointed out, still defending his action and baffled why he was being so hard on himself.

"Think about it, Nora," he said, as always turning it into a lesson. "If I'd stopped when we turned on Hillandale, which we perceived at the time to not have an outlet, we could have blocked his exit. With time to reference a map, we could have directed units to block the other exit we would have realised he was heading for. We know a patrol car could have made it in time, because Didi drove into him. Imagine if we'd stopped chasing? He would have slowed down and almost certainly taken the same route. We would have him trapped. No wild chase through a neighbourhood, with two vehicles travelling at high speed."

"Or maybe he'd have taken to foot and got away."

"Perps rarely leave the car until they're forced to do so," he retorted.

"Well, I was impressed. You're a good driver," I said, hoping the compliment would make him feel better.

"Thank you," he said, almost reluctantly. "Years ago, I took a training course at a high-performance driving school in California. I learnt a lot. But my point remains. Didi would be alive, and we wouldn't have two injured constables or wrecked vehicles."

"It would have been nice to interview Didi."

He looked over at me again. His expression looked pained. "It would have, but more importantly, the man would still be alive. We currently have zero proof David Derrick Antoine was involved in anything illegal."

"He ran," I said coldly.

"Only makes him guilty of resisting arrest."

"Twice. Plus assault."

"True. But that doesn't change the fact he's only guilty of relatively minor violations. Everything else is based on the words of DeWayne and Brenda McGinnis. Didi could have been running because his visa had expired."

My sore ribs didn't consider his bar stool antics minor. He was trying to hurt me a lot worse. But I got the detective's point. "You know he's guilty of more than that, sir."

"I suspect it's more than that, Nora," he said, tapping his finger on the dashboard to emphasise his point. "Everybody is innocent until proven guilty on these islands. Never forget that. We're not the judge or jury. If I had it to do over again, I'd stop on Hillandale."

I wanted to defend his actions further, but I knew from a police perspective, everything he said was correct. I was sure both Haitians were involved in Marissa's disappearance somehow, and Whittaker believed that too. The difference was, he could temper his disgust at these men running free, and stick to procedure. I wondered how many cases he'd had thrown out of court because of screw-ups and technicalities in the way the case was handled? That would be gut wrenching. The other thing I knew far too well was there's no do-overs in this life. Dead people stay dead, no matter how much you wished they weren't.

Well, no smarmy lawyer was getting Didi off, and I couldn't bring myself to feel sorry he was gone, so I guess I was a shitty policewoman. But I was in a position where I could get some of these *drittsekker* out of society, so I didn't need to screw it up.

"You understand what I'm saying, Nora?" Whittaker was asking. "Let my lesson be your lesson. It's one mistake you don't have to make yourself now."

"I get it, sir. Thank you." I said, because I knew I should. "But don't lose sleep over this. What you did wasn't wrong. It may not have been the best solution, given time to reflect, but time wasn't a luxury you had. Besides, it would be a shame to waste all that race car training."

Whittaker rolled his eyes, but he did grin.

29

REMOTE

The Holiday Inn Resort fronted the big, shallow, reef-protected North Sound. It was a couple of kilometres from the bypass along a small road next to a golf course with sleeping policemen every 200 metres. By the time we reached the hotel, my bruised ribs were tired of being jolted. Whittaker parked under the covered front entrance, and we walked inside through automatic sliding glass doors. The chilly air hit us and it felt like entering a refrigerator. It always perplexed me why tourists who come to the island seeking warmth and sunshine like their hotels freezing arse cold.

We both looked to our left where an alcove was marked 'Business Centre' and a desktop computer and monitor resided. Continuing across the lobby, a young Caucasian woman greeted us with a well-practised smile while she looked me over. Her name badge read 'Margo - New Zealand'.

"May we speak with the manager, please?" Whittaker asked politely, showing the desk clerk his badge. "I'm Detective Whittaker, and this is Constable Sommer."

Margo's expression switched to concern. "I'm afraid he's on his lunch break. Is there something I could help you with?" she said with a Kiwi accent.

I looked at my watch. It was 2:35pm. I'm sure my expression reflected my own concern.

"He takes a late break, so he's here during lunchtime for the guests," Margo added, obviously noting my time concern.

"How long have you been employed here, Margo?" Whittaker asked, looking at her tag.

"Near on 18 months, now," the woman replied suspiciously. "Why?" she asked, her front desk greeter veneer slipping.

Whittaker smiled. "Our question regards a situation which took place a year ago. That's my only reason for asking."

Margo relaxed a little. "Oh, okay. I was here then. Don't know what I'll remember from a year back, but maybe it's something I can look up."

Whittaker pointed towards the business centre. "Do any of the employees use the computer in there, or is it strictly for guests?"

Margo looked past us to the little alcove. As with most people being questioned by police, she was trying to figure out where this was going. "It's intended for guests, really, and all the desk staff have a computer terminal we use. So, no, employees don't go in there."

"None of the cleaning staff, perhaps, or other employees who don't have computer access?" Whittaker asked.

"Everyone has a smartphone these days, don't they?" she replied.

"Do you have any long-stay guests in the hotel, Margo? Someone who might use the computer regularly?"

"The place is a timeshare as well as a hotel, so we do have guests who stay for extended periods," she replied. "But a month at the most."

"I see," Whittaker responded, thinking for a few moments. He looked at me, but I couldn't think of anything pertinent to ask. I glanced over at the alcove, looking for a camera. There wasn't one. I turned and checked the rest of the lobby. They had two in the right side corners, covering the lobby. They would also catch the alcove.

"How long do you keep your security camera footage?" Whittaker asked, following my thought process.

"Em… I don't really have anything to do with that, but I think I heard someone say it was a few weeks."

I figured, but worth asking. We were really fishing for clues without any background to go on.

"Who should I contact if we'd like to review the recent recordings?" Whittaker asked, and of course, he was right. This guy tried contacting Patti Weaver a year ago, but his account was only just taken down. There was nothing to say he wasn't still active until then and the social media site had said every login was from this IP address.

"That would be the manager," Margo replied, and handed the detective a business card from a holder on the desk.

"Great, thank you," he said, taking the card and putting it in his jacket pocket. "We appreciate your help."

"No worries," Margo said, looking relieved we were leaving.

As we walked across the lobby, I looked into the alcove one more time, and a thought occurred to me. I paused and turned around. "Margo, do you have an IT person at the hotel?"

She looked up from her computer. "Like a computer geek, you mean?"

"Yeah. Someone who fixes the computers, sets up networks, and all that."

Margo shook her head. "No, we don't."

I looked at Whittaker, who nodded for me to continue.

"So what do you do when a computer crashes?" I asked.

"Oh, right. We have a contract with a tech who comes in."

"How often is this guy here at the hotel?" I asked, thinking we might be on to something.

"Not often really," Margo replied. "Things run pretty sweet most of the time. And it's she, not he."

And there again, maybe we weren't on to anything. Whoever Cayman MY Island was, they were using the computer on a regular basis from what we'd discovered. Maybe not daily, but certainly more than 'not often'. I nodded my thanks, and we turned to leave.

"Of course, she fixes almost everything by logging in remotely," Margo said, and we stopped in our tracks.

"She can log in to all your systems remotely?" I verified.

"Yup. She's pretty whizzy when it comes to the networking stuff. We call her and tell her what's up, then usually she jumps on and takes over the computer. No idea how all that works, but she's a freaking genius."

"But you've met her?" I asked.

"Rabbit? Sure. A bunch of times."

"Rabbit?"

Margo laughed. "Yeah. Her real name is Renee or Rebecca I think, but she goes by Rabbit. Even her business card says Rabbit Thompson."

"Is she a local?" Whittaker asked.

Margo shrugged her shoulders. "I'd say so, but can't say I've ever asked. She sounds like a Caymanian. Cute little thing. Doesn't say much until you get to know her. Always has her hair tied up in different ways."

"You have her card?" I asked.

"Sort of. We have a sticker on the computer with her number. Okay if you just take a pic with your mobile?"

I nodded and leaned over the counter to snap a picture. Maybe we had something after all.

A few minutes later, we were enduring the sleeping policeman and considering the next move.

"You realise this is still a shaky connection, from asking Mrs Weaver to message her, to being involved in anything that concerns us?" Whittaker reminded me.

I'd been thinking that over, and come to the same conclusion.

"If we could show a connection to Patti Weaver, other than the one post, it would suggest Patti's been lying," I said. "She could still be the leak."

We finally cleared the last of the road bumps and met the bypass. Whittaker paused at the junction. "It wouldn't be the first time I've misread a potential suspect, but my gut tells me Mrs Weaver isn't involved in anything more sinister than being patriotic to her island and its people."

"Then let's ask her about this Rabbit chick," I suggested.

Whittaker laughed. "First of all, on official police business, we use the terms female, woman, or suspect, and secondly, the Caribbean Security Systems office closed at lunchtime today. I doubt Patti Weaver will take my call after our last meeting."

"Then let's see if she takes mine," I replied, and dialled the mobile number from Patti's business card I'd kept. Once it started ringing, I put the call on speakerphone.

"Hello?" Patti answered.

"Good afternoon, Mrs Weaver. This is Constable Sommer."

"Oh," was her chilly response.

"Sorry for disturbing you outside of business hours, but I had one quick question."

I heard a sigh. "Okay."

"Do you know an IT tech by the name of Rabbit Thompson?"

The line was quiet for a moment. "I do. Why do you ask?"

"How do you know this woman?" I asked and looked at Whittaker for acknowledgement of my approved lingo. He ignored me.

"She does IT work for us. She has done for years."

"By us, you mean Caribbean Security Systems?"

"Of course. Rabbit isn't in the business of setting up home computers, Constable. Her services are in quite the demand these days. We're lucky to be one of her early contracts. She turns away most new clients now. She's swamped."

"How often do you see her at your office, Mrs Weaver?"

"Not that often these days. She's able to handle most issues remotely," Patti replied. "If you're thinking she had something to do with these break-ins, I think you're barking up the wrong tree, Constable. Rabbit has access to our networking and company systems, but she has nothing to do with the security software. She's never had access to any of that. We use IT support from the alarm company manufacturers for any issues with our products and their monitoring."

I paused and thought for a moment before asking my next question. I was pushing my luck, but as Whittaker had told me, sometimes we have to ask good people shitty questions. "Do you know Rabbit outside of work, Mrs Weaver?"

I'm not sure exactly what the noise was that I heard over the line, but it wasn't a happy sound. "I do not and if that's all, I need to go. You can call me on Monday at the office if you have any more questions."

"Thank y…" The line went dead before I could finish. "I think that's the last time she'll take either of our calls," I muttered.

A car honked its horn behind us and Whittaker waved apologetically in the mirror, pulling out onto the dual carriageway. "This adds another layer, but even if this Rabbit lady is Cayman MY Island, for all we know she's only guilty of violating a social media site's guidelines. She's certainly not the thief, unless she moves like a man and is taller than the average female."

"But we'll still talk to her, right?" I asked. "It's a stone we should flip over."

"Correct," he replied. "When we get to Central, see if you can track down a location for her."

"Do burrows have addresses, sir?" I asked.

He ignored me again and kept driving, but I caught the grin on his face.

30

GOING UNDERGROUND

With two major cases in play, Central Station was busier than usual for a Saturday afternoon. I found an available computer terminal, and fortunately one of Margo's guesses at Rabbit's real name was correct. Rebecca Thompson. Her driver's licence record at the DMV listed an address on South Church Street, not far from Smith's Barcadere, a local's beach spot. There were three Rebecca Thompsons with driver's licences, but the other two were 55 and 71 years old. It surprised me Rabbit was only 27, but the younger Rebecca had to be the one we were looking for.

I walked up the stairs to Whittaker's office where he sat back in his chair, studying several documents.

"I have a location for the bunny," I announced.

"Good. I have a name for The Haitian," he replied. "Jean-René Jérôme. Entered the country at the same time as his unfortunate friend, Didi. Both on work visas listing carpenter as their trade. Their visas are expired, or more accurately, they were cancelled. The sponsoring company claimed they stopped showing up."

"Is there an address with their visas?" I asked, not expecting much.

"They listed Comfort Suites," he replied.

"That place closed down and changed hands, didn't it?"

"Correct. We've given the two names and their pictures to the media. Maybe we'll get lucky and someone will recognise the face or the name."

Whittaker put the papers down on his desk and looked at me. He slipped the glasses from his face. He was building up to asking me something and by the length of time he was taking to mull it over, I started to worry.

"Sit down for a minute, Nora," he said, and I complied.

I noticed the clock on the wall of his office. It was 3:10pm. I hadn't checked exact flight times, but I was sure Randall Cosgrove was either back on the island or getting close. Maybe this was the 'off the case' speech. It wasn't.

"Put yourself in Mr Jérôme's shoes for a minute," he said. "What would your next move be?"

Detective Whittaker and I danced around certain elements of my past. He never mentioned the sailboat that went missing for the same period of time I was off island after the resort bust. My friend Archie, who gave me his shack on the beach before disappearing, was another taboo subject. He undoubtedly had questions, but he was wise enough to not ask questions he didn't want to hear the answers to.

He considered my accepting his offer to join the RCIPS as a clean slate. We had discussed the time I'd spent evading authorities after I'd left Norway as a runaway, and I'd admitted to passing through a few Caribbean islands while skipping customs and immigration, so he knew I'd developed skills for moving about without detection. I was sure he'd assumed I'd broken a few more laws in the process. He was right.

This knowledge I'd accumulated was part of why my mentor had considered me a good candidate for law enforcement. I could think like the people we were often chasing. Hence his question. Which I hadn't been expecting, but I'd already given some thought to the matter.

"Evaporate," I answered. "I would drop off the radar."

"Go underground here on the island," he asked, "or somewhere else?"

"That would depend on his skill sets, contacts, and ties to the Cayman Islands," I replied.

"Flights are out," Whittaker correctly stated. "Even a private charter has to go through immigration, and we only have one airport. To leave the island, he'd have to go by boat."

I thought carefully before my next statement, maintaining the careful dance. "That's where skill set comes in. Can he pilot a boat? Navigate? Sail? If not, he has to involve someone else and the risk factor goes up enormously."

"All we know is that he's a carpenter," Whittaker replied.

"We know he entered the Cayman Islands with the identification of a carpenter," I corrected. "I'll bet you'll find a qualified carpenter is happily working away on Haiti, either unaware his lookalike is here, or a nice payoff richer. I bet neither Didi nor The Haitian have ever built anyone a cabinet."

Whittaker nodded thoughtfully. "Okay, so let's assume he's no waterman. He knows we're on to him, and he knows his friend came to an unfortunate demise. How does he hide on a 22-mile-long island?"

"That would depend on his contacts here. Does he have anyone he can trust? Who was he involved with? Who worked for him or hired his services?" I replied, thinking it through as I spoke. "Assuming he's involved in trafficking young girls, he's either the supplier, or he's doing the legwork for someone else. If he's the supplier, he has somewhere he keeps the girls, which won't be a rented condo or apartment. It will be a remote house, an industrial building, or a boat."

"Seeing the run-down place Didi was holed up in, do you think they were based on a boat big enough to live on and hide victims?" Whittaker asked.

"*Nei.*"

"Agreed," he said. "So, if he's gone to ground wherever it is he's been operating from, it has to be untraceable to him or Didi."

"Ideally," I replied.

Whittaker tapped his pen on his desk. "If she has indeed fallen foul of these two, as DeWayne suggests, what would happen to Marissa?"

I chewed that over for a while. I'd also given her plenty of thought, and my conclusion had been the same every time. "In most scenarios, she's a loose end." I hated to say it, but she'd either be with the end user, or a dangerous witness who needed to be kept quiet. It was hard to see it any other way.

Whittaker went quiet, put his glasses back on, and steepled his hands. His brow furrowed in deep thought. And concern.

"No way The Haitian has an operation as elaborate and well funded as the resort had," I added, feeling I needed to explain my pessimistic view.

Whittaker held up a hand. "I get it," he said, and I was happy to not continue talking about how I came to my conclusion. I felt like I needed a week off in complete silence to make up for all the words I'd been spewing lately.

"Your insight makes sense, and I concur," he continued. "We need to proceed on the assumption Mr Jérôme is still on the island. If he's slipped away, then our investigation may well uncover that fact, but meanwhile, time is still of the essence. Marissa is alive. We'll work from that assumption until proven otherwise."

His logic couldn't be faulted, but we were short on leads to pursue. A lot was riding on Didi's mobile. It may give us someone else to question in our investigation, but I was also praying Randall Cosgrove's number would show up on there.

In theory, the bastard had no reason beyond paranoia to be concerned about his second safe, but my gut told me he'd cover his tracks as soon as he could. Even if it was with his own wife. Surely our conversation, raising the point that she had no access or knowledge of what was in there, would make her curious. I glanced up at the clock. It seemed to punch me in the face every time the second hand moved to another graduation.

"Still waiting on Didi's phone?" I asked, knowing he would have mentioned if he'd already received news.

"I told her she's making overtime until she's cracked it. The RCIPS will feed her until that time, whether it's this afternoon or not until Monday." He managed a smile. "You have an address for Miss Rabbit?"

"I do," I replied, rising from the chair. "I can't guarantee it's current, or where she's located at this very moment, but it's where the DMV thinks she lives."

Whittaker stood up. "We have a phone number for her from the business card, right?"

"We do, but I don't think we should give her a heads-up we're coming. Besides, the Kiwi chick… I mean woman, said she's introverted. I bet she won't answer a number she doesn't know."

Whittaker grabbed his jacket from the back of his seat, "Fine, let's hop along and see if the bunny's in her burrow."

He tried to hide his grin as we walked out, but I caught it.

31

RABBIT

Galicia Apartments was a small, older complex on the inland side of South Church Street. It was on a large piece of land, which, if available today, would hastily see six-storey condos built, jammed shoulder to shoulder with a hundred units. Currently, the two-storey L-shaped structure enjoyed pleasant views over open space and comprising about ten apartments. It reminded me of a travel motel from old American movies.

We parked, and I spotted Rabbit's unit number, second floor on the end, facing the road. Although dated, the building was well maintained. The wooden railings on the stairs and balcony were painted dark brown, contrasting against the white stucco, and potted plants sat outside most people's units. The place had an unpretentious and neighbourly vibe.

I knocked firmly on the front door and listened for any evidence of movement. Nothing. I knocked again, three hard raps. We waited, but still no response.

Whittaker looked over the railing towards the parking spots. "Do you recall her car from the DMV records?"

"It's the yucky green coloured Suzuki thing we passed at the bottom of the steps."

He looked over the edge of the rail to see the compact SUV below us.

"Maybe she's taken a dog for a walk," he said unconvincingly.

I cupped my hands to the window. Sitting at a desk in the living area was a dark-skinned young woman with a mop of frizzy hair. Matting down the middle of her afro was a pair of headphones. She was rocking back and forth in her seat and furiously typing on a keyboard facing a bank of three large monitors. I banged on the window without a response.

"She's in there," I said, and pulled the paper with her phone number from my pocket. I typed a text: 'Open your door.'

I watched her reach for her mobile and casually unlock the screen. She then swung around in her chair, dropping her mobile as she leapt to her feet.

"She knows we're here now," I said.

Whittaker took out his badge and held it in front of the peephole. After a few moments, the door opened a crack, the safety chain rattling until it went taut. A pair of big brown eyes looked us both over. Maybe her name came from the fact she resembled a small mammal caught in the headlights of an oncoming car. But, in her defence, unexpected police on your doorstep tended to surprise most people.

"Detective Whittaker and Constable Sommer," he said in a soft voice. "Miss Rebecca Thompson?"

The young woman nodded, but didn't speak.

"We were hoping to chat with you for a minute. May we come in?"

She made no move to open the door. "What about?" she asked. I was expecting a quiet, shy voice, but her tone was surprisingly forthright.

"Computer and networking questions. We were advised you're quite the expert on these matters," Whittaker explained, using the truth in a slightly ambiguous manner.

"I'm busy right now," she replied. "You need to make an appointment, and I'm booked up for a while."

She spoke with a Caymanian accent, but it was slight, and if I had to guess, I'd say she'd been educated overseas. If she'd studied advanced computer technology, undoubtedly she'd have needed to find a larger university than the island had available.

"Yes, we heard your services are in great demand," Whittaker responded with a smile. "This will only take a minute of your time. We'd prefer to chat now."

"I can't," she said and frowned at the detective. "I'll make some time next week. Call me back on Monday and we'll set it up."

"Tell you what," Whittaker responded, maintaining a friendly tone. "We can have a quick conversation inside, or you can come with us back to the station and we'll talk there. Option B will take a lot longer."

She glared at Whittaker for a few seconds, then pushed the door closed and unhooked the safety chain. When the door swung open, I had my first proper look at Rebecca Thompson. Barely five foot tall, she had a tiny, slender frame and an angelic, youthful face. She wasn't wearing a stitch of make-up, her left nostril was pierced with a small gold stud, and with the headphones removed, her rusty red-tinted hair had expanded to impressive proportions. She wore black leggings and an olive-coloured Che Guevara T-shirt.

She closed the door behind us and pointed to a long couch against the wall. We sat, and I looked around the apartment. It was as though a teenager was living in a space originally decorated by an adult with good taste. A dinette set matched the desk, and the couch was a similar tone to the fabric on the seats of the dining chairs. A patterned rug covered the tiled floor, and a large flatscreen television rested on a wooden stand which also matched the dinette set.

In contrast, she'd pinned a Cayman Islands flag to the wall behind her desk and various science fiction figurines decorated the upper levels of a set of bookshelves, while fantasy novels packed the lower sections. Some of the figurines were the kind with the oversized heads that wobbled about. The computer under the desk was some kind of fancy gaming unit with LED lights and cooling fans I could hear from across the room. On the front face was a small, round decal with a cartoon rabbit giving a thumbs-up. Her company name and phone number were written around the outside, which I couldn't read at this distance, but it was the same sticker I'd taken a picture of at the Holiday Inn. It was a cool logo.

"Okay, what's up?" she asked, remaining standing and glancing at her watch.

"I understand you do contract work with the Grand Caymanian Hotel, Rabbit," Whittaker said. "May I call you Rabbit?"

"Everybody does," she replied, but said nothing else.

"So, do you do contract work for the hotel?" Whittaker asked.

"Yeah. But you didn't ask me that. You stated I did, so why would I reply when you already know? You said you had questions."

I maintained a passive expression, but I wanted to laugh. So far, I really liked this chick. I mean woman.

Whittaker smiled, although I guessed he wasn't as amused as I was. "In the course of your work with the hotel, do you use the business centre computer?"

Rabbit shrugged her shoulders. "I fix any problems it has."

Whittaker sighed, and I could tell he was losing patience. "Are you the person using Cayman MY Island as their screen name on social media?"

The woman's expression morphed from annoyed at the interruption to concerned. "Why you asking me that? What's this all about?"

"I don't believe I made a statement, Miss Thompson," Whittaker said. "How about you answer the question?"

Rabbit's jaw moved several times as though she was about to speak, but thought better of it. She fidgeted and avoided looking at the detective. He left her alone to mull over her options. My money was on her confessing.

"So?" she finally said.

"Is the management at the hotel aware you're using their computer for personal projects?" Whittaker asked.

More shoulder shrugging and fidgeting followed. "Dunno. But it's a computer available for guests and employees and such, so it's no big deal. Besides, I closed that account."

We knew that was a lie. She didn't close the account. It seemed to be the first lie she'd told so far and I wondered if Whittaker would call her on it, but he moved on, no doubt keeping it up his sleeve.

"You also do work for Caribbean Security Systems, is that correct?" he asked, making sure he phrased it as a question.

"Yeah," Rabbit replied, getting more and more uncomfortable.

"Why don't you sit," I said, pointing to her office chair.

She swallowed hard, then spun the chair around to face us, dropping into the seat. I was starting to worry the nerves would get the better of her. I didn't want to see anyone throw up in front of me.

"Describe the work you do for CSS for me," Whittaker continued.

"I maintain and fix their computer terminals and network. Same as I do for most of my clients – they ain't no different."

She'd been eloquent and well spoken, but that had slipped. I didn't think she was putting on a show with her speech, but I guessed she'd grown up in a working-class home, and her vocabulary had improved during years of good schooling. Probably on scholarships if she was as bright as everyone told us.

"We're investigating several burglaries at properties using CSS alarm systems," Whittaker said. "We have evidence of inside information being used in these crimes, Miss Thompson, and we think you can help us with that."

He'd made a statement again, but he was focused on her reaction, so I daren't say anything. Rabbit looked stunned, but she had enough of her wits about her to stay silent. Whittaker let his words hang in the air like an oppressive fog that slowed time.

Finally, he spoke again. "Has anyone approached you asking for intel on the alarm systems?"

I'm glad I'd stayed quiet. As always, he had a method and a

plan. He'd hit her with what appeared to be an accusatory statement and knocked the wind out of her, then followed up with a question which sounded more like an innocent inquiry. The poor woman had no idea where she stood, or what we already knew. If she was guilty, she'd be thinking the worst.

I wondered if she was. I wasn't getting a strong feeling either way. She was terrified, but five minutes ago she was rocking out to some tunes and getting paid a hundred bucks an hour to reboot someone's modem from the comfort of her living room. Now she was undergoing the third degree from a detective who was insinuating she was guilty of a serious crime.

Which she could well be. Was I sitting across the room from someone who knew who'd been in my shack, leaving notes next to my orange juice? That possibility lost her some sympathy with me. I had to go home tonight, walk through the dark woods, not knowing if my visitor had returned. Of course, if anyone should be concerned about running into strangers in remote places, it should be the *drittsekk* who broke into my home. He doesn't want to meet a Viking with a Taser. Just ask Jumbo Flowers.

Rabbit shook her head. "I don't know anything about the alarms. I work on their business systems. They have completely different software for the alarms and the monitoring. I don't have access to any of it," she said with convincing urgency.

"You're avoiding my question," Whittaker persisted.

"No, no one has asked me for anything from CSS," she said, and stood up. "I've answered your questions, and now I need to get back to work."

Whittaker stood and pulled a card from his jacket pocket. "Here's my number. If you think of anything which may be helpful to us, please call me."

Rabbit took the card without looking at it. She walked to the door and held it open for us, staring down at the Darth Vader entry mat.

"Thank you for your time," Whittaker said, as he stepped past her onto the balcony and walked away towards the steps.

I paused for a moment in the doorway. She looked up at me, wondering why I'd stopped.

"Why do they call you Rabbit?" I asked. Because I was curious.

"I could run really fast when I was a kid," she replied, her eyes searching mine as though we might know each other.

"I like your hair," I told her as I walked outside. Because I did.

I met Whittaker at the bottom of the stairs, where he was reading a text on his mobile.

"Anything useful?" I asked.

He looked up. "She's pulled the data from Didi's mobile."

32

CHICKEN AND EGG

Whittaker had me drive while he made phone calls. I was surprised he gave me the keys after the Jumbo incident, but I think it slipped his mind with everything going on. The first person he dialled was Eileen, the lady in TSU. The call played through the speakers in the SUV.

"Most numbers appear to be unlisted pay-as-you-go phones," she explained. "The majority of calls to and from this mobile were to the number you gave me, matching the other suspect. There's a few to the bartender you arrested, several to our buddy DeWayne's number, and sixteen calls between this phone and a number registered to one Ricardo Ferreyros. He's in our system."

"Rico?" Whittaker said.

"That's him," she replied. "I saw that alias noted in his file."

"Text his number to me, please," Whittaker responded, "and last known address. Great work, Eileen, thank you."

"One more thing, Detective," Eileen said quickly before Whittaker hung up. "There are a couple of calls from a UK number. It'll take us longer to trace, as we have to put in a request to the Met."

That got my attention. I tried to recall if we had a contact number for Randall Cosgrove. I didn't think we did. Only his wife's. It was already a quarter past four, which meant if I was right, that prick would be home and clearing out any evidence. I didn't know what I'd do if he slipped out from under this, but I knew what I wanted to do.

Whittaker hung up. "I know what you're thinking," he said, looking over at me.

I nodded. "Could be him," I replied, admitting he knew part of what I was thinking. Best he didn't know the rest.

"That'll still be thin evidence to justify a warrant," Whittaker pointed out.

"It'll have to be enough if we stand a chance," I said, being careful in choosing my words. "If he gets wind about Didi and knows we're after The Haitian, he'll bury any evidence he has at the house."

"If any of this actually leads to Marissa or other girls," Whittaker said. "With your thief targeting resort members theory out the window, Cosgrove's only connection in all this would be if his number's on Didi's mobile. Which means the odds are against it."

He was right. I was trying to make the evidence fit my narrative for the case. Except, I knew Randall Cosgrove had The Haitian's number and a mysterious list of dates in his safe. If Whittaker was privy to the same information, he'd have no problem getting a warrant. Chicken and egg, I believe is the phrase in English.

"Got the address for this Rico guy?" I asked, changing the subject. The phone number either was or it wasn't Cosgrove's. Unless we were wagering on the fact, talking about it served no purpose anymore.

"I do," he said, reading off the location, which was back in Dog City.

I'd been heading for Elgin, so I continued past the station and turned right on Harbour Drive at the waterfront. Whittaker dialled another number.

"Weatherford," came the other detective's voice. "What's up, Roy?"

"We have an address for an associate of these guys in the missing girl case," Whittaker explained. "Are you busy?"

"Not if you have a reason for me to leave this paperwork behind," he answered with a chuckle.

"I'm texting you the address. It's close by," Whittaker said. "I'm in my SUV, which'll stand out like a sore thumb in Dog City. See what's in the pool. We had that old van earlier today, but I don't know if Williams brought it back to Central."

"I'll go look," Weatherford replied. "If not, I drove my daughter's car today. She took mine. It's a little piece of crap that should blend in just fine. Just don't ask me to go chasing anyone in it."

Whittaker laughed. "We'll see you there."

We drove along the waterfront in silence, and just past the traffic lights at Eastern, I turned into Bay Town Plaza, a small strip mall of businesses. Dog City was behind the long building.

"What did you think of Miss Rabbit?" Whittaker asked casually as we sat and waited for Weatherford.

"Unless she was wearing a wig and can stretch herself a lot taller, she's not the thief," I replied. "In theory, she doesn't have access to the information the thief needed to get past the alarm, but I'm guessing she has the skills to look in places she's not supposed to."

"Do you think she was lying to us?"

"Everybody does. So yes," I responded. "But on which subject it's hard to say. I guess the important point is whether she's helped the thief in some way. It appears her motivation would be her concern over Caymanians losing possession of the land. She's strong willed enough to act rather than just hold a sign and put posts on social media. Be tough to pinpoint exactly when and how she compromised CSS, if she did."

The detective thought for a few moments. "I think that's a pretty good assessment. I have a feeling she carefully avoided a lie when I asked about her being approached." He looked over at me. "What if she approached someone?"

The idea that little Rabbit with her cool hair and sci-fi dolls could mastermind a series of burglaries seemed unlikely, but we didn't get a chance to further the conversation. Whittaker's mobile rang. He hit the accept icon on the SUV's command centre screen.

"Detective Whittaker," he answered.

"Hello, Detective," came a voice that sent chills through me.

"This is Randall Cosgrove. I'm calling for an update on the burglary at my house. My wife tells me you don't have a suspect."

His tone was irritation, and he came across as demanding rather than requesting an update.

"Hello, Mr Cosgrove. Are you back on the island?" Whittaker asked.

"I am. So what's happening?"

"We just left an interview with a person of interest. We have several lines of inquiry we're following, but as Mrs Cosgrove correctly reported, we don't have anyone in custody at this stage."

"How the hell does a burglar waltz into my home, clear out my wife's jewellery and disappear on this small island without you having any real leads?"

Whittaker was half listening and half focusing on his mobile, where he sent a text without disconnecting the phone call.

"Sometimes these things take time, sir," the detective replied. "The thief seemed to know what he was doing and what he was after. It was well orchestrated. Made easier by the fact the alarm system wasn't set."

"The damn alarm being on or off has no bearing on the fact someone broke in and stole from us," Cosgrove ranted. "This is supposed to be a safe island."

"And it is, sir," Whittaker patiently responded. "But nowhere on the planet is crime free. I'm afraid we have thefts like any other Caribbean island. Fortunately, we experience a lot less than most."

My mobile buzzed, and I looked at the text. It was an international phone number. I looked at the SUV's LCD screen, which displayed Randall Cosgrove's number. They matched. My heart skipped. I figured out Whittaker had asked Eileen to send me the mystery UK number from Didi's mobile. I gave Whittaker a thumbs-up and pointed to the number on the screen. He nodded as he listened to Cosgrove drone on about the incompetence of the police in his posh English accent.

"How about I come over to see you," Whittaker suggested, once the man had drawn breath and he could break in. "I understand your frustration, sir, so I'd like to sit down and go over the case in more detail with you. How about in one hour?"

The line went quiet for a few moments. "I just landed from a long flight, Detective, and I need to take my wife out to dinner. We haven't seen each other for some time."

"I won't keep you long, but I'd be more comfortable explaining our investigation face to face," Whittaker insisted. "I'll see you at 5:30, Mr Cosgrove."

Before the man could protest, the detective ended the call.

"I knew it!" I blurted. *"Faen ta deg,* you shithead."

Whittaker looked at me with a mixture of surprise and concern. I think. I was just glad I'd sworn a bit in English and spoke the worst part in Norwegian.

"Sorry, sir," I muttered.

"Understandable," he replied. "But you realise I do have to take you off this case now."

I nodded. "I know."

The next few minutes were a whirlwind of phone calls and orders relayed to different departments. The most important call was to a judge. Whittaker's first choice didn't answer, but his second option fortunately did. He was very persuasive putting forth his case as he asked the judge to create a warrant. She pointed out how thin he was on hard evidence.

"Do you have anything else, Detective?" she asked. "I don't think I can issue a warrant based on the man's number being on someone's mobile phone. Any lawyer worth his salt will toss that out in a heartbeat."

Whittaker took a deep breath and looked at me. I guessed what he was asking, and I nodded.

"I have a witness who has identified Randall Cosgrove as a

former member of the Fellowship of Lions resort, My Lady. That places him in the middle of a group we booked for trafficking underage girls. We think there's a strong chance he's the client again in this case. I don't need to remind you that fifteen-year-old Marissa Chandler is still missing."

The judge took a few moments to reply. "No, you don't. Okay, I'll email it over. But Roy, please don't make me regret this."

"Thank you, My Lady," he said, and they ended the call.

Weatherford pulled up alongside us and wound down his window. He hadn't lied. His daughter's car was a piece of crap.

"We have another lead," Whittaker shouted across the SUV through the window I'd put down. "I have a warrant coming for this guy in West Bay. Can you handle Rico for me?"

"Sure," Weatherford replied. "What's the plan?"

"We're after Jean-René Jérôme, the guy known as The Haitian. Rico came up on the mobile phone of The Haitian's partner," Whittaker explained. "It's a long shot Rico has him hidden here, but tread carefully, check out his place, and see what shakes. If all looks quiet, see if you can talk to Rico and get a read."

"You got it," Weatherford said, and rolled up his window by hand. I could hear the mechanism creaking.

"Central," Whittaker told me, and I wasted no time backing out of the parking space.

It was finally happening. Cosgrove would go down. I thought about the other girls from the resort and wished I could share this moment with them. It was a long time too late for Carlina, but Hallie and I could celebrate. He was only one of so many, but it felt like a tremendous victory. If the *drittsekk* hasn't cleared out the safe.

33

THE SECOND SAFE

We spent half an hour at Central Station, where Whittaker collected the warrant and organised Williams and one of his men to accompany him to the Cosgroves'. The warrant included computers and mobile phones, which we'd bring back to be searched by Eileen.

I helped where possible and mulled over different approaches for asking Whittaker if I could go with them. Finally, when he was getting ready to leave, it was now or never, so I made my case.

"I should be there, sir," I began. "Not inside with you, but observing from the vehicle outside. I can verify in person he's the man from the resort."

Whittaker shook his head. "That can be done from behind the one-way glass back at the station, Nora. It's not a good idea."

"I need to be there, sir," I pleaded.

"You want to be there. I don't think there's a need," he said, but not unkindly. "I can't risk compromising the case."

"I swear, I'll stay in your car, regardless of what happens," I persisted. "You're right. There's no need, but I would be there for all the girls he abused. One of us will get to see him marched out of his fancy home in handcuffs."

"If that's what happens," he responded. "There's no guarantee."

"Either way, I'll stay in the car and drive back here with you."

Whittaker sighed. "I need to go. Darn it, Nora, fine. But if you so much as roll down a window, you'll be on graveyard shift for the rest of the year, and you can kiss detective training goodbye."

He didn't wait for my response, and I didn't blame him. Words were worthless. Action would speak for me, or in this case, inaction. I followed him out to his SUV, telling myself over and over not to fuck this up. This was one time I couldn't go all Viking and start causing chaos. I noticed he glanced at the dent in the tailgate of his Range Rover, so I hurried to the passenger side and got in.

Williams followed in a patrol car and the drive took longer than usual as we hit rush hour traffic. It was amazing how a small island could have such a problem, but morning and evening commutes were becoming brutal. It was right on 5:30pm when we pulled through the gates into the Cosgroves' residence and parked in front of the main house.

A slender man in his late fifties with greying hair opened the front door. He was wearing a pale blue Oxford shirt with the sleeves rolled up, dark blue trousers, and loafers.

"That's him," I confirmed, feeling anger and disgust welling from deep within me.

"Nora," Whittaker said, and waited for me to look his way. I didn't want to take my eyes off the man I'd hoped I would never see again. Visions of smashing his arrogant face flashed through my mind, and my jaw ached from clenching my teeth.

"Nora," Whittaker repeated, and I forced myself to look his way.

"Stay in the car. Okay?"

I nodded. "I will."

"Thank you," he said as he climbed from the Range Rover.

Williams and the other officer, who I recognised but whose name I didn't know, joined Whittaker at the front steps. Cosgrove gave them a slightly confused and irritated stare. He raised his hands and spoke, but I couldn't make out what he was saying. The Range Rover was ridiculously well soundproofed.

Cosgrove didn't look happy. Whittaker spoke for a moment before taking the warrant from his pocket and handing it to him. The man shook the piece of paper and wagged a finger at the detective. After some more animated complaints from Cosgrove, they went inside and closed the door.

I sat in silence, wondering what was going on. It was killing me. Whittaker had left the keys, but I didn't want to run the engine just for the AC. Carbon footprint and all that. I had to make up for driving a 1986 CJ-7 Jeep, which wasn't the cleanest burning vehicle on the road. It was getting stuffy inside the SUV, but I daren't put the windows down.

I heard a vehicle behind me and turned to see Estelle's Porsche pull up to the garage. Instead of raising the garage door and parking inside, she hurriedly got out and marched towards the house. She looked worried. Police vehicles in your driveway do that to a person. She was amazingly adept at rushing around in heels and I wondered how the hell she drove in them.

Before she reached the house, she spotted me in the Range Rover and came straight over, knocking on the window. How on earth do I explain through a closed pane of glass that I'm not allowed to roll it down, or get out, or talk to her? Whittaker never specifically said anything about talking to anyone, but as confinement was very clear, conversation was inferred.

Estelle gave me a puzzled look. I hit the button and lowered the window.

"What's going on?" she asked.

"Detective Whittaker is inside, Mrs Cosgrove," I replied. "He can explain."

She didn't leave, looking towards the house, then back to me. "Why are you sitting out here?"

"Because the detective asked me to," I said, telling the truth.

I felt bad. She looked really worried, and she had good reason to be, which I knew better than she did. Her husband was a creepy piece of shit hiding behind the veneer of a successful businessman and loving husband. Estelle's world was about to come unravelled.

"I just ran out to get some wine for later," Estelle said, bewildered. "We're going out to Ragazzi's at seven."

"You should go inside, Mrs Cosgrove," I urged her.

"Estelle. Please, call me Estelle," she said, once again staring at the house as though she knew setting foot inside would be life changing.

We both watched the front door open and Whittaker appeared, followed by Cosgrove. I quickly hit the button, putting the window back up, and slapped my police cap on my head, keeping my chin low. Whittaker came over to Estelle, right beside the Range Rover, and I heard him explain they had a warrant to search the premises. Her jaw hung open and her gaze switched to her husband, who began ranting and telling everyone how ludicrous this was.

Whittaker shepherded them both towards the garage building, but Cosgrove glanced at the SUV and looked surprised to see another constable in the vehicle. I tried to keep my head down, but I had to see what he was doing – and what he was doing was staring at me. He was three steps away. I could tase the shit out of him and be back in the Range Rover before he hit the ground.

Detective Whittaker herded the Cosgroves away towards the other building, and the *drittsekk* went back to complaining about the incompetent RCIPS. I watched them leave and returned to nervously waiting.

They entered through the same door I had at the end of the building and I watched them move past each window on their way upstairs to the office. I could see three silhouetted figures move across the room. I presumed Williams and his man were still going through the house, which I was sure would turn up nothing. Everything was riding on the second safe.

The sun was setting by the time Whittaker reappeared, its flame-coloured glow casting long shadows from the people as they walked towards the cars. The two policemen had joined the detective a while back and now carried a desktop computer, a laptop and two evidence bags, which I presumed contained their mobile phones.

Randall Cosgrove was red faced, livid, but free of handcuffs. I dipped my head again in case he looked my way and waited to see if they guided him to the police car. They didn't. With another barrage of complaints, he opened the front door for him and Estelle to step inside. The Cosgroves' front door closed just as the driver's door to the Range Rover opened.

"Nothing?" I asked, needing to hear the words to believe it was true.

Whittaker started the car and shook his head. "The safe contained business papers. I looked at every page."

"*Jeg visste det!*" I growled angrily. "*Vi er faen meg for sent ute, han kommer til å slippe unna med det!. Jeg rota det til.*" I held my head in my hands and tried not to scream.

Whittaker backed up and turned the SUV around.

"I'm guessing I'm better off not knowing the translation," he said. "I'm sorry we didn't come up with anything more, but maybe the computers will yield fruit."

He was right. He didn't want to know what I'd said in my outburst. I was mad at myself. If I'd had the guts to tell him what was in the safe, maybe he could have come up with a way to search it before Randall had time to move everything. It didn't matter now. Time had no rewind button. All I could do was look forward.

"Anything even suspicious?" I asked.

"I asked him about his number showing up on Didi's phone, and he told me they hired the guy to do odd jobs around the property," Whittaker replied. "Without Didi's comment on the matter, we have no proof to the contrary."

My frustration was boiling inside, and sitting in the car, trundling along back to the station with our tails between our legs, was making it worse. I needed to run, jump up and down, or punch things. The calm and inactivity was amplifying the point that Randall Cosgrove had remained in his home. He would take his wife to an expensive restaurant for dinner, enjoy the fine wine she'd bought when they got home, then sleep in his own bed.

"The office above the garage is big," Whittaker said, and just in time to not react or say anything, I remembered I shouldn't know that. "There's a full bathroom and a bedroom up there."

There was the answer to the locked door. It was a bedroom. But who locks a bedroom from the outside in their own home?

"What was in the bedroom?" I asked, trying to sound mildly interested.

"Just the normal furniture," he replied. "Nothing much in the closet, just a few items of clothing. He said he sleeps there sometimes when he works late or needs to operate on UK time."

Whittaker seemed like he was going to say more, but he paused and looked thoughtful.

"What?" I asked. "What did you see?"

The detective took a few moments, choosing his words. "We found no… paraphernalia, or what have you," he said, searching for words. "But the metal-framed headboard and footboard had marks on them."

He looked over at me to see if I was following what he was suggesting. Unfortunately, I did.

"But no handcuffs or straps anywhere?" I asked.

He raised an eyebrow as he realised I was very aware of what he'd been inferring. "No. Nothing."

"He got wind of Didi and our hunt for The Haitian," I said firmly. "He cleared out the place of anything incriminating."

"Possibly," Whittaker replied solemnly. "I'm sorry. Nora."

I tipped my head back and drew in a long, slow breath, trying to cleanse my mind of the poisonous shit people like Cosgrove deposited in my head. Images of the foul man refused to leave my thoughts. I wondered what the conversation was like when the door to their home closed.

"How did Estelle react?" I asked.

"None too good," he replied, cringing. "She seemed annoyed to start with, then once she heard why we had a warrant and what we suspected her husband of, she stopped complaining at me and went very quiet. The looks she was throwing him were like daggers."

Maybe their dinner and fancy wine wouldn't go on as though nothing had happened. I hoped Estelle tore him apart.

Whittaker's mobile rang, and he accepted the call from Detective Weatherford.

"Rico's on the move. He picked up groceries, but he's not taking them home. He's heading towards the industrial area by the airport."

Whittaker pushed the throttle pedal a little harder as he turned onto the bypass. "We're on our way. Text me a location when he stops."

34

BULL IN THE CHINA SHOP

We twisted and wound our way through George Town's industrial area north of the airport, until the buildings became more run down, and shipping containers seemed to be scattered everywhere. The street was called Blue Lagoon Drive, but nothing was blue and there certainly wasn't a lagoon. Brown, grey, rusty and abandoned seemed to be more of the theme. I'd never been to this part of the island, but Whittaker knew where he was going.

Weatherford waited for us at the end of the road where it turned ninety degrees right and continued. He was parked with his lights off, but we spotted his daughter's car. Whittaker parked farther around the corner, out of sight. We met at the street corner and looked back along the unlit road.

"See the old Honda back there?" he said, pointing in the direction we'd arrived from.

There was only one building on the west side of the street and I'd seen a car parked alongside.

"Rico went inside that shack?" Whittaker asked in reply.

"Took the groceries in with him," Weatherford replied. "He's either staying there himself for whatever reason, or he's bringing supplies for someone. You have back-up coming?"

"I do, but we can't wait. Let's take a look," Whittaker said, and borrowed my handheld radio to let dispatch know we were on the move.

We began walking down the road, staying against a wire fence on the east side. "Nora, go past the building and through the trees on the far side. Get behind the building in case anyone bolts," Whittaker ordered, and I trotted ahead of the two detectives.

The sun had set, but low in the sky, the last traces of daytime lingered in a deep blue hue. With no streetlights, I was glad of the faint glow. The small building sat askew in a large patch of dirt where the trees had been cleared. Metal shutters covered the few windows I could see, so if lights were on inside, I couldn't tell. Behind the building, two rows of shipping containers rested where, by the weeds growing around their edges, I guessed they'd lived for quite some time.

I was rapidly losing all light, which was good for concealment and bad for seeing my way through the trees and shrubs. Scratched and prodded, I made it through and hoped I hadn't dragged too many bugs and spiders with me. I moved over to the first container and crouched down. Something scurried away underneath, and I willed myself to ignore it. I texted Whittaker, letting him know I was in place. He returned a 'thumbs-up' emoji.

The only door I'd seen was on the side where Rico had parked. If there was another on the opposite wall, it was nestled into the trees where I couldn't see it. I made out movement and picked up the silhouette of the two detectives between the car and the shack. I heard a rap on the door and Whittaker shouted, "Police! Open the door."

Everything fell still around us for a few moments, cicadas and distant cars creating a backing track, emphasising the lack of activity. And then everything happened at once. I heard doors opening and Whittaker barking orders, while the brush rustled and someone came running from the trees. I couldn't make out who it was, but they were sprinting behind the container where I was hiding in the dark.

Realising I couldn't head him off before he went behind the big steel box, I set off the other way, running parallel to him along the opposite ends of the containers. In the gap between the first two containers, I glimpsed movement and wagered on him running until he reached the end of the row. I sprinted for all I was worth, no longer looking left as I went.

I cleared the final container and cut hard to the left, running down the long side, hoping I'd guessed correctly. The ground was uneven and scattered with small rocks and what I guessed were bottles and cans from careless workers' lunch breaks. The man had slowed to a jog, knowing he was reaching the last container and when I sensed more than saw him, my timing was spot on.

Barrelling into him at a full run, I hit him just above the shoulder with my forearm extended. We both went tumbling and my arm hurt like crazy from his hard head. I rolled to my feet and, with my eyes adjusting to the low light, I could just make out the figure before me. He'd recovered quickly. His arms were flared, ready to fight. Two seconds later, the man rolled on the floor in the darkness, with the two barbs from my Taser in his torso.

"Nora!" Weatherford shouted from somewhere distant.

"Behind the last container," I yelled back.

The detective heavily plodded around the corner with a torch in his hand, blinding me with the beam.

"Shine that thing at him, not me," I complained, ejecting the Taser cartridge before handcuffing the man I could now see was The Haitian.

"You got him," Weatherford said, sounding surprised.

The man lying on the floor groaned and curled his legs up into the foetal position.

"Yup. Sometimes it's good to be the bull in the china shop," I said, wishing AJ was here so I could remind her it's not always bad to run up the beach on your own.

"Huh?" Weatherford said, looking at me with a puzzled expression.

"Is Marissa in the building?" I asked, not bothering to explain myself.

"I don't know. Whittaker has Rico and I think there's someone else in there, but he sent me after you."

I dragged The Haitian to his feet, where he struggled to stand.

"Apparently, I needn't have bothered," Weatherford said, shining the torch ahead so we could see our way back. My antics hadn't improved my bruised ribs, and I winced as we walked with the adrenaline wearing off. I'd added another bruise or two to the collection.

By the time we reached the building, back-up had arrived and by the wailing of sirens in the distance, more were on the way. Rico was already in the back of a patrol car and Weatherford held Jean-René Jérôme, otherwise known as The Haitian, off to one side.

"See what Whittaker wants to do with this one," he said, and I walked over to the open door of the building.

A single bulb hung from the ceiling of the main room, which appeared to have been used as a residence. Tatty-looking kitchen cabinets lined the front wall on my left, with a sink, two-ring stovetop and refrigerator. A threadbare sofa was pulled away from the far side wall where a door hung open as evidence of Jean-René's escape route. The only other furniture was a small table and two chairs to my left. The grocery bag sat on the table.

To my right was a partition wall with two doors, one of which was open. I noticed several latches and padlocks had been used to secure the room. Whittaker poked his head out of the room and saw me.

"Put on gloves, then come in here, quick," he ordered.

One of the other constables must have heard him and handed me a pair of nitrile gloves. I thanked him and slipped the awkward material over my sweaty hands as I walked into the shack. I paused at the doorway to the back room. Two young girls, probably fourteen or fifteen years old, sat huddled together on the bottom level of a metal-framed bunk bed. A similar set of beds occupied the opposite wall; otherwise the room was bare, beyond a plastic bucket in one corner. The room stank of human waste.

Both girls were dark skinned, barefoot and filthy, their clothes dingy and ragged. One girl, with straight black hair, was lighter toned. They both bore marks around their mouths and I noticed rolled-up pieces of duct tape on the floor, next to large, severed zip ties. Both girls had abrasions around their wrists.

"Neither speaks English, but one of them sounded like she spoke Spanish," Whittaker said. "See if you can understand her."

"*Tu hablas español?*" I asked, and the paler girl looked up at me.

"*Si,*" she replied. "*Ella solo habla frances,*" she added, nodding to the second girl.

"*Dominicana?*" I asked.

"*Si, si.*"

For the next five minutes, I translated as best I could what the girl, named Ilaria, told me. They'd been in the shack for about a week, but she wasn't sure exactly. They'd lost count in the dark room, unable to tell night from day. By the time they'd figured out to count by the sounds from the trucks outside, it had already been a few days. They'd been grabbed weeks ago and spent a long time at sea. I had to tell them which island they were on, as they didn't know. The second girl was from Haiti. On the boat, there'd been many more young girls, but they were the only two dropped off here as far as they could tell. They'd been brought to shore on a smaller boat, blindfolded and bound.

They were allowed to shower, but only with one of the men watching them, so they'd both refused. They'd been treated like animals, but fortunately, neither of them had been violated. My guess, which I expressed to the detective, was they were being saved for some foul creature to grant them their first sexual experience. People like Randall Cosgrove paid handsomely for the privilege.

They'd only seen two men since they'd been in the building. We'd verify at the station, but based on Ilaria telling me they both spoke the same language and the other girl, Millie, apparently understood them, I presumed they were Didi and Jean-René.

"You're sure it's only been the two of them?" Whittaker asked.

"That's what she said," I confirmed.

"Then where is Marissa?" he asked, more to himself than asking me.

"*Escuchaste el nombre de Marissa?*" I asked Ilaria and watched Millie in case she reacted to the name.

"*No*," Ilaria replied, and the other girl showed no signs of recognition. Ilaria then went into a longer explanation, which I struggled to follow perfectly.

"What did she say?" Whittaker asked.

"We need a better translator than me, but I think she was saying they had the impression someone was being taken back out to the boat when they arrived," I explained. "She heard a female voice, but it wasn't clear. Whoever it was spoke English, though, and didn't sound happy. They were both hooded, gagged and terrified, so she can't tell us much more than that."

"Damn," Whittaker cursed. A very rare occurrence for him. "If they've already taken Marissa off the island, we'll never find her."

35

SPILLED NUTS

It was nearing 8:00pm by the time we were back at the station with Rico sitting in an interview room. The girls had been taken to hospital, along with The Haitian, who'd whined like a little sissy about being tased. We all knew he was just buying time, but protocol dictated we had to oblige him with a medical examination. He was well guarded and kept away from the girls.

Rico looked like an antelope who'd lost his herd in the savannah. His leg was tapping up and down like an epileptic typewriter, and he couldn't sit still for a second. Based on what Whittaker had told me and a quick check of his rap sheet, trafficking young women was way out of his league, but somehow he'd got himself caught in the middle.

Detective Whittaker asked me to sit in on the interview again. I stifled a yawn and gladly accepted. I was knackered, but we couldn't delay if Marissa had any hope. Although the chances she was already gone seemed high.

"Looks like you've elevated your game a few notches, Rico," Whittaker began. "Frankly, I'm surprised at you. I thought you were smarter than to play errand boy to men like this."

"I don't have anything to do with these people," Rico replied with panic in his Hispanic-accented voice. "I just met them around town. The guy calls me and says he'll pay me a hundred plus cost to grab him some groceries."

"Do you not watch television or listen to the radio?" Whittaker asked. "It's all over the news about these two Haitian guys."

"Nah, I don't own a TV," he replied.

"I believe you when you say you don't own a TV," Whittaker said. "But I guarantee there's several in your home, Rico, all previously paid for and owned by someone else."

The suspect held up his cuffed hands. "No way, man. I'm legit these days."

"Arresting you while harbouring a fugitive and imprisoning two underage girls says different, Rico."

"Shit, come on, Detective! You know that ain't me."

"Rico, my main concern is finding Marissa Chandler," Whittaker said, tapping a finger on the table. "Help me find Marissa, and we'll work things out for you. If you've got nothing, then you'll roll through the system as Jean-René Jérôme's accomplice."

"Who?" he asked, looking genuinely confused.

"Marissa Chandler, the missing girl," Whittaker said.

"No, I heard about her. It's the foreign guy I don't know."

"The man you were found with, The Haitian. Jean-René Jérôme is his name," Whittaker explained.

"See, I don't even know the guy's real name."

"Marissa Chandler, Rico," Whittaker repeated. "Where is she?"

"Hey, just 'cos I heard of her doesn't mean I know anything about her! Try that deadbeat DeWayne. He's been banging the girl's mother."

I imagined it wasn't the first time a Dog City resident had thrown another one under the bus. The area was well known for fights amongst the residents. The emergency room had stitched up plenty of them.

"DeWayne claims he sold Marissa out to The Haitian, and now we find you're partners with him," Whittaker retorted. "So how about you help yourself by helping us find the girl?"

Rico shook his head and stared at the table. "Lawyer," he finally said.

I sat across the desk from Whittaker and we both sipped coffee. Me from a paper cup, him from a mug with AJ's 'Mermaid Divers' logo on it. I'd already had too much caffeine and the shitty office coffee tasted, well, even shittier than usual. We wouldn't get to interview The Haitian until the morning, and Rico had clammed up until his lawyer could get there, which would also be in the morning.

Ilaria and Millie were safe, so the day wasn't a loss, but Marissa was still out there, and as we turned over rock after rock without finding her, the chances were getting slimmer. Whittaker's desk phone rang and he put it on speaker as we were the only ones left in the offices.

"Whittaker."

"It's Eileen. Check your email. The mobile you found at the scene was the same pay-as-you-go brand as the other bloke had. I was able to get into it quickly, having done it before."

"Great work, Eileen, thank you. I hope you enjoy your Sunday, and I promise I'll try not to ruin it for you."

Eileen laughed. "So you don't want those seized computers and mobiles examined tomorrow, after all?"

"That's right," Whittaker said, shaking his head. "I'm really sorry, Eileen. I do need those as soon as possible."

She laughed again. "I'll see you tomorrow."

Whittaker hung up the phone, so I stood and walked around the desk behind him. He pulled the Excel file from his email and copied the names and phone numbers into the spreadsheet he'd already made with Didi's information.

"Without looking through every line, how can I see which phone numbers appear in both mobiles?" he asked me.

"Use a conditional format for duplicate values," I replied.

He stood up and stepped aside. "How about you use a conditioning duplicate thing, and I'll watch?"

I dropped into his chair, which was warm. I don't know why, but sitting somewhere another person had just vacated always felt strange to me. Oddly uncomfortable. Maybe because we associate another's body warmth with intimacy. Or maybe because I'm weird.

I copied the two columns of numbers into another worksheet. Selecting the first column, I used 'Delete Duplicates', and then did the same for the second column. The list reduced considerably as all the repeatedly called numbers disappeared.

"Huh, that was neat," Whittaker muttered over my shoulder. "But there's still a lot of them."

"I'm not done," I told him.

"Sorry. Carry on."

With all the remaining cells selected, I clicked on 'Conditional Formatting', hovering over 'Highlight Cells Rules' from the drop-down menu, then selected the 'Duplicate Values' option. I chose a yellow highlighted cell for the format, and hit 'OK'. The screen lit up with a bunch of yellow cells.

"That's much easier," Whittaker said.

"I'm not done."

"Okay," he said. "You're doing good."

I selected the first column and clicked 'Sort', chose 'Cell Colour', and 'Yellow'. Adding a second tier, I chose 'Smallest to Largest Values'. Hitting 'OK' put all the yellow highlighted cells at the top of the list in numerical order. I scrolled down, selected the non-highlighted cells and hit delete. I repeated the same procedure for the second column. Everything remaining was highlighted and lined up.

"There, that's the same numbers that were used from both phones," I said, sitting back so Whittaker could see the results.

"Great, that would have taken me an hour or three," he said. "Now we just need to look back at the lists and see if any of these numbers were saved with a contact, or have one traced by Eileen."

"That's easy." I leaned forward and typed a 'Lookup' formula in the cell next to the top phone number and used the array from the original worksheet which had the contacts next to the numbers. I locked the array in the formula using '$' signs by the cell references and dragged the formula down the column. All the phone numbers with identified contacts now had the contacts' name next to it.

"How on earth did you just do that?" Whittaker said, peering over my shoulder.

It was easy to pick out Randall Cosgrove's number. It was the only UK number on the list. He had appeared on both phones. I clicked back to the worksheet with the complete call log and sorted the lists by 'Smallest to Largest' number.

"Cosgrove called them, not the other way around," I noted aloud. "Twice to both mobiles."

With the list sorted, we could see which numbers had the greatest number of calls. On both phones, the two Haitians spoke to each other more than anyone else.

"There's another unidentified number with the second highest number of calls from both of them," I pointed out.

"Maybe someone else they're working with," Whittaker suggested.

"Or working for."

I got up from the detective's chair and went around to the front of the desk, trying to decide whether to sit down or go home and sleep. "I wish we could have interviewed The Haitian tonight," I mused. "Maybe there'd be a chance to find Marissa. Poor kid is spending another night… wherever the hell she is."

I was exhausted. The idea that Cosgrove was getting away scot free was grinding my insides up. Now that he'd buried the slim evidence we would have had from the safe, The Haitian was our only hope. And that was a long shot. Unless he gave us hard evidence of wrongdoing, useable in court, Cosgrove would still walk. Hanging all my hopes on Jean-René Jérôme felt desperate at best.

Maybe we shouldn't hang all our hopes on him, I thought. Maybe it was my tired, muddled mind, but I threw the thought out there anyway.

"The Haitian could give us Cosgrove," I said, and Whittaker looked up from behind his computer.

"He might, but until we speak to him, we won't know."

"But Cosgrove doesn't know we haven't interviewed him," I pointed out.

Whittaker sat back in his chair and rubbed his chin. "Are you suggesting we arrest Cosgrove?"

"Yup," I replied, drumming up more conviction than I really felt. "We tell him we have new testimony from The Haitian who was arrested with two underaged girls held captive."

"Still, we have nothing to hit Cosgrove with. All he has to do is say nothing and his lawyer would have him home by sunrise."

"Unless he thinks he's fucked…" I quickly stopped myself. "Sorry, sir. Unless he thinks he's being set up as the ringleader for the whole thing. What if that burner phone is his? The one with all the calls. A pay-as-you-go service probably doesn't work overseas, so the couple of calls on his personal mobile may have been from the UK. We tell him The Haitian has spilled the nuts, and we know Cosgrove was running the entire operation."

"Spilled the beans," he corrected.

"Shit, I always get that one wrong. Nuts, beans, whatever he spilled, we tell Cosgrove they're all over the floor."

"I think that's a touch more literal than the phrase warrants," he said, absentmindedly as he mulled over the idea. "He could be the man in charge, or he might simply be a client."

"Doesn't matter," I persisted. "Either way, he'll want to bargain his way out of it."

"Only if he thinks we actually have a case against him," Whittaker reminded me. "Which we don't."

"But we can hold him for 24 hours without charging him, right?"

"We can, and as this is a serious crime we're talking about, I could apply for an extension for up to 96 hours, but I wouldn't get it based on the lack of evidence we have. Especially as the house search was fruitless."

"In 24 hours we will have interviewed The Haitian, and we should have DNA results from the shack, which will likely give us a match for Marissa," I campaigned. "We'll have more evidence to build a case. He's guilty as f... Guilty for sure, sir."

Whittaker sighed. "In for a penny, in for a pound," he said, punching keys on his computer.

"We're arresting him?" I asked excitedly.

"We're not," he said, lifting the receiver on his desk phone and punching in an extension. "But someone is."

I was confused, wondering what the penny business he mentioned was all about.

"Dispatch, this is Whittaker. I need a patrol car on North West Point Road looking for one of two vehicles." The detective read off the description for the Cosgroves' cars from the DMV records he'd pulled up, including number plates. "We're looking for a male driver, 50s, slightly greying hair, slim build. We have a tip he's been drinking."

"Ragazzi's!" I blurted, and Whittaker looked at me.

"They had a reservation for seven at Ragazzi's," I explained, recalling Estelle's comment.

Whittaker relayed the information to Dispatch and asked for one car to check the car park at the restaurant and one to wait on North West Point Road in Pearl Divers' car park.

I sat back, smiled, and contemplated another cup of shitty coffee.

36

A LIFEBOAT FOR ONE

I sat on the carpeted floor and leaned against the wall in the corner of Whittaker's office.

"Why don't you go home, Nora?" he said from his chair. "I'll call you when I know more."

"I'm good," I replied, and was glad when he left it at that.

I'm sure it wasn't standard procedure for constables to take a nap in the lead detective's office, but no way was I leaving before I knew Cosgrove had been arrested. We didn't have to wait long. I'd barely dropped off to sleep when the handheld radio on Whittaker's desk sprang to life. The detective had kept the volume low while the usual chatter went back and forth between Dispatch and officers on duty, but turned it up when a report came in of a Porsche with a male driver suspected of driving under the influence. I stayed on the floor, but I was wide awake again.

"Whisky 3, this is Whisky 1. Possible DUI heading north on West Bay Road. Over."

"Roger, Whisky 1. Whisky 3 in position."

Everything stayed quiet for a few minutes while the Cosgroves made their way towards their home. I wondered if they were rolling along in blissful oblivion, looking forward to their wine at home, or if their dinner had been a tense affair, fraught with questions and lies. I hoped she was making his evening miserable.

"Dispatch, this is Whisky 1. Possible DUI pulled over on North West Point Road just beyond West Bay Road. Whisky 3 also on scene. Over."

The call sounded mundane and routine. For those constables, it likely was. Every Saturday night, they pulled over and arrested at least one driver for DUI. Often, the RCIPS used sobriety checks in key locations, which always yielded several cases until word got around through social media and friends texting friends. Traffic would magically dry up after that.

After five minutes of silence, the radio squawked once more. "Dispatch, this is Whisky 1. Transporting DUI suspect to Whisky station. Car is in safe location, no tow required. Over."

Whittaker reached for the radio, but before he could speak, it lit up again. "Whisky 1, this is Dispatch. Negative on Whisky station. Transport to Zulu. Copy?"

Whittaker put the radio back on his desk. The constables from West Bay were planning on taking Cosgrove to their station, but Dispatch told them to bring him to us at Central.

"Dispatch, this is Whisky 1. Understood. Over."

We were back to waiting. I leaned my head against the wall and closed my eyes.

"Now you can go home," Whittaker said.

"I'm good," I replied again.

"You know you can't see him or be anywhere near him once they bring him in?"

"I know."

"You really should go home, Nora."

"I'm good, sir," I said again without opening my eyes.

Whittaker didn't say any more, and when I woke up, he was gone. I looked at my watch. It was almost nine.

"*Faen*," I mumbled, getting to my feet.

I'd intended on staying until it was confirmed the arsehole was here and being interviewed. My guess was he'd lawyer up and nothing would then progress until the morning. Now I didn't know where things were in the process. I walked downstairs to the reception area. It was strange being in Central during the evening when everything was so quiet; I'd only ever been here during the day. West Bay was much smaller and quieter at any time of day. This was like being in a bar before it opened. The silence and echoed footsteps didn't fit the location.

I started towards the front desk and the duty constable when I noticed one other person. Estelle was sitting in a chair in the waiting area, head in her hands. She looked up at the sound of my boots on the tiled floor. Her eyes were red and puffy from crying, her hair ruffled, and a pair of designer heels were next to the chair, her bare feet on the tile floor.

I was totally crap at the reassuring, patting-on-the-back bullshit. How could I tell her it would all be fine? She'd be better off without the bastard, but that didn't make her world okay at the moment. I sat down next to her.

"I don't understand what's going on," she whispered.

"DUI, I was told," I replied, knowing that was not what she meant.

Estelle shook her head. "That was just a ploy to get him in here. We both know that."

I didn't respond.

"You think you know someone," she said. "We've been married for 22 years. I can't believe all these things about young girls could be true."

"You had no idea at all?" I asked.

She turned and looked at me. "You think it's really true, then?"

I nodded.

"Bloody hell." She let out a long breath and wiped her eyes. "There's been a few times over the years that I wondered if there was someone else. But not like this. We spent a lot of time apart with work, but we spoke every night, and I never had proof he was cheating, just an odd sense occasionally. He's been a loving husband. I was looking forward to when he retired and we could be together all the time."

A tear escaped from the corner of her eye, and I put a hand on her arm. "Has he admitted anything to you now?"

"No," she was quick to reply. "He denies everything. Says he's being set up or framed by someone. I quizzed him over dinner and he got all defensive and mad, saying I'm not being supportive. I feel bad that we argued. He swears it's all lies."

It was my turn to take a deep breath. Everything was likely to come out eventually. His membership at the resort; my witness to his actions; his involvement with The Haitian. I wondered if they could keep my name secret. I doubted it. Estelle would find out that I was the one her husband requested every month. For almost a year. My skin crawled at the memory. Maybe, if I told her, she could accept the truth about the man she didn't really know, and the healing could begin. For us both.

"I'm going to the UK," she said, before I could speak. "I need to get as far away from all this as possible. Away from Randall. At least until the truth comes out, whatever it may be. I need to be with my family. People I trust without any doubt."

"There's something you should know, Estelle," I began nervously. "I *know* these things about your husband are true."

She looked at me again, her brow furrowed. "What do you mean?"

"I know, because…"

Footsteps approached, and I swung around to see Whittaker striding into the lobby. He slowed when he saw us both. Estelle stood up.

"What's going on, Detective? Where's my husband?"

"Mr Cosgrove is being detained for further questioning," Whittaker replied in a firm tone. "His lawyer won't be here until tomorrow morning. You should go home, Mrs Cosgrove. Call me mid-morning tomorrow for an update." He handed her a business card, which she stared at as though answers would leap from the printed words and numbers.

"Has Randall been charged?"

"Not as yet, Mrs Cosgrove," Whittaker replied carefully. "But we expect he will be."

"Oh my God," Estelle gasped under her breath. "Can you keep him here without charging him? I thought there were rules about that?"

"There are, and we can. Standard time is 24 hours, but that can be extended to as much as 96 hours in certain circumstances."

Estelle was an astute businesswoman who'd held high rank in the corporate world before she'd successfully retired early, but it was clear these circumstances were beyond the scope of anything she'd dealt with before. She looked at me. Her eyes seemed to plead for help, but I had no help to offer. I'd started to tell her about the resort, but I'd been interrupted and I daren't say anything in front of Whittaker. She reached down and picked up her shoes.

"I have no way of getting home," she said, remembering her car was in West Bay.

"I could..." I began, but the detective quickly cut me off.

"I'll have a constable take you, Mrs Cosgrove. Please wait here just a few minutes while I organise something." He turned to me. "Constable Sommer, if you'll wait in my office, I'll be up shortly."

I was about to tell him I was on my way home, but the look he gave me made it clear this wasn't a suggestion or request.

"Yes, sir," I replied, and touched Estelle's arm. She gave me a strained smile as I walked away.

"What was that about?" Whittaker asked me, pushing his fingers through his closely cropped hair.

"I was leaving, and she was in the lobby," I replied. "She was upset. I thought I might learn something from her."

"That's hardly taking 'off the case' and 'stay away', seriously, is it?" he said, with less annoyance than I was expecting.

"Sorry, sir." I spoke the words, but I wasn't sorry. It was what he needed me to say, so hopefully we could move on. I was far more interested in how the interview went.

"Did you?" he asked.

"Huh?"

"Did you learn anything?" he repeated impatiently.

"Oh, no. Well, a little. She seems genuinely shocked and upset. One second she can't believe any of it, and the next she's talking about going to England to get away from him. She said they argued over dinner and he denied everything."

Whittaker nodded while he tidied his already tidy desk. "I wish she did know something. Maybe she'd tell us," he said. "Her husband clammed up from the get-go. Apart from yelling about slander, he hasn't said much. I told him The Haitian had spewed his guts and fingered him, to which he replied he was being played, and he wanted his lawyer. Looks like he's going to stick with denial."

"Let's hope The Haitian does give us something tomorrow. He doesn't strike me as the honourable type," I offered optimistically.

"I'm sure he'll gladly throw anyone else out of the lifeboat," Whittaker agreed, shutting down his computer. "But he can only do that if Randall Cosgrove is actually involved."

"He is," I responded confidently.

"Let's go home, Nora," he said, leading me down the hall. "By this time tomorrow, I'm sure we'll know more." He paused at the top of the stairs. "You don't have a shift tomorrow, do you?"

"No," I replied cautiously, guessing where this was going.

"Then take tomorrow off, Constable. You've earned it."

"What about Marissa? I can't take time off while she's still missing."

Although he smiled, his expression seemed sad. "You'll learn. Our work continues twenty-four-seven, and if you don't force yourself into taking a break now and then, you'll quickly burn out."

"But this case is different," I responded, truthfully.

"It is, and you're emotionally embedded in the outcome. Which makes it even more important to step back and take a breath or two. We'll make progress tomorrow, I promise."

We walked down the stairs and I pictured myself sitting on my porch, looking at the ocean, balling my hands into fists while I wondered where Marissa was.

37

SPOILT MILK

On my ride home, I almost called AJ a dozen times. But I didn't. Usually, my default was to be alone to figure things out for myself, but lately I'd found myself leaning on my friend more and more. Often, she pissed me off and told me things I didn't want to hear, and often, she was right. Regardless, she would be at home with Jackson, enjoying their Saturday evening, and didn't need me barging in.

Whittaker was annoyingly right as well. I'd become so immersed in both cases, I was having a hard time keeping all the threads straight. They were still two cases, but interwoven to such an extent they'd blended into one in my mind. I wasn't sure I could verbalise everything buzzing around in my head, even if I tried. I needed sleep, that was for sure.

I parked on the verge outside the tall wire fence that the dickhead who owned the land formerly containing the Spanish Bay Reef Resort maintained around the woods. The resort had been demolished years ago, my shack being the only remaining building. It sat on its own small lot, which Mr Dickhead had tried to swindle away from my friend Archie. Fortunately, he failed, and I wasn't certain who actually owned the resort property now, after various charges had been filed.

I hated the fence, but it gave me a layer of security. In theory. I had no direct access to my home, so I parked and walked, clambering through a gap I'd made in the fence along the side of the property. I shone my torch on the narrow path I'd beaten clear through the woods, and for the first time since earlier in the day, I wondered what, or who, might greet me.

Switching off the torch, I paused at the edge of the clearing where my shack stood facing the ocean. A first quarter moon shone between banks of cloud and my eyes quickly adjusted. The main pathway ran to the west of the building with more open space, so I chose the narrow and shadowed east side. Carefully placing my footsteps in the brush I'd been remiss in clearing, I reached the porch and took a tentative look around the corner.

From my acute angle, I could tell that the front door was closed, but there was no way to know if the pebbles were in place. I was certain I was being overly cautious, but in the back of my mind, the paranoia which had kept me safe during most of my travels nagged and begged not to be ignored. I was tired and the bruises on my ribs were ready for an ice pack and some aspirin, but the penalty for taking my time was only a minute or two.

I slowly moved around to the front steps. No lights were on inside, and resting my hand on the wooden planks of the old deck, I couldn't feel any vibrations from movement. I took the first step, staying to the edge where the treads were screwed to the stringers to avoid creaking. A rumble emanated from the side of my home and I froze in place, my heart thumping faster.

I realised it was the air conditioner compressor kicking on, and shook my head. Stepping onto the porch and moving towards the entry, I looked carefully at the gap between the door and the jamb. I squinted in the low light, searching for the little stones. The moonlight wasn't enough to make out anything but a dark line, so I turned the torch on with my other hand over the lens. By splitting my fingers, a slot of light illuminated the edge of the door and I carefully scanned from top to bottom. I didn't see any pebbles.

Bent over, looking at the lower part of the door, I was poorly prepared and vulnerable. The door swung away from me, and for a moment my brain thought I was falling forward. Whoever ran out of my shack hit me a glancing blow, which from my prone position, spun me around and bowled me over. Stunned and disorientated, I gathered up the torch I'd dropped and swung the beam across the open space between the deck and the shoreline. A figure glanced back before disappearing beyond the trees, running west towards my neighbour's house. It was definitely a man, wearing all black, including a mask. Beyond that, the only thing that registered was bright blue eyes as my light had caught his face.

Leaping down the steps, I sprinted after him. Somewhere in the back of my mind, I knew it was the thief, but rage was consuming me and all I could think about was getting my hands on him. The shack, my home and private escape, was a precious sanctuary this guy had violated. Again. The only way this would stop was to catch him.

I rounded the corner and shone the light ahead while running as fast as I could. It was a narrow trail where dirt met the ironshore, weaving back and forth as it followed the rugged coastline, bordered by woods on the left. I caught glimpses up ahead of the intruder when the trail took him closer to the water, clear of the trees. He had the same build as the man in Cosgrove's security footage.

At the next outward curve, which should have revealed the man once again, the trail was empty. We were short of my neighbour's property, so he had to have gone into the woods, or the Caribbean Sea. Slowing to a jog, I ran the light across the water and saw nothing. He must be in the dense woods. If he could find his way through the thick brush, casuarinas and sea grapes, he would come to the road. I hadn't noticed any unusual cars, but presumably he'd arrived in a vehicle, which meant it had to be hidden along Conch Point Road.

Rather than enter the woods where he could easily evade me, I killed the torch and kept running down the path to the large home next door. The owners were rarely on the island and were nice people who I'd met several times. They allowed me to park my Jeep in their driveway, which I often did if I planned on not going anywhere for a few days. I wished I had tonight.

I turned inland across the edge of their property and kept running past the house, down the long driveway to the road. Panting, I looked both ways, trying to see a car I may have missed. There was still nothing out of the ordinary. Sprinting to make sure I reached my Jeep before the man could exit the woods, I hid behind the rear tyre so he wouldn't see my feet underneath.

I was out of breath. The blow had knocked the wind out of me before I'd started the chase. My panting was the loudest sound on the quiet roadway, and I focused on calming down while keeping an eye along the trees beyond the fence to the west.

Twenty minutes later, the adrenaline had worn off, and now I was fed up with waiting. He'd either backtracked to the coast trail, stayed in the woods and gone west, or was waiting and watching to see what I'd do next. In which case we were in a stand-off. I should call it in, and we'd have constables and dogs combing the neighbourhood all night, but I didn't know what waited for me in my shack. Another note? I suspected there was, but why he'd decided ten o'clock at night was the best time was puzzling.

Sod this, I decided, and walked out into the open. "Instead of leaving stupid notes in my refrigerator, why don't you tell me what you want me to know?" I shouted into the night.

A dog barked from somewhere down the road, but no one emerged or answered me.

"Seriously? This is bullshit. Talk to me!" I yelled. Nothing. Now I felt like a nutter, standing by the side of the road screaming at the moon. "Fine. I'm going home. If you surprise me in the woods, I'll tase the shit out of you."

But instead of taking my usual path through the fence and the woods, I backtracked down the neighbour's driveway to the water's edge and followed the trail home. I wasn't a jumpy person, but the dense, dark woods didn't seem appealing.

The ocean breeze had kept the front door swinging wide open, so I reached in and turned the light on. The sudden brightness made me blink, but I couldn't see movement, so I stepped inside and locked the door behind me. First thing I did was draw all the curtains closed. The idea of someone watching me from outside crept me out. When you don't know where somebody is, the brain tends to go loopy. They're not where you can see them, which means they have the rest of the planet to hide. Of course, that's not reasonable, but my imagination was having fun with the concept at my nerves' expense.

Confirming it was the same person as before wasn't difficult. The refrigerator door was open. The bastard was going to spoil my milk as well as my evening. I guess I'd surprised him in the act of note leaving. There was no piece of paper in the fridge itself, but on the floor there were two. I picked them both up. The first had the same 'Good evening, Nora' typed on the front, and inside were the words, 'Don't believe Cosgrove – put pressure on him'. Apparently, he wanted me to interfere now, but he was behind the times. I'm not sure what more pressure we could put on the *drittsekk,* and I certainly wasn't believing a word out of Cosgrove's disgusting mouth. Not that I was privy to his interview.

I opened the second note, which had nothing typed on the front. Inside, the words were handwritten: 'Go see Chesterton-Clark'.

Chesterton-Clark was the name of the old widow who'd been robbed. I stared at both notes. It dawned on me why the intruder was there so late. He'd already left the first note about Cosgrove, then found out we'd arrested him. He'd been forced to return, and thinking I was still at the station, he replaced the note for the second one, which he'd hurriedly written by hand. I'd walked in on him mid exchange.

Why he couldn't find a better way to tell me this stuff, I had no idea. Trust, I supposed. He couldn't be sure I wouldn't arrest him. And he was right to be wary. The bugger kept breaking into my home, so he was pissing me off no matter how much he was trying to do some good in the big scheme of things. If that was even true. I'd thought the thief was targeting resort members, but that no longer seemed true. The old lady, Chesterton-Clark, certainly had nothing to do with the International Fellowship of Lions. But now he was sending me to investigate her? Or just talk to her?

I had no idea, so I bagged the fresh notes with the first one and hid them again. I couldn't do anything more until the morning. Undressing, I washed, cleaned my teeth, then took an ice pack from the freezer. Usually, I slept naked, but tonight I threw on an oversized T-shirt which hung to mid-thigh on my tall frame. I triple checked my Taser was in easy reach on the bedside table, and my extendable truncheon sat propped up, ready to grab.

Lying in bed, I rested the ice pack on my ribs and wished I had a few more as various other body parts ached. I stared at the ceiling I couldn't see in the dark. I spent the night dozing in short bursts, which all ended in me jolting awake, either fretting over where Marissa was being held, or hearing strange noises outside. At one point I considered tasing myself to see if that would knock me out for a while, but the vision of poor Jumbo flopping about like a breakdancing bear brought me to my senses.

38

SHAKING HANDS AND ACCEPTING AWARDS

Dawn was a long time coming. I'd given up on meaningful sleep and the clock seemed to laugh at me as it refused to keep up with the planet's rotation. Sitting on the couch, I was halfway through a mug of coffee when the sky finally eased from pitch black to indigo. I'd opened the curtains on the north-north-west-facing front windows, where in the evening I was regularly gifted with colourful displays of tangerine sunsets. The beginning of each day was more akin to the dial of a dimmer switch being slowly turned up on the world.

With fins and mask in hand, I took the trail by the water in the opposite direction from where I'd chased the thief the previous night. A tiny marina was one of the few traces remaining of the old resort. A rock wall protected the entrance to the inlet, which had been used to pick up guests for diving and sunset cruises.

Small crabs scurried away down the vertical side of the concrete dock as I stood near the edge and slipped my fins on. Stepping forward, I dropped into the balmy, refreshing water. The ocean wrapped its arms around me as I closed my eyes and welcomed its comforting embrace.

Swimming on the surface, making long easy strokes, I made my way towards deeper water against the soft, incoming swells. With little wind, the surface had a glassy shine which rolled with the gentle waves as they made their way towards shore. Breathing through my snorkel, I kept my face in the water and watched the silent world below me grow busier as I approached the reef.

It reminded me of when I was a child and my parents took me away on weekend trips to the countryside. I loved the outdoors, but when we returned, a feeling of comfort and anticipation would build as we passed through smaller towns and the scattered suburbs of Oslo. The closer we came to the city, my excitement grew with the traffic and activity. Once home, I would enjoy a sense of relief before longing to be outside in the open space once again.

My home in Norway was an anchor, a safe place where no harm could come to me. A cocoon I felt forced to leave behind me, although looking back, it was a choice I made. Since that day, I had been adrift without prongs buried deep in the sand to hold me in place. Until Archie gave me his shack. Now, the thief threatened to rob me of that security, casting me loose to flounder aimlessly, exposed from all sides.

The coral spread out before me in a vibrant display of abundant life. A calm descended as the entanglements of unimportant details were thrust aside, opening a focused pathway forward. In an instant, all became as crystal clear as the water below me.

Find Marissa.

The young girl held the key to both cases, I was sure of it. Everything else swirling around in my mind was causing me to lose sight of the singular and most important goal. Finding Marissa had been top of the list every time I paused to consider the priorities, but Cosgrove, The Haitian, my fears, all of it, kept clouding my vision. They were all pieces of a puzzle which led towards the girl. She would tie everything together.

Diving smoothly down to mingle with the residents of the underwater metropolis, I felt relieved, refreshed, and centred. But in the back of my mind I knew everything now hung on Marissa still being on the island. And alive.

Rosemary Chesterton-Clark lived in an ocean-front home on Boggy Sand Road, down the street from AJ's place. Of course, AJ didn't own her little cottage. It was on the grounds of a large multi-million-dollar home, which she kept an eye on for the actual owners. I presumed Mrs Chesterton-Clark held the title to her impressive home.

It was single storey, with a Spanish tiled roof, and a pillared porch over double entry doors. I rang the doorbell and heard a dog barking. It was more of a yip than a bark. If I did ever get a dog, it would be a proper-sized one with a real bark, not one you had to carry around. But I understood the appeal of a cat-sized pooch for older people who couldn't walk them far. They probably wanted one who'd curl up on their lap in the evening. I just couldn't take the shrill yipping. I'd have a rabbit instead. My aunt had one. They don't make any noise, litter train easily, and shit little pellets that don't stink.

The door finally opened, and a lady in her seventies smiled at me. She was wearing something white and frilly, with various forms of gold jewellery attached to her body in every available location. The dog was an equally white and fluffy little beast, which jumped around her feet and continued to make a noise that made me want to stick pencils through my eardrums.

"Good morning, Mrs Chesterton-Clark," I greeted her. "I'm Constable Sommer. I'm sorry to disturb you on a Sunday, but I wondered if I may ask you a few follow-up questions?"

"Of course, my dear. Come inside," she replied in a posh English accent. "I was just making tea. Would you like some?"

"No, thank you," I replied. I hated tea, hot or iced. Although I was certain an upper-class Englishwoman would slit her own throat before drinking cold tea.

"Coffee?" she offered. "I have coffee if you'd prefer?"

"Coffee would be good," I replied. I'd had another cup at home, after my swim, and figured I'd need one an hour to make it through the day ahead.

I followed her through the entryway to a large living area with the kitchen to the right, a dining area to the left, and in the centre, three large sofas forming a semicircle facing the Caribbean Sea through tall, arched, floor-to-ceiling windows. The decor was fragile looking. Lots of china, figurines, and glass shelves. I was already nervous the mere presence of my inner bull would break something.

"Have you made any progress finding who this burglar might be?" she asked as cups were brought out and a kettle set to boil.

"We have a few promising leads, ma'am," I replied. "But it's early days."

"Hm," she murmured. I never knew such a simple sound could be overloaded with that much judgement and comment. "So, what questions did you have, young lady? I believe I told the other police chaps all I knew."

I stood by the broad kitchen island, and also wondered what questions I had. A cryptic note had guided me there, as though all would become clear when the front door opened. I should have thought about a plan on my way over, but that notion had escaped my sleep-deprived brain.

"Has there been any sign of entry at any other time, ma'am?"

She looked over at me with one of those 'are you simple' stares. "I didn't know the burglar had ever been here at all," she replied. "I only found out when I opened my safe and all my best jewellery was gone. As I explained to those other fellows."

I almost raised an eyebrow as I tried not to stare at the gold, diamonds and other precious stones she deemed appropriate for wearing in an empty house on a Sunday morning. I couldn't imagine her insurance had paid out already, so this display of opulence must be her 'everyday cheap stuff' she left lying around.

"Have you had any issues or interruptions with your alarm service?"

She handed me a cup of coffee and slid a bowl of sugar and a little silver jug of milk my way, neither of which I needed. "I hadn't set the alarm that evening, as you'll see in my statement, but no, the system has worked well as best I know."

She picked up her cup of tea and offered me a seat in the lounge. I was terrified I'd spill my coffee or leave a dirt mark from my backside on her white sofa. The Jeep's seats weren't always perfectly clean since it lives outside with the top down. She sat, so I quickly brushed the seat of my uniform trousers and followed suit.

On the glass-topped coffee table sat three picture frames. One held a wedding photograph, clearly from a long time ago. Rosemary was a good-looking woman in her day, and her husband appeared proud and regal in a military uniform. The second was a family shot with layers of offspring lined up in rows. From what I could make out, she had three children who had all married and reproduced. The third was a more recent photograph of an older man I could only guess was her husband.

"That's my Roly," she said. "The middle picture was taken a year and a half ago. That was the last time our whole family was together before he died."

"I'm sorry for your loss, ma'am," I said, as that's what you're supposed to say.

"Thank you. It's been difficult, I must say, but one must go on. And that's our wedding day back in 1971," she continued. "He was Captain Rowland Chesterton-Clark at that time. He looked so handsome in his uniform."

But my gaze had wandered back to the photograph of her husband. He was sitting in the cockpit of a luxurious-looking boat under blue skies, a cigar in one hand and a tumbler of amber liquid in the other. I picked the frame up and studied it more closely.

"I love that picture of him," she said nostalgically. "That was taken about six months before he died."

"Is that your boat?" I asked, certain I already knew the answer.

"No, no," she replied. "We never bothered buying one. They're such a large expense, and a lot of work. We chartered if we felt like a day on the water, but Roly was far keener than I." She sighed and sipped her tea while I continued to stare at the picture. I didn't recognise the man.

"He was a member of a gentlemen's club where he and a few of his friends would meet one weekend a month," she explained. "Play poker, go fishing, and probably drink too much." She laughed as though he was a young boy who'd been a touch overexcited at summer camp.

I didn't recognise her husband, so he hadn't ever requested me, but I knew that boat. The International Fellowship of Lions owned an 80-foot Hatteras named *Cova do Leão*, which translated as *The Lion's Den*. Rowland Chesterton-Clark was sitting on the rear deck of the very same boat. He was screwing underage girls right under his wife's nose, and I was correct from the beginning. The thief was directing the police to these scumbags.

But why worry about a dead man?

I stood and looked around the room at the items on the shelves and the abundant picture frames. Not the large, colourful artwork hanging on display, but the photographs resting in frames on the furniture. Many showed 'Roly', the paedophile, shaking hands and accepting awards from important-looking people.

"He was a very prominent businessman," Rosemary blathered from the sofa. "There's still talk of him being posthumously knighted for his charity work."

"Thanks for your time," I mumbled, as I spun around to leave. I'd seen enough.

The stupid dog chased me, yipping and bouncing along, as I ditched the coffee mug on the kitchen island and headed for the door.

"Thank you," I managed over my shoulder as I nudged the mutt aside with my foot and closed the front door behind me. Gulping in deep breaths, I walked towards my Jeep in the driveway. I felt nauseous, angry, and conflicted. On arrival, I was ready to strangle the thief, but now I was back to wondering why they were tracking down resort members.

My mobile rang as I climbed into the Jeep. It was Whittaker. I hoped the old lady hadn't jumped straight on the phone when I unceremoniously bolted from her home. I answered, expecting the worst.

"Where are you?" he asked urgently.

"West Bay," I replied, without giving too much away.

"Good," he said, sounding like he was walking briskly, his footsteps echoing down a hallway. "The Haitian won't say a word, but Rico has given us the address where he says The Haitian's been staying. It's in West Bay. I'm texting you the address, but don't go in before we get there, Nora."

"I understand, sir. I'll meet you there," I replied.

Find Marissa, and find the truth about both cases. That had been my epiphany that morning when I'd found clarity, and now I drove down Boggy Sand Road faster than I should have, impatiently waiting for the address to one of the few remaining locations where the young girl might be.

39

INCOHERENT BLATHERING

The address was less than half a mile away on Powell Smith Road. I stopped at the entrance to the dirt driveway and tried to see the house set well back from the road. The area was densely wooded, and the driveway curved slightly, blocking most of my view. When Whittaker said, 'Don't go in before we get there', I decided he meant inside the actual building. I drove slowly down the rutted trail with leaves and small branches brushing both sides of the Jeep.

The home was a typical older island dwelling with stucco exterior, small windows, and a corrugated steel roof. It was aged, rough around the edges, but clean and tidy. The yard surrounding the house was surprisingly clear of the usual junk that older locals tended to accumulate. Looking about, I couldn't see any vehicles, dogs, or signs of life. I parked by the trees to the left, leaving room for Whittaker and whoever else was coming.

I stepped out of the Jeep and argued with myself over whether I should have stayed put the whole time I walked around the house. Once I'd finished the perimeter check, seeing or hearing nothing unusual, I stood looking back and forth between my Jeep and the front door. I checked my watch. 9:50am. I knew who wasn't there.

The Haitian was locked in a jail cell and Didi was dead, so the house was almost certainly empty. I walked to the door and tried the handle. To my surprise, it was unlocked.

I could hear AJ in one ear, talking about bulls and rushing in, while Whittaker was barking in my other ear, saying 'Don't go in before we get there'. Their voices blended into an incoherent babble, and I shoved the door open.

"Police!" I called out loudly. "If anyone's home, make your presence known and show yourselves."

Muffled thumps echoed from somewhere inside the home, and at first I thought it was someone scrambling out the back door or window. But the sounds didn't fade.

"Police! I'm entering the premises!" I yelled and stepped inside, feeling around the wall for a light switch while I kept my eyes on the dim interior. All the curtains were drawn, and the interior had a slightly musty, stale odour. Flicking the switch, a single bulb illuminated an old fabric shade hanging from the ceiling in the middle of the room. The furniture was a mishmash of worn and faded old items, and cheap modern replacements. Colour choice was clearly based on price, as nothing matched. The entry led into a living room, with a dining table to the left and the kitchen behind. Across the room was an open door to what appeared to be a hallway. The thumping sound was coming from back there.

Taking out my torch, I shone the beam through the doorway, ready to shift its use from bright light to a hefty club. Straight ahead was a closed door with the hallway extending across the building to my right. There were two more doors on the left side of the hall. The next one was slightly open and the last one closed.

The sound was coming from the far room, so I eased quietly down the dark hallway, peeking into what I discovered was a bathroom on the way. The thumping sound was getting louder as I neared, its rhythm and tone varying enough to know it wasn't anything mechanical. I turned the handle and flung the door open, sweeping the beam around the bedroom.

Lying next to a single bed was a young woman, her ankles bound, lifting and slamming her feet on the floor. She blinked when my bright light hit her face and manically groaned behind the duct tape over her mouth. She rolled to her side and collapsed in exhaustion, looking up at me in relief. I knelt down and quickly cut the zip ties with my pocketknife.

"This will suck," I warned her as I peeled back the duct tape.

She yelped and wriggled, then gasped for deep breaths once I'd removed the tape.

"Marissa?" I asked, to be certain.

She nodded. "Thank you. I thought I was going to die here." Her voice was a hoarse whisper, and she rubbed her wrists, trying to return the circulation.

"I'm Constable Sommer. You're safe now." I knew the emotions behind those weary eyes. I'd seen that look in others, and felt the same way myself. All the fear, anger, and desperation amassed over her time in captivity, and now, the reluctance in trusting the ordeal was really over. I'd leave it for a counsellor to explain to the young woman how it would never be over. The memories and fear wouldn't go away. Finding a path to live with the trauma was different for everyone. "I'm Nora," I added, trying to sound more personable. "It's good to meet you."

The smell of urine overpowered the stale odour of the home. My first reaction was to get her to the bathroom, but we had to preserve any evidence. I stood and found the light switch on the wall.

"How long have you been here?" I asked.

"I don't know exactly. Five days I think." She looked herself over and moaned. "I'm a mess."

Her accent was Caymanian, but she was very well spoken and if I didn't know differently, I'd never believe she'd grown up in Dog City. Helping Marissa to her feet, I supported her and guided her to the bed so she could sit down.

"I know who you are," she whispered, and I looked at her

quizzically. "You're Hallie's friend. She talks about you all the time."

I smiled. "She's my little sis." I looked away as I heard vehicles pull up outside. "I'll be right back. That's more help arriving," I told her. I pulled my radio from my belt, then thought better of it and ran down the hall.

"In the back of the house!" I called out and saw Whittaker cautiously approaching the front door. "House is clear, sir. Marissa is in the back. She's unhurt." Whittaker crossed the living room towards me. "I heard banging from inside, that's why I came in the house, sir," I explained, before he had a chance to chew me out.

He grunted and followed me to the back bedroom.

"Marissa, this is Detective Whittaker," I let her know. The detective stayed by the doorway, careful not to frighten or overwhelm the girl.

"Are you hurt, Marissa?" he asked. "I'm calling an ambulance for you anyway, but do you have any specific injuries?"

Marissa looked dazed, but she shook her head. Whittaker caught my eye, and I knew his concern right away.

"Sir, could you see if there's a large towel or a dressing gown in the bathroom down the hall? We need to get Marissa out of these clothes."

For a second he appeared annoyed I'd given him a task, then the penny dropped, and he left the room. Sometimes, as humans, we ask questions, the answers to which have the power to dramatically change us forever. Marissa's response to my next words would define how this case would live inside of me from this day forth.

I sat next to her. "Marissa, I need to ask you this…"

She shook her head. "No, I'm okay," she replied before I could finish the question. "They were rough with me, but they didn't…" her expression was a mixture of embarrassment and relief. "You know."

I opened my arms, and she threw herself into my embrace. We hung tightly to each other and I let out a long breath, knowing I'd been a part of saving this girl from what would have been a very different outcome. Whittaker poked his head around the door and I managed a smile and gently shook my head. I watched the relief flood through him in the same way.

I helped Marissa change in the bathroom and bagged her filthy clothes for the lab. Rasha, the scene of crime officer, or SOCO, joined us and took scrapings from under her fingernails, a mouth swab for DNA, and checked her over for bruising or other marks. Once she left, a female EMT helped Marissa clean up at the sink and provided a gown for her to wear.

She'd already guzzled two bottles of water and was desperately hungry. She said they'd fed her, but only once a day and it hadn't been much. As we walked through the house, I nipped into the kitchen and with the nitrile gloves still on my hands, I opened the fridge to see if there was anything I could steal. There wasn't much in there, but I found a packet of Pop-Tarts in one of the cupboards, which were also sparsely stocked. Hardly great recovery food, but she inhaled them before we made it to the ambulance.

The EMTs had Marissa lie down while they started a saline IV, and Whittaker and I loitered outside. I had a thousand questions I wanted to ask her, and I was sure Whittaker did too. I'd restrained myself from inundating her as we'd been cleaning up, but at some point, we needed all the details she could provide. With the players sitting in jail cells, or the morgue, I guessed it could wait until she'd been checked over at the hospital.

"Marissa," Whittaker said, leaning into the ambulance. "We'll catch up with you and get your full statement once you've recovered a bit, but may I ask you a couple of quick questions?"

She held her arms up as the EMT put safety straps over her body for the ride to the hospital. She nodded her consent to the detective.

"Nora tells me you've been held for about five days. Is that correct?"

"I think so," she replied. "I kinda lost track of time."

"That's okay, I understand," he responded. "Do you know who took you?"

"I don't know his name, but he never hid his face from me," she replied. "My mother's boyfriend gave me a number to call. He said the guy wanted girls to serve drinks and stuff on a boat. We don't have much money, so I'm always trying to find work doing anything I can. He sounded okay on the phone, so I met with him." She paused and checked her emotions for a second. "He threw me in a car and brought me here."

"How many people did you come in contact with while you were here?" Whittaker asked, and the female EMT turned to the detective.

"Sir, we should be gettin' her to da hospital."

"Absolutely," Whittaker said. "But could she just answer that last question?"

The EMT nodded.

"The man who took me," Marissa began. "He was a small, older guy, and then he had a friend who was taller and younger. They both spoke a foreign language I didn't understand."

"Thank you," Whittaker said, and the female EMT sat down on the opposite side from Marissa, checking everything was secure. Her partner stepped out the back and began closing the doors.

"Oh, and the woman," Marissa said.

I reached out and grabbed the door, surprising the EMT, who was trying to close it.

"Woman?" I asked, pulling the door back open so I could see the girl.

"She came by one time. They blindfolded me, but I heard her voice. Sounded like she was in charge."

My first thought was Marissa's mother. I wouldn't be surprised if she'd sold out her daughter, but of course Marissa would recognise her own mother's voice.

"Anyone you knew?" I asked. "Could you tell an age, accent?"

Marissa thought for a moment while Whittaker and I exchanged a glance. We didn't have any females in custody. Patti Weaver and Rabbit were suspects in the robbery, but we didn't even have a female person of interest in the kidnapping.

"She sounded older, you know, like a businesswoman or something," Marissa said. "And she was definitely English."

40

CRYPTIC BS

For a few moments, Detective Whittaker and I both stared at the back doors of the ambulance, getting smaller as it carefully trundled down the narrow dirt driveway towards the main road. Nothing made sense. Surely it couldn't be Estelle?

"Do you think it's Cosgrove?" Whittaker asked without hiding his surprise and disbelief.

"She's been on island," I began, thinking through all the events over the past five days. "She could have emptied the second safe before her husband even came home…" I realised my stupid big mouth a moment too late.

"What's that?" Whittaker asked, frowning at me.

"We think the thief missed something that was probably in the second safe," I replied, hurriedly wiggling my way out of the hole I'd just dug. "But she could have moved any evidence before you were able to look."

Whittaker nodded. Fortunately, he was focused on any angle which tied Estelle to the case instead of dwelling on my rambling.

"You suspected some kinky shit was going on in the office bedroom," I added, keeping his thoughts away from my blunder.

Whittaker put a hand on my shoulder and steered me away from the other police personnel. "Cosgrove was alone when he visited the International Fellowship of Lions resort, correct? You didn't hear of, or see, anyone else with him, did you?"

"No," I replied. The direct reference to my presence at the resort was a thorny and uncomfortable reminder. "I would have said if I knew she was involved."

"Of course," he murmured. "I'm just trying to place Estelle Cosgrove into this puzzle in some way, and honestly, I'm struggling."

I was having a hard time figuring it out too, but more than that, I was getting really pissed off. It appeared inevitable it was Estelle, which meant she'd played all of us, especially me. Did she know I was her husband's favourite underaged girl when I'd walked into her home after the robbery? When she'd let me console her at the station?

My anger was growing so intensely and quickly I was in danger of losing control. I turned away from the detective, clenched my fists, and closed my eyes. With deep breaths, I brought myself back in check and channelled all the energy into rolling back through the facts that we knew. She must have left some clues. The notes? She didn't leave them, but the thief had been directing me with them.

'Don't believe Cosgrove – put pressure on him.' The 'him' had been underlined. What if the note really meant 'Don't believe *Estelle* Cosgrove – put pressure on *Randall*'? Was the thief telling me to pressure Estelle's husband into cracking and giving her up? Why the fuck couldn't he just tell me this instead of making up cryptic bullshit notes?

"*Fy faen,*" I blurted out loud. "She was going to leave!"

"What?" Whittaker asked, as I spun around to face him again.

"She talked about going back to the UK. She was probably testing me to see if I'd tell her she needed to stay on the island while the case was in process."

"Did you?" he asked, as we both started towards the cars.

"No, I didn't say anything," I groaned. "Now I bet she's running."

Whittaker went into full tactical mode while I looked on my mobile for flights to the UK. He contacted Weatherford and directed him to Owen Roberts International Airport, then called someone at the Cayman Islands Immigration Department and warned them to look for Estelle Cosgrove.

He finished the call by saying, "Do not let her board a plane, private or commercial, under any circumstances."

"There's a UK flight at 11:30am," I said and looked at my watch. "It's quarter to eleven now."

Whittaker opened the driver's door to his SUV. "Follow me," he ordered a constable, who was standing next to a nearby patrol car.

I opened the passenger door, but the detective leaned over from the driver's seat. "No way, Nora. I'm going to the Cosgroves' house in case she's there. Weatherford has the airport covered, and you can't be in either place."

I started to complain, but he held up his hand and interrupted me. "Go to the hospital, Nora. Be there for Marissa."

I closed the passenger door with a little more enthusiasm than I'm sure Whittaker appreciated. Now I needed to see Estelle Cosgrove in handcuffs as badly as I'd wanted to see her husband arrested. Whittaker left, followed by the patrol car, leaving me, Rasha, and another pair of constables at the scene. It would be a while before Marissa would be done with the doctors prodding and poking her, so I was in no hurry, but staying at the house was a waste of time.

I said goodbye to Rasha and climbed into my Jeep. Taking my time, I drove down the dirt trail and sat at Powell Smith Road, contemplating my options. Finally, I turned left and made my way through town, passing the West Bay station and continuing to Batabano Road. As I reached the right turn onto the beginning of the Esterly Tibbetts Highway, I glanced in the rear-view mirror and noticed a red car speeding towards me.

I quickly cancelled my turn signal and slowed, but stayed on

Batabano. Watching in the mirror, I saw a familiar Porsche whipping around the turn onto the bypass. I braked hard and made a U-turn, accelerated back to the junction, and squealed the tyres around the corner onto the bypass. My CJ-7 was no match for her sports car, but if I could keep Estelle Cosgrove in sight, maybe I could see where she was going.

Her Porsche was probably capable of going a zillion kilometres an hour, but she was smart enough to stay around 15kph over the speed limit, and not draw unwanted attention. Still, she zipped around the first roundabout and accelerated hard on the other side, leaving me lagging behind. My Jeep wasn't made for tarmac performance.

I could see her way up ahead, entering the next roundabout where West Bay Road met the bypass. The red Porsche veered left into the large traffic circle, then disappeared from my view behind the trees. The raised centre of the broad roundabout and trees on either side of the bypass obscured my sightline completely. I had no idea if she stayed on the bypass or took one of the other two exits.

Arriving at the roundabout, I drove slowly and surveyed the options. The Yacht Drive exit was a small road into a wooded area which curved almost immediately. She would be well out of view if she'd gone that way. I arrived at the far side of the roundabout and stared along the bypass. Late morning on Sunday, there was very little traffic, and I couldn't see the Porsche. Continuing, the West Bay Road seemed like an unlikely choice, so I kept moving. I was pretty sure she'd taken one of the side roads, but if she'd gone down West Bay Road towards her house, Whittaker would be waiting for her. The Yacht Drive exit led to several expensive housing estates on canals, and the marina.

I accelerated, the old CJ-7 leaning over as I turned left onto Yacht Drive. Once the road straightened, I grabbed third gear and the big V8 rumbled as I pushed the pedal to the floor. If I needed to get off the island, and the authorities were looking for me, I'd be heading for the water. My guess was Estelle Cosgrove was doing the same.

A voice over my handheld radio startled me and reminded me I should be calling this in. I awkwardly unhooked the radio from my belt as I sped down the road.

"All units, this is Dispatch, be on alert for female suspect driving a red Porsche…"

While waiting for Dispatch to finish giving the registration plate details, I arrived at the turn for the marina. I braked hard and swung the Jeep into the turn, almost dropping the radio in the process. As I slid around the corner and accelerated away, I spotted the Porsche way over to my left across the open, cleared land, entering the marina car park.

"PC277, I have eyes on the suspect entering the Cayman Islands Yacht Club Marina. Over."

I made the next ninety-degree left with the big off-road tyres complaining as they drifted across the dusty tarmac. As I straightened the wheel, I tossed the radio out of the right side of the Jeep, just as Detective Whittaker's voice began telling me something about waiting for back-up.

As the call had gone out about the Porsche, it meant the detective had already discovered Estelle was not at home, and her car was missing. There was a chance they'd missed her by mere seconds. They obviously hadn't found any trace of her at the airport either, otherwise they wouldn't be looking for her car. Plus, of course, she was here, although I bet she'd booked a flight to throw our focus on the airport.

The main marina was on the left behind a fence with gates the slip owners had keys to, but on the right was a handful of buildings, a large parking area, and a sea wall where larger boats could tie up. All the tour boats which used the dock were out on the North Sound, so the car park was full of customer vehicles, but the dock itself was empty.

Estelle pulled her Porsche up to the dockside and stopped a few feet from the edge. The buildings blocked my view for a few moments as I tore down the road towards where she'd parked. As I made the last turn, I could see an 18-foot RIB approaching, and I instantly knew I'd been right. It was probably the same launch that had delivered the two girls, Ilaria and Millie, to the island. The larger boat was undoubtedly waiting offshore, ready to whisk Estelle away to freedom.

There was no way that was going to happen.

41

TOO MANY WORDS

The driver's door of the Porsche swung open as I arrived and braked hard, ready to pull alongside. But, as I slowed, instead of steering around the back of the shiny red sports car, I stayed straight... and released the brake pedal.

The impact jarred me forward in my seat, slamming my already bruised body against the seat belt. If the old Jeep had been equipped with airbags, I'm sure they would have deployed. As my vision cleared and I lifted my head back up, I could see I'd punted the Porsche to the very edge of the dock. The hefty aftermarket steel bumper bar across the front of the CJ-7 had caved in the tail of the pretty car, shoving the rear bodywork into the rear-mounted engine. The jolt had also slammed the driver's door closed.

Fortunately, I'd instinctively dipped the clutch, keeping the engine running. I selected four-wheel drive low on the transmission, and crept forward until I nudged the back of the Porsche. Revving up the V8, I slipped the clutch and used the torque of the crawler gear and the traction of the oversized tyres to shove the Porsche forward.

The sports car's front wheels dropped over the edge and the car became a sled as it bellied out, and a loud scraping sound emanated from underneath, as metal graunched across concrete. I saw the driver's door open again, and I pushed harder on the accelerator to keep the Porsche moving. A foot appeared, adorned with a high-heeled designer shoe with a red sole, but before Estelle could step out, the car had enough mass hanging over to pivot on the edge of the dock. Grinding free of my bumper, the rear of the car rose above the bonnet of the Jeep as I quickly dipped the clutch and braked to a stop. The underside of the Porsche loomed large before my eyes, then slithering away like a boat being launched down a ramp.

I took the Jeep out of gear and set the handbrake. Running to the edge, I watched the expensive motor car quickly filling with water and sinking like a stone. The impact with the ocean had pushed the driver's door closed once again, but it appeared the front windows were open, letting the water flood in.

The RIB had turned and was making a hasty retreat, the pilot glancing back over his shoulder. I wished I'd hung on to the radio, but distant sirens told me that help would soon be here. I unbuckled my duty belt and dropped it on the seat of the Jeep, then took off my boots. Looking at the water, I could just make out the red roof below the surface, still dropping. All around the vehicle, air was bubbling and gurgling to the surface as the water pressure invaded every available space.

With long, careful breaths, I steadied my heart rate and filled my lungs with fresh oxygen before diving into the harbour. With no mask, it was hard to make out much except the large red object before me. I swam to the right side of the Porsche as it settled on the bottom. Estelle was thrashing madly, half out of the open window. The onrush of water would have prevented her escape until the inside was full, and now she was likely running out of air in her lungs and panicking.

She seemed to relax when I placed my hand on her shoulder. Why she thought I'd be coming down to save her sorry arse was beyond me, but maybe she'd banked on her guy in the RIB being a hero. He was at wide open throttle, making his escape. I was here to make sure Estelle Cosgrove never saw the light of day again. I took a firm hold of the top of the door frame before shoving the woman back inside her precious German car. Estelle wasn't so relaxed after that.

As the woman who'd deceived us all struggled for her life beneath my hand, a million thoughts, emotions, and faces rushed through my mind. Poor Carlina, whose body had been found, floating in the open ocean. My beautiful dark-skinned little sister, Hallie, who'd narrowly been saved from the fate which befell the rest of us at the hands of animals like Randall Cosgrove. And facilitated by people like the woman who was losing strength below me.

I wasn't naïve enough to think I would feel any better with Estelle Cosgrove dead, and her husband behind bars. But it wasn't about me. It was about what I was taking away from them. They'd robbed a piece of our souls from so many of us, a piece we would never get back. I wanted to take away their chance of ever doing that to anyone else. Remove every ounce of pleasure their futures held. All decisions, actions, or words. From this moment forward, their lives would be irrelevant. No opportunity at regret or redemption. There was no forgiving what they'd done. Ever.

Taking another's life was no simple task for anyone with a conscience. Rarely does anyone surrender their existence easily or simply. But more than that, regardless of the circumstances, there's a cost involved. Often punitive, but always emotional. Could I be sure this woman was guilty of all she appeared to have done? Her running told me yes, but a court was supposed to make that decision. There was a risk I'd regret my action, for many reasons.

But none of what I felt allowed me to release Estelle Cosgrove and let her breathe again.

I surfaced and sucked in as much air as I could flush through my lungs. Lights were flashing and sirens wailed from the dock.

"Is the car down there?" Whittaker shouted to me.

I nodded. "She's unconscious, but I can get her out," I gasped. "Get an ambulance here!"

There was no time for the breathe-up exercises I used in preparation for freediving. I needed to get back down there and I didn't want anyone else joining me. I took in a long inhalation, and dropped below the surface, inverting and kicking down to the open window of the Porsche. Estelle's lifeless body swayed inside the car. Fumbling with my blurry vision, I found her chin and lifted it up, opening her airway as much as possible. With my other hand, I shoved against her chest as hard as I could, using the door top against my shoulders as leverage. A string of bubbles wriggled past her lips and joined the thin layer of air trapped under the roof.

I pumped my palm between her breasts again and again, with Carlina's beautiful face clear in my mind. I forced the life from Estelle with a blind determination, wishing it was my friend I was resuscitating. But it wasn't. Carlina was dead, and this woman didn't deserve to live.

I finally realised no more bubbles were escaping her mouth. Grabbing her under an arm, I began dragging her body out of the car. My efforts had dearly robbed me of oxygen and my lungs burned, but I needed to get her topside. Too soon, and they might revive her, too long and help would be down here. I'd prefer the events be described by me, rather than witnessed.

Finally freeing her high-heeled feet from the window, I kicked for the surface, but went nowhere. It was a lot harder raising a body void of buoyant air in their lungs, than a live, struggling diver or swimmer. I managed to find the roof with my foot, and pushed off enough to send us up, breaking the surface. I gasped for breath as a life-ring landed next to me and Williams swam over. Between us, we looped the orange ring over Estelle's head and pulled her arms through, keeping her face out of the water.

Once to the side, several men, including Detective Whittaker, dragged her body out by the rope attached to the life-ring. Someone began CPR, while Williams and I swam over to a ladder and climbed out. I dropped to the hot concrete and caught my breath. The sirens had been silenced at the scene, but in the distance I could hear the ambulance wailing a warning as it rushed our way, intent on saving the woman I'd gone to great lengths to drown.

I looked at my Jeep sitting six feet from the edge of the dock. A pair of black tyre marks ran from under my tyres in a perfectly straight line to the water, as though I'd spun my tyres in reverse. This was going to be hard to explain. The Porsche had its brakes locked as I'd shoved it over the edge, and the physical evidence displayed that perfectly. Add that to the marks on my bumper and the damage to the Porsche's tail, and there was no doubt about what happened.

Williams stood next to me. "You okay?"

I nodded. "Shit, grab a radio," I blurted, remembering the RIB.

He found his clothing and gear he'd stripped off before jumping in and snatched his radio from the belt.

"Have the Joint Marine Unit look for a dark grey RIB heading out across the sound from Governor's Creek," I instructed. "He'll be heading for a larger boat outside the reef."

Williams keyed the mic and relayed the information, then looked at me. "Helicopter?"

"Yes," I replied. "I only saw one male at the helm, but he has a head start."

A few moments later, the ambulance arrived, and the EMTs took over attempts to revive Estelle. She looked sad and bedraggled, lying on a concrete dock, her expensive dress clinging to her pale, wet body as they broke rib after rib in attempts to pump life back into her lungs. I remembered the first night I'd met her after the robbery. She was vibrant and alive. But death was never glamorous.

They carried her into the ambulance, one of the EMTs continuing CPR the whole time. Once the doors were closed and the sirens faded, Whittaker made his way over to me. He stood there looking around and contemplating for a while before he spoke.

"I ordered you to wait for back-up."

"I'm afraid I dropped my radio, sir. It flew out of the Jeep."

"Seriously, Nora?" he said. His tone was that disappointed crap again.

"I had just called it in, sir, and skidded around the corner over there, when it fell out of my hand."

"Skidded around the corner? You were in a high-speed pursuit?" he asked. "Did my error yesterday not teach you anything?"

"She didn't go very fast, sir. It wasn't really high speed."

"You caught up with a Porsche in your Jeep, and you're telling me you didn't drive fast to do that?"

Whittaker may have taken race car driving lessons, but my father taught me to drive on an icy lake when I was fourteen. I could handle a vehicle just fine. But I was going to be on the losing end of every point he could make. I felt like a child being literally talked down to by their parent. I wished I was still a kid and he would just send me to my room, but that wasn't how it worked when you're a responsible adult. And a police constable.

He shook his head. "Just tell me what happened here."

I stood up. This wasn't going to go well, or be easy, so I'd rather look him in the eye. "I spotted the Porsche getting on the bypass at Batabano. I followed to make sure it was Cosgrove's vehicle. I heard the radio call from Dispatch and verified the registration plate. She took Yacht Drive off of the West Bay Road roundabout, and that's when I called it in. When I made the left turn towards the marina, I was trying to make a second call when I dropped the radio. You'll find it in the grass back there somewhere."

"No. You'll go find it in the grass back there somewhere," he corrected. "Carry on."

"The suspect pulled up to the edge of the water, and I spotted a RIB approaching from the south," I explained, telling the truth. Apart from the dropping the radio part. "The suspect began getting out of the car. The RIB reached the dock, and it was obvious she was planning to leave on the boat. I arrived and didn't feel I had time to stop her on foot, so I bumped the car with my vehicle and it went into the harbour. Sir."

Whittaker turned and looked at my Jeep and the dark black skid marks leading to the edge of the concrete dock. I now noticed the chipped and gouged corner where the Porsche's underbelly had ground along.

"Bumped?" he repeated, and put his hands on his hips.

"Well, she was trying to get out, and the RIB was right there, so I kept pushing to stop her from getting away. And then the car plopped into the water."

"What happened to the boat?"

"He took off, but Williams called it in while you were…" I stopped myself before 'trying to save the bitch' came out of my mouth. "Doing CPR. Hopefully, the Joint Marine Unit will pick him up and the boat he was heading for. I bet it's the boat that brought the two girls here."

I looked past the detective to where a constable was taking a series of photographs of the scene. He was spending more time than I liked on the tyre marks and my Jeep.

"You understand this looks a lot like excessive force, right?"

"I figured she'd swim out. It's not deep here, sir. I was trying to stop her from getting on that RIB."

"Was she trapped inside when you got down there?" he asked.

"She was panicking," I replied honestly. I was trying to stick with the truth as much as possible. "The window was open, but she couldn't get out of the seat belt, and she was flailing so badly, I couldn't undo it for her. When I finally did, I had to come up for a breath. I thought she'd follow. That's when I saw you'd arrived. When I went back down, she was unconscious, and I pulled her out."

I didn't do so well with the truth on that part.

Whittaker sighed and scratched his chin stubble. "You can't use vehicles as weapons, Nora. That's not how we do this."

I knew better than to say anything. If I wanted the conversation to stop, any comment, whether it was apologetic or defensive, would only lead to more words. I'd been using far too many words lately.

"Do you need to go to the hospital?" he asked me.

"I do," I replied. "I need to go and see Marissa."

He looked me over. "You'd better clean yourself up before you do."

"Yes, sir," I responded, already two steps towards my Jeep.

"And don't forget that radio," he called after me.

"Okay, sir."

42

ALARM BELLS

I took my second shower of the day. Standing still, with my eyes closed, I let hot water cascade down my body in the hopes it would cleanse me. The salt and sweat washed away easily, but the life I'd taken and the lies I'd told clung to me like a second skin. A marred and scar-ridden skin. They would stay with me for the rest of my life.

Not that I regretted my actions. Estelle Cosgrove was supplying underage girls to sexual predators, including her husband. But that didn't mean I was free of guilt or pain.

Towelling dry, I sipped coffee and took bites of toast with Gudbrandsdalsost, a traditional Norwegian cheese. For some reason, I felt rushed to see Marissa. Perhaps it was the chance to remain involved before the unavoidable review of the incident. Usually I'd be confident Detective Whittaker would have my back, but I wasn't so sure this time. I think I'd pushed my luck, and his tolerance, too far. If he'd lost faith in me, then his mentorship would fade, along with my relatively new career.

Out of habit, I was about to hunt down a clean, or clean-ish uniform to wear, then realised I was officially off duty the rest of the day. Maybe the beginning of many days off. Instead, I chose black leggings and a Mermaid Divers T-shirt. I didn't mind slipping on flip-flops instead of strapping on boots, either.

Testing the waters, I sent Whittaker a message before I left the shack. 'Heading to hospital. Anything from The Haitian?' I'd reached the Jeep out by the road, and had given up hope of a reply, when my mobile buzzed. 'Call you in a minute.'

What did that mean? I scolded myself for poking the bear when I should have left him alone. Tomorrow was Monday, and I was back on duty, working days for the coming week. If he didn't have me moved to graveyard shift. Or park my arse altogether.

I drove the long way around West Bay, keeping to the coast road. I didn't consciously make that decision when I left home, but as I approached Reg and AJ's dock, I realised why my subconscious had steered me that way. AJ's van was in the little car park and I could see her dive boat, *Hazel's Odyssey*, moored offshore. Apparently, she didn't have afternoon customers.

"We were just talking about you," AJ said cheerily when I found her, Reg, Pearl, and Thomas sitting on deck chairs looking out over the ocean, eating lunch.

"Hey," I replied. My name was the centre of attention far too much lately. Probably in direct correlation with the number of words I'd spewed. Actions may have come into it as well. Either way, it made me uncomfortable.

"We haven't seen you all weekend," AJ pointed out. "I thought you were off work?"

"I didn't have shifts, but I've been helping," I replied, certain the detective wouldn't describe my involvement as help at this very moment.

"You'll be making detective in no time," AJ enthused.

"What were all the bloody sirens about this morning?" Reg asked. "Sounded serious."

I wondered which set of sirens he was referring to. I went with the better news. "We found the girl, Marissa Chandler."

"That's brilliant!" AJ enthused. "Is she okay?"

"Yeah. I'm on my way to see her," I replied. "She'll be fine."

"Was that both sets of sirens?" Reg asked. "There was some mid-morning, then more not long after."

"A car fell into Governors Creek," I replied.

"Fell in?" AJ laughed. "How does a car fall into the water?"

"Long story," I said. I didn't want to hide anything from my friends, but right now, I couldn't talk about it, or use lots of words. I would tell AJ the story when we were alone some time. Maybe. Or maybe it would be another secret I held inside, liked a caged leopard clawing at my guts.

Seeing everyone going about their normal Sunday, enjoying everything our beautiful island had to offer, made me smile. I had taken on a job that had me dealing with the worst side of people. It seemed so contrary to be exposed to crime and wrongdoing in a place which exuded peace and tranquillity. Such was the nature of human beings. There's always someone who wants to take someone else's stuff, or turn paradise into hell.

My phone rang, and the caller ID told me it was Whittaker. "I have to answer this. I just wanted to say hi," I said, and they all smiled and said nice things as I walked away.

"Hello, sir."

"Are you at the hospital?" Whittaker asked.

"On my way."

"Okay. It was easier to call you than text, although there's not much to say about Mr Jean-René Jérôme, or whatever his real name is. We've sent details to the authorities in Haiti to see if they can verify. Anyway, he's lawyered up and given us nothing useful. Unfortunately, he knows he'll be extradited, so he has little incentive to talk. Of course, he claims to know nothing about Marissa at his house, but he also said he didn't know the other girls were locked in the bedroom of the shack where we arrested him. Claims he hired young ladies to waitress at special events, and they all had to be over eighteen. He's sticking with the story that Marissa never showed up for the meeting DeWayne organised."

I was interested in the details of the case, but more than that, I was relieved by Whittaker's attitude towards me. He sounded normal.

"We're still short on evidence against the Cosgroves, aren't we?" I asked, not really wanting to bring up Estelle, but her husband was now the focus. I doubted I'd get the chance to give him what he deserved, so he needed to end up in jail.

"We are, and that's where The Haitian's testimony would be crucial."

"Do we have to extradite him?" I asked.

"We don't, but the court certainly will. Our system is already stretched, and as a violent crime offender, we'd send him to the UK."

"But he doesn't know that, right?"

"His lawyer will tell him," Whittaker replied. "We've set precedent numerous times."

"All we need is doubt in his mind. Or hope," I suggested. "I guarantee a prison cell on Grand Cayman or the UK will be preferable to one in Haiti. Tell him you'll press for the trial to be held here, as a local girl is involved. If he doesn't talk, he'll be extradited for sure."

"Worth a shot," Whittaker agreed. "Good thought. I'll give it a try."

"I guess if he's denying kidnapping any of the girls, there's no point asking him why Marissa was at his house instead of with the others."

"I'll ask if he does start cooperating," Whittaker replied. "On a better note, Ben's men picked up the man in the RIB. He's another Haitian who doesn't speak a word of English."

"What about the boat he was from?"

"It made it to international waters, but the helicopter took video and we have the name, so the boat will have trouble finding a dock anywhere in the Caribbean without a welcoming committee."

"If that's the guy who brought the girls to shore in the RIB, then he met Estelle," I pointed out. "Maybe he can ID her?"

"We'll try, but if he has an ounce of sense, he'll realise his only offence we can prove was he skipped customs and immigration," Whittaker said. "He'll be shipped back home."

The detective was right. Knowing he'd be extradited back to where his employers could reach him, he'd be terrified to say anything to the police. His bosses were likely the men responsible for finding the young girls throughout the Caribbean islands – the Cosgroves bought from them and supplied the local demand on Grand Cayman. It made me sick to imagine there was a 'demand' for destroying these kids' lives.

"Divers pulled two bags from the Porsche," Whittaker continued. "They contained clothes, a lot of cash, and a pay-as-you-go mobile phone."

"I bet you've found the other number from The Haitian and Didi's mobiles," I suggested.

"Likely," Whittaker responded in a stern tone. "But as everything was submerged in sea water, we may never know."

"Eileen works wonders, sir," I said optimistically.

The line went quiet for a few moments and I held my breath. I didn't want to hear what was coming next.

"You understand there'll be an inquiry into the incident, Nora?"

"Of course, sir."

Another prolonged silence.

"You've had my support, because I believe in you and your potential, but we can't turn our peaceful island into a Wild West show, Nora," he said. "I led with a poor example yesterday, and now we have a second suspect in the morgue today. We're going to have a lot of fingers pointed our way. I expect us both to be under scrutiny over this, and we'll both be deserving of whatever disciplinary action comes our way."

"I understand," I responded, guessing there was more to his point.

"In the future," he continued. "I need to know I can trust you to do the right thing. I'll say this again; we have lines we cannot cross. If those lines are grey in your mind, then this isn't the career for you."

The full impact of my actions and the effect it had on those around me hit home. Detective Roy Whittaker had put a lot on the line. He helped any constable who came to him for advice, but he'd gone several steps farther on my behalf. There were many who took umbrage at the fact he was mentoring a foreigner over a local officer, and it was hard to blame them. He'd certainly taken many local policemen and women under his wing in the past, but that was quickly forgotten when a young, blonde Norwegian became his new charge. I'm sure there were some who harboured suspicion over his motives. As unfounded as I knew that to be, it still took a brave and committed man to shrug off such rumours.

He appeared willing to believe that whatever transgressions I'd made weren't too far over the line for me and my career to be unsalvageable. That was the misplaced trust and faith he put in me. I couldn't even see the line from where I'd been during these cases, and I felt incredibly guilty. Not for taking the life of a scumbag, but for doing things Whittaker could never forgive if he knew.

I faced a difficult decision. I could confess everything and end my career, tarring his reputation in the process, or stick to the lies, and try to be a better policewoman in the future. Both options left me in anguish. I wasn't sure I could be the person he wanted and needed me to be. But I could try.

"I have a lot to learn, sir," I said, speaking truthfully. "I've made too many mistakes, but I want to be a good detective one day. You've done more for me than I could ever ask for, but I understand if that can't continue."

I heard a deep breath over the line. "Later this week, let's meet at my office. I have a couple of training courses I'm putting you through. You'll hate them, because they'll want to talk about your feelings and motivations, but they'll be good for you."

He was right, as usual. I would hate them. But the fact he was talking about ways for me to improve meant the world to me. "Thank you, sir. I promise I'll try my best."

We hung up, and I was flooded with a sense of relief. I swore to myself that I would stop doing crazy shit, like breaking the law to uphold the law. As I drove towards George Town and the hospital, the rush of emotions slowly calmed and I faced reality. I was making promises I doubted I'd keep. But I did want to be a detective. Taking bad humans off the streets made me feel good. It gave me purpose and accomplishment, two things I'd desperately lacked in my life since Ridley's murder. But to make it that far, I had to clean up my act.

I made a promise with myself to try. A real effort to work within the confines of what the badge allowed me to do. If I failed, I'd be the one inside a jail cell, and my friend and mentor, Roy Whittaker, would forever be tainted with my blemished brush.

But first, we had to move beyond these two cases, where my lies and deceit would need to be upheld.

Marissa was sitting up in a hospital bed looking much perkier than when I'd found her that morning. Beyond a heart rate monitor, she was free of wires and tubes, so I presumed she was medically fine. She smiled as I walked in.

"Hey," I greeted her.

"You clean up nice," she said, and I remembered I was in civilian clothes.

"You too," I replied with a laugh. "How are you?"

I dragged a chair over to the side of the bed.

"I'm fine," she said. "Looking forward to getting out of here."

"Where to?" I asked, wishing I'd not said that so bluntly.

Marissa looked at me carefully, as though she was sizing up my intentions. Maybe she thought I was still in police mode despite being out of uniform. She was partly right.

"I met your mother," I added in a softer tone. "And DeWayne is currently in one of our cells."

"I can't go home," Marissa replied, her eyes alive with defiance. "She's never going to change, and he'll be out again soon. He was willing to sell me to a stranger, and she'd allow him to do that."

"Do you have other family here on the island?" I asked, trying to think of a way of keeping her out of the Department of Children and Family Services system. The DCFS did a great job, but life was much simpler if a relative could become her legal guardian.

"No, but I have friends I can stay with."

That wouldn't satisfy the legal side of her problem, but I didn't want to disappoint her while she sat in a hospital bed. I glanced up as I heard footsteps enter the room, and a young man abruptly stopped. Something about his face looked familiar, but I couldn't place ever meeting him before. He was a nice-looking guy with a mixed-race skin tone like so many Caribbean islanders. His colour was that of a heavily tanned Caucasian, but his features clearly held African influence. But his eyes stood out the most. He had piercing blue eyes.

The young man and Marissa looked at each other in a mixture of surprise and concern.

"Sorry, wrong room," he said with an Hispanic accent, then quickly left.

Marissa shifted and fidgeted in her bed. "Have you caught everyone involved?" she asked.

"Boyfriend?" I responded, not letting her steer me away from the subject of her visitor.

"I don't know him," she said. "He said he was in the wrong room."

"Bullshit." I smiled to let her know my curiosity meant no harm, Hallie's theory of a boyfriend in the back of my mind.

Marissa nervously rubbed the palms of her hands on the sheets. "You never saw him," she said, and the fire was back in her eyes. "Okay?"

I guessed the young man to be early twenties, and I knew Marissa was only fifteen. That was a big age gap for a teenager, and statutory rape if they were having sexual relations. My internal alarm bells went off in a fury. We'd just pulled her in the nick of time from the clutches of sex traffickers. I hoped she hadn't already been in a compromised relationship. She must have seen the concern on my face.

"I promise. He's not a boyfriend."

"So why all the secrecy?"

She shrugged her shoulders, searching my face again.

I held out my hands. "I'm off duty, and here as a friend. As someone who's gone through something similar to your experience."

Marissa sat in her bed, deep in thought. I couldn't know exactly what she was processing, but I gave her time to do so. I looked around the hospital room. She'd only been there for a few hours, but there were no flowers, items from home or anything personal. Or anybody. Although I wasn't surprised her mother hadn't bothered to come by, it was odd nobody had. I guessed Hallie didn't know she was here yet.

I spotted what appeared to be a sports jersey, folded on the second chair in the room. The corner of a laptop computer poked out from underneath. I stood and went over to the chair, picking up the shirt. It was a Dominican Republic national football team jersey. And it was too big to be Marissa's. I laid it over the back of the chair and looked down at the laptop. It was covered in stickers from various football teams from around the world.

"Nora," Marissa called to me, and I heard her swing her legs out of bed.

One sticker in the corner caught my eye. I turned and stared at the young girl I'd rescued from a dark bedroom that morning. Her mouth was open and her eyes had lost their ferocity and determination. She looked scared.

The sticker was small, round, and had a cartoon rabbit in the centre.

43

UNBALANCED

I marched over to the door.

"Don't leave," Marissa pleaded.

I wasn't about to leave. Swinging the door closed, I wheeled around. "You'd better start explaining."

Tears rolled down the young girl's face, but she gritted her teeth. "You of all people should appreciate this."

"Appreciate what?" I spat back. "A woman is dead based on your word that she was involved in your kidnapping."

"She was!" Marissa shouted. "She was, you have to know that," she repeated, in a quieter voice.

"That guy who came in here, he's the thief, isn't he? He's the man who's been breaking into homes. Including mine!"

"Yours was different. We tried to keep you out of it, but you couldn't stay away. You risked screwing everything up when you broke into Cosgrove's."

Fy faen, she knew. They knew. I was at their mercy as much as they were at mine. We were in bed together now. I sat back down in the chair and tried to fathom all the threads which ran intertwined throughout both cases.

"How do you know anything about the International Fellowship of Lions?"

"Hallie told me," Marissa replied. "We're best friends."

"You involved Hallie?!" I groaned, rising to my feet.

"No, she doesn't know," she said, waving me back to the chair. "We met in school. She's older than me, but we had advanced classes together. There's only a few of us, so we study together, just working on different curriculums. She told me all about it one day. She said you were her big sister now."

Hearing the way I felt about Hallie mirrored in her own words meant a lot to me, but I wasn't ready to let my sentiment get in the way of this situation just yet. "What about Rabbit?"

"She's a genius. She taught me everything I know about computers," Marissa explained. "So when I wanted to find out more about the resort, I asked her to help. She can get access to files and secure stuff I could never find. She's the one who got the list."

"The list?"

"Yeah. The list of resort members that was suppressed in court."

How on earth Rabbit managed to get that file I had no idea, but I was glad she'd found it. And terrified what else she could see in police records.

"It was impossible to hide what I was looking for from Rabbit, and she's pretty active in human and citizens' rights movements, so she wanted to help. The story which really stood out was Carlina Arias, the girl they found in the water."

My heart skipped at the mention of her name. "Carlina was my best friend at the resort," I said softly.

"Well, we found her half-brother in the Dominican Republic. He plays football for a team there. I guess he was a few years older and got away from the home when his stepfather, who was Carlina's father, became abusive. He'd planned to get his sister out of there too, but she went missing before he could. As far as he knew, she was never found. He hadn't spoken to his mother from the day he left, so it seems she never bothered to find him and tell him when the Cayman Islands police contacted her."

"So he came here?" I asked.

"Like I said, Rabbit's a genius, and she found him. We contacted him and he flew over here. We met with him before he went to the police to talk to them," she grinned at me. "You, I guess."

I shook my head. "Not right now. There's no police in this room."

"Good," she said, then continued. "The people who'd run the resort were all in jail, but the customers weren't. We had the list, and most lived abroad, but we identified three men who lived on the island, at least part time. These men were walking around as though nothing had happened, so we decided to go after them."

"Why start with the dead guy?" I asked.

"Because we had to see if we could do it, and the old lady seemed to be the easiest one of the three. Rabbit gave us the details to get past the alarms and the idiot had a stupidly easy passcode for the safe."

"Does Rabbit have inside help at CSS?"

"No, it's all her," Marissa said, clearly in awe of the woman's abilities. "She can see all the servers at CSS, but she also figured out how to intercept the live feeds from the cameras at the homes. She saw the odd time of day you'd turned off the alarm at the Cosgroves', so she checked the camera files for that time frame. That's how we knew you'd been in there."

"But how did you know it was me?" I asked, wondering why my brilliantly pieced together disguise hadn't thrown them off.

"Because there aren't too many tall, slender females with a reason to break into that home," she answered. "Plus Rabbit matched up footage of you from when you'd been in the house the night of the robbery."

I felt like an amateur in front of the fifteen-year-old, so I moved on. "Then you went after the Cosgroves?"

"We weren't, we were going after the third name, but then that arsehole DeWayne tried to set me up with The Haitian. My brain had been immersed in all this sex trafficking stuff, so I guess I was supersensitive to it, but I smelled a rat."

"You didn't meet with him, did you?"

Marissa shook her head. "But we followed him and found where he was staying. That night, he went to a quiet jetty on the North Sound and met a boat. It was a small rubber dinghy. It brought two girls ashore, tied up and hooded."

"Ilaria and Millie," I said. "We found them."

"You would have found them sooner if we didn't lose the Haitian and Didi that night. We were too slow getting back to our car after they left."

"The woman," I said, recalling the girl's comment about hearing a female voice.

"Estelle Cosgrove," Marissa confirmed. "She was clearly in charge."

I took a few deep breaths and put the puzzle together in my mind. "So you robbed Cosgrove, hoping to find something incriminating, but Estelle came home before Carlina's brother could find the second safe."

"That's right. And his name's Fernando."

"Then I screwed it up by breaking in. Estelle moved all the cash and the notebook with The Haitian's number and a bunch of dates."

"We saw the cash on the security feed, but couldn't tell what else you found," she said.

"I hope you're the only ones who ever see that footage."

"No one else will," Marissa replied. "Rabbit erased it that night."

I was stunned. They'd erased their only true leverage on me. There was nothing stopping me turning them in, and doing my job as a policewoman. The scales had gone from perfectly balanced to completely one sided. Yet that had already been done, so why was she confessing all this to me? She was leaving three people's futures in my hands. All Marissa knew of me was what Hallie would have told her. That was the only way she'd be trusting me now, I was sure.

"I rammed Estelle Cosgrove's Porsche into the bay earlier today, then dived and made sure she couldn't get out." There. The scales were balanced again.

"Shame her husband wasn't in the car with her," Marissa responded, surprisingly calmly.

"That was my thought, too."

We grinned at each other for a few moments.

"And you were never kidnapped, right?" I surmised.

"Right. I'd been hiding with Fernando. Once you arrested The Haitian, we tied me up at his house and waited." She rolled her eyes. "You took a long time to get there, by the way."

"Sorry," I said, as thoughts raced through my brain. "You said there's one more *drittsekk*, here on the island?"

Marissa nodded.

"We have to wait. It'll be a miracle if Whittaker doesn't figure all this out," I said, and I certainly meant it. Working with the man, I had seen how clever and resourceful he could be. He was brilliant at reading people, and now I'd have to hide a mountain of secrets from him. So much for turning over a new leaf. That would have to wait.

"Does that mean you're not turning us in?" Marissa asked.

"I wouldn't have told you about Estelle if that was my plan."

She nodded. "Then we both pledge to stay quiet and help each other, no matter what?"

"Okay," I agreed. "But on these conditions. First is Hallie stays out of it and never knows."

Marissa shrugged her shoulders. "That's easy. She knows nothing now and never will from us."

"Two. I get the name of the third person."

Marissa let out a sigh. "Okay," she relented, and reached for a pad of paper and a pen from the bedside table. She wrote down a name and handed it to me. I read the note.

"*Fy faen*," I muttered. "Seriously?"

She raised her eyebrows and nodded. "We can help."

"You and Rabbit, maybe, but condition three is Carlina's brother needs to leave."

"He won't want to."

"He must. He can't risk staying here any longer. If this goes pear shaped, he'll be tried as an adult, but you won't be. Plus, you're on the hook for a lot less than him."

She nodded.

"You need to tell Rabbit to behave herself now too," I added, and leaned back in the chair to reach for the laptop. I peeled the incriminating sticker off, wadded it up, and threw it into the rubbish bin next to the bedside table.

When I turned back around, Marissa was texting someone. A few moments later, Fernando came into the room. He closed the door behind him and looked at me nervously.

"It's okay," Marissa told him, but his expression didn't change.

I looked him over. He was athletic and very handsome. His eyes were so familiar. "You look a lot like your sister," I said. "She was my best friend."

His face broke into a broad smile, and I pictured Carlina's pretty face, laughing in the sun on the deck of the Hatteras as we enjoyed a day on the water. The hopes and dreams we'd spoken about at length came flooding back. How our lives were going to be so different with the resort behind us, and the money they'd promised us. She'd been paid with a rope around her ankle, tied to a heavy weight.

"She knows everything," Marissa added.

"There's one more," Fernando said, with urgency in his voice.

I held up the piece of paper. "Don't worry. I'll take care of him."

I would put my new leaf on hold until some point in the future.

ACKNOWLEDGMENTS

My sincere thanks to:

My amazing wife Cheryl, wonderful friend James, and my family, for their unwavering support, advice and encouragement.
My marvellous editor Andrew Chapman at Prepare to Publish for his diligent work and wise suggestions.
Lily at Orkidedatter for her Norwegian advice.
Casey Keller, Craig Robinson and Alain Belanger for their help with all things Cayman Islands related.
Shearwater dive computers for their friendship and support.
The Tropical Authors group for their advice, support, humour and, most importantly, rum. Visit and subscribe at www.TropicalAuthors.com for deals and info on a plethora of books by talented authors in the Sea Adventure genre.
My beta reader group has grown to include an amazing cross section of folks from different walks of life. Their suggestions, feedback and keen eyes are invaluable, for which I am eternally grateful.
Above all, I thank you, the readers: none of this happens without the choice you make to spend your precious time with my stories. I am truly in your debt.

LET'S STAY IN TOUCH!

To buy merchandise, find more info or join my newsletter, visit my website at
www.HarveyBooks.com

If you enjoyed this novel I'd be incredibly grateful if you'd consider leaving a review on Amazon.com
Find eBook deals and follow me on BookBub.com

Find more great authors in the genre at TropicalAuthors.com

Visit Amazon.com for more books in the
Nora Sommer Caribbean Suspense Series,
AJ Bailey Adventure Series,
and collaborative works;
Graceless - A Tropical Authors Novella
Timeless - A Tropical Authors Novel
Angels of the Deep - A Tropical Christmas Novella

ABOUT THE AUTHOR

Nicholas Harvey's life has been anything but ordinary. Race car driver, mountaineer, divemaster, and since 2019 a full-time novelist. Raised in England, Nick now lives next to the ocean in Key Largo with his amazing wife, Cheryl.

Motorsports may have taken him all over the world, both behind the wheel and later as a Race Engineer and Team Manager, but diving inspires his destinations these days – and there's no better diving than in Grand Cayman where Nick's *AJ Bailey Adventure* and *Nora Sommer Caribbean Suspense* series are based.

Printed in Great Britain
by Amazon